IN
HER
GRAVE

BOOKS BY WILLOW ROSE

IN HER GRAVE

WILLOW ROSE

bookouture

Published by Bookouture in 2024

An imprint of Storyfire Ltd.
Carmelite House
50 Victoria Embankment
London EC4Y 0DZ

www.bookouture.com

ISBN: 978-1-83525-466-0
eBook ISBN: 978-1-83525-465-3

PROLOGUE

My feet pounded against the pavement as I raced toward the cemetery gates. The hammering of my heart was so fierce it felt like it would burst through my chest at any moment. I scanned for any sign of danger, my breathing quickening into short, sharp gasps. Time was running out—I knew I had to get there before it was too late.

Ivy crept up the wrought-iron fence, casting eerie shadows on the decaying brick walls. The thought of what lay beyond that threshold made me pause for just a second, but then determination took over.

I pushed open the creaky gate and crossed into the graveyard. A dense mist rolled in, obscuring everything more than a few feet away. Shadows danced between headstones, and I couldn't tell if they were just tricks of light or something else entirely. Fear pulsed through me, but I kept moving forward.

I could feel beads of sweat dripping down my forehead.

I was terrified, but I had to find what I came for, no matter how dangerous it might be.

I quickly swept over the rows of headstones. Then, I saw it. Etched into the stone.

Wilde.

A cold shiver ran down my spine as I gazed at the tombstone in disbelief. How could this be? Was I losing my mind?

I rushed toward it. The dust that rose from beneath my feet seemed to follow me. My hands were trembling when I reached the grave. I took a deep breath. And I started to dig.

The dirt flew in the air as I clawed at it with my hands, my fingers quickly becoming raw from the rough earth, catching on sharp stones; I cut myself and began to bleed in places.

But then, I touched something. I grabbed it and pulled at it, panic setting in. It was a small limb, a foot, protruding from the soil. Without hesitation, I reached farther down and pulled at it, my heart beating so fast that I could feel it in my throat.

Suddenly, my eyes locked onto my little boy lying in the grave. His clothes were dirty and disheveled, his skin pale. He was lifeless. My heart felt like it was going to explode as I scrambled over to him, scooping up his small body into my trembling arms. Tears of sorrow mixed with dust and dirt smudged my face as I sobbed uncontrollably.

"Zack, my boy." My voice was choked with emotion. "What have they done to you?" I looked around the rows of graves, searching for any sign of the monster who had done this to my sweet child.

But all I saw was the empty graveyard, the silence broken only by my own sobs. I clutched Zack's body tightly and rocked back and forth.

"Zack, oh no, Zack!"

I cried out, my voice echoing into the emptiness around me. The moon was high in the sky, illuminating the grave beneath my knees. I had no idea how long I had been digging, or how long it had been since I had last seen my son alive. It was all a blur.

Zack's body was cold and stiff in my arms, and the sight of

him had brought me to my knees. The weight of what had happened crashed down on me, and I knew that I would never be the same again.

Neither would the people who had done this.

ONE

CHARLIE

Four Days Earlier

The moon was full, and the air was warm and humid as Tommy and Charlie made their way through the entrance of the Haunted Jail Trail. The sound of rustling leaves and branches breaking underfoot made Charlie jump even before they entered through the gate. He had never done this before, and it terrified him, but he couldn't tell that to his friend, who had been every year for the past three years, usually coming here with his older brother.

"Oh, this is going to be so much fun, aren't you excited?" Tommy exclaimed, his eyes big and wide.

Charlie answered with a cautious nod, then looked down at his feet as they moved forward.

Tommy and Charlie crept along the overgrown path, the sharp edges of the tall grass brushing against their legs. The sky above was clear, the moonlight giving just enough light to navigate. As they stepped inside, a chill ran down their spines. They could hear people screaming ahead of them and saw beams of light darting between the trees.

The trail became more and more sinister as they traveled deeper into the forest. They could make out mummified figures in tattered clothing hanging from trees and witches cackling beside bonfires. They held each other close as they watched a skeleton with glowing red eyes rotate eerily on its platform. Another skeleton leapt out at them from the bushes, displacing cobwebs with mechanical screeches, while fake body parts hung in display cages among the foliage. Every now and then, an unexpected jump scare startled them.

Charlie was especially frightened; he had never been to a haunted trail before, and he couldn't shake the feeling of unease. Tommy, on the other hand, was having the time of his life. He laughed every time he jumped and urged Charlie to keep moving forward. "Come on, Charlie, it's just for fun!" he exclaimed.

But Charlie wasn't so sure it was all fun. He dreaded what was around the next corner. He wondered for a second if he should go back, but how could he? It would be too embarrassing. He would never hear the end of it from Tommy. So, he continued.

Every time a monster or a ghoul jumped out to scare them, he flinched. The first time a zombie came shambling out of the bushes, Charlie jumped back. Tommy laughed and grabbed him, pulling him forward, just as a man in a white mask and black cloak rushed toward them, swinging an axe. Charlie gasped and ducked, then ran toward Tommy and grabbed his arm. They took off toward a bridge in the middle of the forest. A dead body lay on the path, covered from head to toe in blood and grime. When Tommy started to walk toward it, something rose from the torso. Tommy gasped as a rotund zombie stepped into view. It reached for them and snapped its teeth together.

Up next was a slaughterhouse. They walked inside and a little girl rushed toward them, her skin painted white, blank eyes staring into the air, growling sounds coming from her mouth. Nothing terrified Charlie more than little girls, so he jumped to the side with a shriek. But as he did, arms grabbed for him from behind the walls, bloody fingers touching his skin, and he screamed loudly.

Tommy laughed at Charlie's frightened reactions. "Come on, man, it's just for fun," he said, trying to reassure his friend.

Charlie tried to keep up, but the fear and anxiety were starting to get the best of him. The two boys approached a darkened path, where a figure suddenly lunged out at them.

Tommy laughed, but Charlie's fear only intensified. He didn't like the feeling of being scared and vulnerable. It was too much for him. He knew the trail ended with a maze that he risked getting lost in. Charlie was very claustrophobic and feared that part more than anything.

"Tommy, I don't know if I can do this," Charlie said, his voice trembling, as they reached the entrance of the maze. The sound of people screaming came from all sides, but the loudest was from inside of the maze.

"What are you talking about? We're almost at the end, Charlie. Don't be such a wimp," Tommy replied, a hint of annoyance in his voice. "Now I will go into the maze, and you will follow me. Stay right behind me, okay?"

"O-okay."

Charlie watched as his friend entered the maze, and then he walked up to the entrance and peeked inside. There was a fog in there, making it impossible to see where you were walking. And lights, strobe lights that confused him. He stood at the entrance, letting people behind him walk past, seeing them disappear into the infinity. He took a few more steps inside, then came to a narrow section where he had to walk sideways in order to pass. He turned around and took a left instead, but as he walked down that path, a group of people came toward him, giggling and talking in loud voices. They said it wasn't the way out. It was a dead end.

Charlie felt his heart rate go up. He turned around and couldn't see Tommy. He saw people disappear in all directions and didn't know where to go, which path to choose. It felt like the walls were closing in on him.

"Tommy?" he said. "Tommy?"

But no answer came. Screams emerged from inside of the maze, loud and scared screams, and he didn't know what to do. He turned around and ran back the way he had come in. Or at least he believed that was the way, but he had lost his sense of direction.

Charlie ran blindly through the maze, his heart pounding in his chest. The sound of his own ragged breathing filled his ears as he stumbled over someone crawling on the floor, her bloody face looking up at him, letting out a cackling laugh. He ran farther, his fear propelling him forward. He didn't know where he was going, only that he needed to get away, to get out of there as quickly as possible.

Just as he thought he had escaped the maze, a hand reached out from the darkness and grabbed him by the shoulder, pulling him violently backward.

Was this another cruel part of the show?

Charlie was pulled into the darkness, and he looked up, his eyes widening in terror as he saw the figure in the white mask from earlier looming over him. He felt a knife as it touched his skin. Around him people were screaming in fear and joy, running from one end to the other in the fog.

Charlie tried to scream from the top of his lungs, even though he knew it was in vain. It was too late.

TWO

BILLIE ANN

I stood in front of the full-length mirror, staring at my reflection, as I tried on another pair of black pants. My blonde hair was growing out after I had shaved it the year before, but I had just styled it into a pixie cut that framed my face. I tried to put on makeup, but I had never been good with that sort of thing, so I ended up looking like a raccoon and wiped it off. Then I changed the top I was wearing. And the pants. Again.

"Maybe I should wear a dress?" I said, looking inside of my closet. "Maybe she'll like me to be more feminine?"

I shook my head. No, I had to be myself. I couldn't wear something I didn't feel comfortable in. I sighed, letting the nerves get to me.

My parents, who had come over to look after the kids, watched me with concern. My mom came up to me and tilted her head. "I don't think I have ever seen you like this."

"Maybe I should just cancel," I said with a sigh, trying on a blue blazer. I stared at the missing left breast beneath it, then touched the area. I had been wanting to have it reconstructed after my cancer had been removed, but for some reason hadn't done it yet. Even if my insurance would pay for it. I think maybe I wasn't sure I wanted to hide that part of me. The scar, the battle wound I was proud of. It proved that I had overcome cancer. That I had won. But the missing breast did make my clothes look strange.

"Take it easy," my mom said, patting me awkwardly on the back. Her face held a mixture of concern and apprehension, but she did her best to hide it behind a forced smile. I could sense the tension in her voice, but I appreciated her effort, nonetheless. My mother had always been proud of me, but this part of my life challenged her beliefs in ways she struggled to comprehend. "You'd think you've never been on a date before."

"I haven't," I admitted, feeling my cheeks flush with embarrassment, and I turned to hide them from her. I didn't want her to feel any more uncomfortable than she already did. "Not like this."

My dad came closer. "Leave her alone, she's just nervous. We'll take care of the kids while you are out."

I nodded, grateful for their help, despite their beliefs. I knew it took a lot on their part. My parents were very religious people and me being a lesbian wasn't an easy pill to swallow for them. I knew they hadn't told anyone about it yet, especially not their friends from the church, and perhaps they never would. They had tried their best to talk me out of it and make me believe that it was just a silly phase, and I'm sure they still believed it was, but I knew it wasn't. And lately I had needed them to help me with the kids.

These past few months hadn't been easy. My ex, Joe, was trying to take the children away from me, looking for proof that I was an unfit mother, so I didn't dare to leave them alone at the house anymore when going out. Not even if Charlene had turned seventeen and was perfectly capable of caring for her brothers, who were fifteen and ten. My ex believed I wasn't there for them, and he and his lawyer were still debating with my lawyer about the conditions of the divorce, and who got the

children. And the house. So far, we hadn't reached an agreement, and it was dragging on forever. It left me in this weird
vast space that I had to figure out how to navigate. I couldn't
mess up, or he would take the kids. I had to be very careful and
responsible, considering my every move. One more mistake and
that would be it. In Joe's eyes, just the fact that I was now living
the "gay lifestyle" was enough for him to declare me unfit.

I turned back to the mirror, trying on yet another outfit. "Do
you think Danni will like this?"

My mom's eyes avoided mine, and she shrugged. I hated
how me being myself for the first time in my life made her
uncomfortable. It made me feel wrong. But I also knew she was
doing her best to support me in any way she could. I had to
remember where she came from. And despite that she was
actually trying. She wanted me to be happy. And going on a
real date with Danni, my best friend and the greatest love of
my life, had been my dream for ages. She had told me she loved
me. She had said it in the hospital as she grabbed my hand, and
I still remembered it like it was yesterday. She had been hospi-
talized for months after she had been in a fire the year before,
and I had sat by her side every day, reading to her or enter-
taining her with stories from my colleagues at the police
station. Once she finally came home, she had trouble walking
and needed rehabilitation, and her children were demanding of
her as well, as her soon-to-be ex-husband had left to be with his
girlfriend, and taking care of the twins by herself was quite the
challenge. I had helped her as much as I could with the daily
chores, and that had been the extent of our relationship so far.
But I wanted more, a lot more, and now it was finally time. She
had agreed to go on a date with me, a real date to a restaurant,
and I was ecstatic. No, make that terrified. I had never wanted
anything more than I wanted her, and I was so afraid I would
blow it.

"Danni has known you for years, Billie Ann," my mom said.

"She knows what you look like. It's not like you're a surprise to her."

"No, maybe not, but I want her to think I look good. I want her to be attracted to me." I almost whispered the last words.

My mother sighed and her eyes hit the floor in embarrassment.

My dad sent her a look. "Maybe we shouldn't disturb her any longer. Let's go check on Zack and see what he is doing."

He grabbed my mother's hand and they left, walking down the hallway to my youngest son's room. I felt relieved. Now I could focus properly on what I was wearing.

As the sun dipped below the horizon, casting a warm golden glow over our small town and our house that was already dressed for Halloween, I nervously adjusted my outfit in front of the mirror. I looked at myself, then realized this wasn't it. It was all wrong. So once again, I redressed. This time I put on a pair of jeans and a button-up shirt and a blazer. Then I nodded, satisfied. This was me. My mom was right. Danni knew me, and she wanted me to be me.

I looked out the window and into the street, anticipating her arrival with the sound of every car entering our cul-de-sac. Jack-o'-lanterns with sinister grins lined the porches all around, casting an eerie glow that danced across the dimly lit street. A large cobweb was stretched across the front porch at our neighbor's house, its sticky strands coated in a glistening dew of silver glitter. Fake spiders of all shapes and sizes clung to its threads, as if frozen in a terrifying moment. The porch was transformed into a spooky graveyard, with tombstones protruding from the ground at odd angles; parts of skeletons were sticking up from the ground, pretending to be reaching for people passing by. My own house was well decorated, but it was nothing compared to the neighbor's.

I glanced at my reflection in the bedroom mirror one last time, trying to tuck and tame a few stray strands of hair.

Then I heard it—the familiar chimes of the doorbell echoing up the stairs. It was her. I knew instinctively that it was.

"I'll get it!"

A wave of anticipation swept through me like an electric current as I raced down the stairs taking two steps at a time, feeling like a kid going to prom for the first time. I passed my work phone and badge on the way to the door, then paused for a second, before picking up both and taking them with me.

THREE

TOMMY

Tommy couldn't believe he had finally made it to the end of the maze. He had been lost for what had felt like hours.

But now, as he stood at the exit, he felt a sense of pride wash over him. He had conquered the maze, and he felt like he could conquer anything else that came his way.

Looking around, he saw other people coming out, their faces etched with different emotions. Some were laughing, others were breathing heavily, clearly exhausted. But there was one face he was looking for, and it was nowhere to be found.

He turned around, hoping to see Charlie emerge from the maze as well. But as he watched the people streaming out of the exit, his heart began to sink. Where was Charlie?

Tommy checked his watch, realizing that his parents would be arriving any minute to pick them up. He couldn't leave without Charlie, but he also didn't want to risk getting lost in the maze again.

Tommy felt a cold shiver run down his spine. He had been so focused on getting out of the maze that he had lost track of his friend. He had assumed that Charlie would have followed him closely, but now he wasn't so sure. And he knew Charlie was scared. He felt terrible.

The minutes stretched as Tommy waited for his friend to emerge from the maze. But he still didn't. Tommy felt a pang of guilt in his chest. He should have waited for Charlie. He shouldn't have left him alone in the maze.

Tommy's mind churned through different scenarios. What if Charlie was lost? What if he had gotten hurt? His parents would be furious if they found out he had left his friend behind.

Tommy decided to take action. Without a second thought, he plunged back into the maze.

The twists and turns seemed even more confusing now, and Tommy's heart was beating fast. But he kept going, calling out his friend's name and listening for any response.

"Charlie!"

Tommy turned another corner, trying to find his friend, calling out his name desperately. But what he found was not what he was expecting.

There, lying on the ground, was Charlie. His body was still, and he was pale, blood was pooling around his head. Tommy's stomach turned as he rushed to his friend's side.

"Charlie!" he screamed, his voice echoing off the maze walls. But there was no response.

Tommy could see the lifeless look in his eyes. He gasped, his hands shaking as he reached out to touch Charlie's arm to feel for a pulse. There was none. He knew then it was too late. Charlie was dead.

As he knelt by his friend's side, he heard laughter coming from behind him. With a gasp he turned to see a flock of teenagers staring at Charlie's body, and the blood, pointing fingers and laughing. Tommy stared at them, unable to speak, then looked down at the blood on his hands from touching Charlie. More people walked past them, thinking that Charlie's body was just another part of the show.

Tommy's mind went blank, he didn't know what to do. How to get help.

Charlie was bleeding from a deep gash on his throat, and his eyes were void of life. Tommy fell to his knees beside him, shaking him gently, but he knew in his heart that it was too late. His friend was gone.

More people came, giggling and laughing at the display.

Tommy wanted to scream at them, to tell them that this was real, that his friend was really dead. But he couldn't find his voice. It felt like the entire world was spinning around him, and he was the only one standing still.

Slowly, he rose to his feet, his eyes still fixed on Charlie's lifeless body. He knew he had to do something. He couldn't just leave his friend there.

Slowly, Tommy picked up Charlie's body, holding him close to his chest. He didn't know where he was going or what he was going to do, but he knew he had to get Charlie out of the maze. He had to find help. As he stumbled through the exit, clinging to Charlie's bloody body, getting it smeared all over his favorite shirt, he let out a small cry.

"Please, please help."

A man walked past him, then told his friend that this one really looked real, that it was an awesome show this year. Tears streamed down Tommy's face as he frantically looked around for anyone who could help, but all faces turned away, still thinking this was all an act, a show.

Tommy let out a sob and crumpled to the ground, burying his face in his hands. His anguish reverberated through the air, and he screamed so loud that it finally silenced everyone around him.

FOUR

BILLIE ANN

The restaurant was dimly lit, the soft glow of candles on each table casting shadows onto the walls. Danni sat across from me, her eyes sparkling in the candlelight. She was beautiful, as always, but tonight was different. Tonight, we were on a date.

As I sat across from Danni at Pompano Grill, a nice Italian restaurant in downtown Cocoa Beach, I felt the overwhelming awkwardness between us. We had been best friends for years, but now that we were attempting to have a romantic relationship, everything felt different. Was it really possible to make that shift? What would we talk about? We already knew everything there was to know about each other.

I nervously fiddled with my fork, twirling it around on my plate as the silence between us got to me. I could feel myself about to say silly things, then stopped before I did. No matter how hard I tried to control my nerves, they seemed to be getting the best of me. I felt so awkward and unsure. How do you go from being friends to being more than that? I fidgeted with my napkin, trying to think of something to say. Should I grab her hand? Would that be too forward? Maybe I should just try talking to her and let things flow naturally.

"So, um, how's work been?" I asked, wincing inwardly at the lameness of my question. "Are you happy to be back?"

Danni smiled, a small grin quirking up the corners of her mouth. "It's been good," she said. "Busy, but good." She paused for a second before she continued. "This place is really nice, I've always loved it here, especially since they renovated it. Thanks for bringing me."

I nodded, feeling my heart race with nervous energy. "Yeah, I thought it would be a good spot for us to, you know, hang out."

Danni raised an eyebrow. "Hang out?" she repeated with a chuckle. "Is that what we're doing? Just hanging out?"

I felt my cheeks flush with embarrassment. "No, I mean, I was hoping... I mean, I want this to be a date," I said, stumbling over my words.

Danni's face softened, and she reached across the table to take my hand. "I know," she said. "And I want that too."

I felt a surge of relief and happiness flood through me, and I squeezed her hand back, intertwining my fingers with hers. She looked up at me, surprise and curiosity in her eyes.

"I know this might seem sudden, but I've been wanting to do this for a long time," I said, my voice barely above a whisper. "I don't know what the future holds, but I do know that I want to be with you, Danni. I want you in my life."

She nodded, then looked down. "I love you, Billie Ann, I truly do. I can't deny the strong feelings between us. I know it's more than friendship. But we need to take it slow. I'm just about to start my divorce, and you... you're still going through yours, fighting with lawyers and everything. And the children"

"Hey, it's okay," I said, stopping her. "Let's just be here, right now, and not overthink everything, okay?"

She swallowed, then nodded, pulling her hand out of mine as a couple passed our table. Then she sent me a smile, it was soft and gentle and had everything of her in it. It melted my heart. I knew this was all a little much and a big change for her.

I had been through it myself and struggled with my own sexuality for years. It wasn't easy, so I knew I had to go easy on her, take it very slow.

I poured her a glass of wine, trying to act suave and sophisticated, but ended up spilling some on the tablecloth instead.

Danni burst out laughing, and I couldn't help but join in.

The tension between us finally dissipating, it felt like we were back to our old selves, enjoying each other's company without any added pressure or expectations.

As the evening went on, we talked about everything and anything, from our favorite childhood memories to our dreams for the future. It felt like we were discovering new sides of each other, even though we had been friends for years.

As we finished our meal and walked out of the restaurant, Danni slipped her hand into mine. It was a small gesture, but it meant the world to me. I knew we still had a long way to go, but I was willing to take it slow and be patient. Who knew what the future would hold for us? But for now, I was just grateful to have Danni by my side as my best friend and maybe, just maybe, something more. Eventually.

But it didn't take long for her to release her grip as she felt my phone begin to ring in my pocket. I sighed and pulled it out. And saw Chief of Police Becky Harold's name lighting the screen. My heart sank. There was only one reason she would call me on a Saturday night.

"What's going on?" I asked.

"We have a body. At the haunted trail by the jail. It's a kid. I'm on my way there. I need you ASAP."

My heart sank at the news. A child.

"What's going on?" Danni asked, her voice shaky.

I didn't want to tell her. Just as things were finally starting to go right for Danni and me, the reality of my job as a detective came crashing back in. I knew I had to go, but I didn't want to leave Danni alone. I looked at her, her eyes filled with concern.

"It's work," I said, trying to keep my voice calm. I wasn't on call this weekend, but as the head of the homicide department I had to go to this one because it was a child. "There's been a homicide. I have to go."

Danni nodded, her expression understanding. "Go," she said. "I'll be okay. Just be careful, okay?"

I nodded, feeling a pang of guilt in my chest. This was supposed to be our night, and now I was leaving her alone. But I had a job to do, and I couldn't let my personal life get in the way of that.

"I'll call you as soon as I can," I promised, giving her hand a squeeze before letting go.

FIVE

Then

Betty was wiping down the stainless-steel countertop as the smell of bacon sizzling on the griddle filled the air. She had been working at the diner for years, serving the same regulars their usual orders day in and day out. Just as she thought this day would be like most others, the door opened and a tall, handsome man walked in. His uniform was crisp and clean, and Betty couldn't help but stare at him as he approached the counter.

"Morning, ma'am," he said with a smile, tipping his cap to her.

"Morning," she replied, biting her lip. "What can I get for you?"

"I'm Officer Travis Walker. Just wanted to grab a quick cup of coffee and a bite to eat before heading out on my patrol."

Betty smiled back at him. "Of course, Officer Walker. I'll get that for you right away."

As Betty poured him a cup of coffee, she couldn't help but steal glances at him. He was so handsome, with his chiseled jawline and piercing blue eyes. And something about him made her feel safe, like he could protect her from anything.

Travis noticed Betty's lingering gaze and smiled at her again. "So, how long have you been working here?"

Betty blushed, feeling a little embarrassed. "Oh, I've been here for a few years now. It's not the most exciting job, but it pays the bills."

Travis chuckled. "I know what you mean. Sometimes the daily grind can get a little monotonous. But I have a feeling that things are about to get a lot more exciting around here," he said, nodding toward the door.

Betty followed his gaze and saw a group of six teenagers strutting into the diner, chuckling and shoving one another. One of them tipped over the sign she had put up inside, telling customers about today's special. The others laughed as he kicked it across the tiles of the diner. They threw themselves in a booth and one of them yelled at her to come over and give them food. Then he told her to move faster as she approached them.

"What can I get you?" she asked nervously.

"I know what I ought to get you," one of them said. "A new face. Dang, you ugly, girl. They should be keeping you in the back."

They laughed, and Betty's heart sank. But just as she was about to turn and walk away, Travis stood to his feet.

"Don't worry, ma'am, I'll take care of this," he said, his hand resting on his gun holster.

Impressed by his confidence, she watched him approach the group. "I'm going to have to ask you to apologize to the lady," he said sternly.

The group of teenagers looked up at Travis in surprise, but quickly regained their confidence. "Who are you to tell us what to do?" one of them sneered.

"I'm Officer Walker. And if you don't apologize to the lady

and leave this diner immediately, I'll have to take matters into my own hands," Travis said, his voice low and threatening.

The teenagers looked at one another nervously. Travis said something further in a hushed voice, and then the group quickly apologized to Betty before scurrying out of the diner, tripping over one another to get out first.

As Travis returned to his seat, Betty couldn't help but feel grateful for his presence. "Thank you for handling that," she said, smiling at him.

Travis grinned back at her. "No problem. It's all part of the job."

They continued to chat as Betty served him his eggs and bacon, and she found herself enjoying his company more and more. There was something about his easy smile and confident demeanor that drew her in.

As Travis finished his meal and got up to leave, Betty was a little disappointed.

"Will I see you again?" she blurted out before she could stop herself.

Travis turned back toward her, his eyes lighting up. "I hope so," he said. "Actually, I was wondering if you'd like to go out for dinner sometime?"

Betty's heart skipped a beat. She had never been asked out by a police officer before, but she felt like this was an opportunity she couldn't pass up. "I would love to," she said, smiling back at him.

Travis grinned. "Great. How about tomorrow night?"

Betty nodded eagerly. "Tomorrow night works for me."

As Travis walked out of the diner, Betty couldn't help but feel like she was walking on air. She had just been asked out by the most charming man she had ever met, and he was a police officer to boot. She knew that things were just beginning for her and Officer Walker, and she couldn't wait to see where this new adventure would take them.

SIX

BILLIE ANN

I parked at the police blockage, showed my badge, and made my way toward the entrance of the haunted trail. The air grew thick with humidity, and an eerie silence engulfed the area. The surrounding swamps looked ominous, especially when lit up by the lights from emergency vehicles. I couldn't shake off the feeling that something sinister was lurking in the shadows. The forested and swampy area around Brevard County Jail was eerie normally, but with the added horror of what had just happened, it was almost foreboding.

When I got closer, the sound of people crying filled my ears. The sobs grew louder with every step. It was as if the very ground was alive with fear. I saw faces distorted in pain and agony, tears streaming down their cheeks. People were gathered everywhere, hugging one another, holding hands over their faces, their eyes distorted in fear and pain. People had been carelessly enjoying the night, but now their expressions were full of anguish and misery as I overheard them recounting what they had just witnessed. Others had been working inside of the trail, enjoying scaring people, dressed as zombies, or witches, or the grim reaper, and never for a minute thought anything bad could happen. It had all just been fun and games till now.

I watched as the little boy, no more than nine or ten years old, shook with sobs that he couldn't contain. The officers on the scene towered over him in their uniforms looking like giants in his unsteady line of vision. His parents stood behind him, their faces drawn with worry and grief. His mother reached out a comforting hand, placing it heavily on his shoulders as tears streamed down his dirt-smudged face and dripped onto his bloody hands.

I froze when I saw the boy lying on the stretcher. A pool of blood had formed around him, and his clothes were soaked with it. His skin was pale, almost gray, and his throat had been slashed deep enough to expose the veins. I could see it even from the distance where I was standing. I felt my stomach turn and my heart race, but I could not make myself look away. As I walked closer my heart began to race even faster. I realized I knew this boy, and the horror of it made me sick to my stomach.

Oh dear God, no!

When a voice called my name, I turned toward it.

"Detective Wilde."

It was Chief Harold. She had spotted me and came closer. "You look pale. What's going on?"

I swallowed the lump in my throat. "H-he's my nephew."

Saying it out loud made the tears roll down my cheeks, faster than I could wipe them away.

The Chief let out a deep sigh. "Oh, dear lord, I'm so sorry, Wilde."

"I... I haven't seen him in years. My oldest brother Peter and I aren't close. But... it's definitely him. His name is Charlie Wilde. His family lives in St. Cloud, about a fifty minute's drive inland from here."

I said the words, even if it was breaking my heart. My oldest brother and I had never seen eye to eye on many things, but I knew this was going to break him. And my family. My mom and dad especially.

"Can I tell them?" I asked. "My brother and his wife?"

"It's too late," she said, placing a hand on my shoulder. "A patrol has already been there and notified them. They're on their way here now."

I nodded. Perhaps it was for the best. I would only break down if I had to tell my own brother his son was dead. It would be unbearable.

"What happened?" I asked, wiping the tears away, trying to remain professional.

"I can't have you take the lead on this case, Wilde," she said, and I nodded. "But Big Tom and Scott aren't here yet, so I can let you help with the scene, if you're up to it?" she asked.

"Yes, please," I said, grateful. "I can control my emotions," I confirmed, but the Chief knew this. I'd proven myself to the Chief in the past. I'd been connected to several cases I'd worked on over the years and never let my emotions get in the way. I'd saved lives. And a scene like this was a ticking clock. With every second we lost, another victim was in danger, or our evidence, our trail to finding the killer, was running away from us.

She gave me a look, then nodded. "You have the most experience, and Tom and Scott are both still in training. That's the only reason I'm allowing this. Okay?"

I sniffled then nodded. "Okay. Just tell me what happened."

The Chief called over the responding officer and asked him to review what had happened.

"Charlie Wilde, our victim, was here with his friend Tommy Kent. Tommy and Charlie went into the maze between six and seven p.m. We know they arrived at around six as one of the workers remembers them purchasing their tickets. Tommy has confirmed they went on a few rides before heading for the maze itself," he said. "Tommy said they walked around together at first, but then parted ways. He says he exited the maze, waited for Charlie and when he didn't come out, he went back in. He said Charlie was a bit scared of the special effects. He found his friend Charlie on the ground in there, his throat slit. Dead. He then carried him out and got help from some of the security guards. That's all we know so far. Since it's so close to the jail, we have confirmed that no prisoners have escaped."

I nervously glanced toward the entrance of the maze. I had a fear of closed-in spaces, and the idea of having to traipse through that labyrinth made my stomach churn in dread. I swallowed down my anxiety and asked, "Has he told us precisely where his friend's body was discovered?"

"No." The police officer looked over at Charlie. "I'll ask him to tell us."

Chief Harold and I watched as the officer approached the boy and his parents. The little boy looked up. Tears were rolling down his cheeks, and he looked like he was about to break down into sobs, but he managed to hold them back. His parents stood behind him, anxiously looking over his shoulder at his response. He glanced toward the maze that had been blocked off by police tape, and I could tell the very sight of it filled him with a deep fear. I couldn't even imagine what was going through his mind at this moment, being asked to face what he had seen in there again. Then he nodded. Seeing this I walked closer and bent down in front of him, swallowing all my anger and fear.

"What's your name?" I asked.

"T-Tommy," he said. "I'll have to show you where I found him. I can't remember exactly."

"All right, Tommy. I know this will be hard, okay? We all know that. What you saw in there must have been pretty scary. We understand that. The officers and I will be with you all the time, okay? You can bring your mom as well, and your dad if that helps you. You have nothing to fear. We just need to take a closer look. It will help us get justice for Charlie."

He sniffled, then nodded. "O-okay."

"You're a very brave boy, Tommy," I said.

He nodded, then put his hand in mine as we walked toward the maze.

SEVEN

BILLIE ANN

Tommy and I walked forward, with the officers behind us. The Chief asked me to take this one, as I was better with children than her. I was a mother and she wasn't. I could feel his hand tighten. The maze was a dark, damp place, with vines hanging from the trellis and leafy bushes lining the pathway.

The haunted trail was created by volunteers in the area, and it ran every year from the first of October till Halloween. It raised a lot of money for the sheriff's department and the local animal shelters that the sheriff supported. He had made this program where inmates took care of the rescue animals and bathed and fed them till they could be adopted. The maze was a new addition this year. It had been set up by poles all over the area, and then covered in black plastic, so you couldn't see anything as you walked through it. Not even see the sky above. It ended with a very tight space, where you had to walk sideways in order to get through. It looked extremely claustrophobic to me as we approached it.

We pushed through it and ended up inside of the maze, the long dark tunnels ahead of us. They had turned off the fog machines, and the area had been searched by the officers who had been first on the scene. But this place was just perfect for anything or anyone to hide, and I felt a shiver run down my spine as I walked deeper inside.

"I walked through the tight space here, and then took a left here," he said. "I then went the wrong way and turned around here, before taking a right, I think."

I was impressed with the young boy. Even if he was visibly terrified of having to go back in there, he moved confidently and surely, whereas I was hesitant and tentative with every step. I saw fear in the eyes of the parents as they watched Tommy lead the way through the twisting maze. I couldn't blame them. I could still hear the cries and sobs of the people outside and that didn't make it easier.

"I called his name many times," Tommy said, clutching my hand tightly. "And then when I reached this corner here, and turned it... that's when..."

We followed him around the bend, and he stopped. He stared emptily into the dark corridor, and I felt him tightening his grip on my hand.

"Is this where you found him?" I asked.

He nodded anxiously. Then he pointed. "At the end of this one. He was lying on the ground by the bottom of it. There was blood. It must have been his."

I looked at the ground beneath us. There was fake blood smeared everywhere. It would have been impossible for people to distinguish between the fake and the real. We would need the forensic team to do that. Tommy didn't want to walk any farther, so I continued into the corridor and reached the bottom of it, then lit up the area with my flashlight. There was a lot of blood, and the soil was still wet from it, reflecting the light, glistening. This was real blood. It wasn't red like the fake stuff. It had turned brown, almost black as real blood does when it oxidizes.

Oh dear God.

I took pictures of the area using my phone, careful not to touch anything. I stared at the ground and the walls that were covered in plastic. There was definitely blood splatter on them, but again, it looked like it was intentional. Like it was part of the display. I knew the forensic team from the sheriff's department was on the way, but I needed to see it for myself, the way it looked when Tommy found his friend. I had to picture it exactly the way it was for him, before they tore it all down. And standing there, I could see it. I could see the terror in my nephew's eyes as he was grabbed by someone and pulled back there. I could see the faces of anyone who might have seen it and thought it was just a show. I was just hoping that some of the testimonies we got here today were helpful to us. This was going to be very hard to figure out. It could be any one of the maybe three hundred people out there. Anyone could have paid for the entrance, then walked in there and done this without being seen. Maybe even dressed up. Most people who came here were in costumes. Not just the people working here. This person could just as easily have slipped out before it was all closed down, before the body was found.

I looked at the Chief coming up behind me.

"It could be anybody," I said. "He could be long gone."

"The perfect murder," she said, and as the words hung in the air, I felt like the walls were closing in on me.

I couldn't believe we were dealing with this. It was a nightmare. A young boy had been murdered, and we had hundreds of suspects and no eyewitnesses, no CCTV. Tickets were all paid in cash so there was no credit card trail. It was like trying to find a needle in a haystack. I rubbed my forehead, trying to ease the tension building up in my head. I couldn't even imagine how Tommy was feeling right now, knowing that he had been so close to the murderer, but not close enough to see their face. And I couldn't even begin to comprehend the pain and suffering the victim's family—my family—was going to go through.

I closed my eyes and let out a slow exhale, trying to dispel the nerves that were buzzing through me. We had to find this person before they could strike again. My instincts told me this was a killer with planning and experience. Right now, this guy felt like he had gotten away with it, and that he was invincible, almost on the verge of immortality. I had seen this type of murderer before and knew his profile. It was the worst kind. This powerful feeling, he was enjoying right now would only lead him to kill again. He had probably already planned it out. I had a sick feeling we were chasing someone devious; someone with the potential to simply slip away.

EIGHT

Then

Betty looked around the small backyard that had been transformed into a wedding venue. Her eyes sparkled with joy as she took in the sight—the marquee, the flowers, the chairs that Travis had borrowed from his uncle's lawn, and the altar that had been decorated with pictures of the couple. It may not have been a grand wedding, and maybe not what she had dreamed of, having it in her parents' backyard, but it was perfect in its own way.

Betty was the happiest she had ever been in her life. As she walked down the makeshift aisle in her mother's backyard, she couldn't help but feel grateful for everything that had led her to this moment. She looked up and saw Travis standing at the altar, his eyes locked on hers, and the love she saw in them made her heart swell with happiness.

Betty's mother, who had been skeptical about the wedding arrangements, was now beaming with pride. She had never seen her daughter so happy and in love. Betty's father, who had passed away a few years ago, was missed, but his presence was felt in the air as the couple exchanged their vows.

As the ceremony continued, Betty couldn't help but think about all the sacrifices they had made to be together. Travis had worked tirelessly to save up enough money for a ring, and Betty had sold most of her belongings to contribute to the wedding.

But despite all the hardships they had faced, they knew that they were meant to be together. As the officiant pronounced them husband and wife, they shared a passionate kiss that left them both breathless.

The reception was held in the same backyard, with a small tent set up and fairy lights strung up everywhere. As the sun set, the atmosphere became even more magical. They danced to their favorite song, holding each other close and swaying to the rhythm. Betty couldn't believe how perfect everything was. She had her loving husband, her family and friends around her, and the sun was shining on them all through the trees as it went down. Betty danced with Travis, and the guests cheered them on in tune with the music. Betty laughed and looked lovingly at her husband, feeling the cool breeze in her hair as the sun disappeared behind the tall trees.

Soon the guests started to dance to the music, and everyone seemed to be having a spectacular time. The couple danced together, their eyes locked, their hearts beating as one. It was a moment that they would cherish for the rest of their lives.

As the night wore on, the party grew wilder. Travis' best man, Damian, a rowdy college friend, brought out a bottle of whiskey and started pouring shots for everyone. Betty had never been much of a drinker, but she couldn't resist the excitement of the moment and soon found herself dancing on the table with her new husband.

The whiskey burned in her throat, but it only made her feel more alive. As the night wore on, they drank more and more, and the party became more and more raucous. The music got louder, the dancing more intense, and the guests wilder.

Betty felt herself getting drunk and giddy, and she couldn't help but let loose. She danced with everyone, from her mother to her best friend's boyfriend, and didn't stop until her feet ached and her head spun.

It wasn't long before Betty found herself in the center of a circle of people, doing shots with Damian and Travis. They laughed and cheered as the music blared, and the night seemed to go on forever.

Soon the guests started to leave one by one until only a few of them were left. Travis' best man, Damian, was still there, along with a few of his college friends. They were all drunk and laughing, and Betty couldn't help but feel a little uneasy around them.

But Travis didn't seem to notice. He was too busy drinking and laughing with his friends, and Betty felt a pang of jealousy. She wanted his attention, but he was too preoccupied with his buddies.

So, Betty continued to drink, and as the night wore on, Betty started to feel the effects of the whiskey. She stumbled a bit as she danced, and her head started to spin. She felt dizzy and disoriented, but she tried to push through it. She didn't want the night to end. She realized suddenly that she hadn't seen Travis for quite some time and started to search for him. She went back into the house and, just as she did, he came rushing out toward her. His hair was tousled and his tie undone. Seeing her swaying on her thin legs, he laughed.

"Where were you?" she asked, her voice slurred.

"Just hanging out with my buddies," he said.

"What were you doing in there?' she asked, trying to look past him inside of the house. She could see Damian in there and a couple of others.

"You're drunk," he said and laughed again. "I think we should call it a night."

He led her inside to the bedroom, and they collapsed onto the bed, laughing and giggling as they snuggled up together. Her mother had let them stay in the house for the night of the party while she would sleep at a friend's place. This way, they didn't have to pay for a hotel room and could save a little money. They slept in her parents' bedroom that her mother had decorated with rose petals; she had left a bottle of wine out for them along with a box of chocolates. The whiskey had made them both feel warm and fuzzy, and they were incredibly happy and content.

"The best day of my life," Betty sighed.

She would say those words for many years to come, sticking to it, even after she stopped believing it.

NINE

BILLIE ANN

I emerged from the maze, gasping for air as I took in the sight of the open starry sky above me. The claustrophobic walls of the labyrinth had seemed to press in on me, tightening my chest until I thought I would suffocate. I took a deep breath, feeling a sense of relief wash over me.

The area was still packed with people, with the police talking to each and every one that had been there at the time of the murder. I spotted Big Tom in the distance talking to one of the volunteers, and Scott was talking to the Chief, gesticulating wildly as he spoke.

And then I heard it. The distant sound of someone shouting. I turned to look in the direction of the noise.

I saw him right away. My older brother Peter, running toward me as if all the demons of hell were chasing him. I could see the panic in his eyes, the wild look that came over him when he was scared or worried about something. I recognized it from our childhood, and it broke my heart. As the middle child, and the only girl, I knew my brothers better than anyone. I felt a jolt of fear run through me. How was I going to deal with this?

"Billie Ann!"

I braced myself as Peter approached me, his face twisted in agony and tears streaming down his cheeks. I knew instinctively that all his anger and resentment toward me was forgotten in this moment.

"Billie Ann, oh God, Billie Ann," he cried out, his voice choked with emotion.

I could feel the weight of his grief bearing down on me, and I struggled to keep my own emotions in check. My brother, who was always so emotionless, so cold. I had no idea how to deal with this.

"I'm so sorry, Peter," I simply said, taking a step toward him. I hadn't been this close to him in many years, and it felt strange. My arms hung heavily down my sides, and I didn't know what to do with them. Did I hug him?

"My boy, Billie Ann," he sobbed, clutching at my arms. "He's gone. He's dead, Billie Ann."

I felt a surge of pain and heartache at the mention of Charlie. I knew how much Peter loved him, and the thought of him losing his child, his youngest son, the baby of the family, his pride and joy, was almost too much to bear. "I'm so sorry, Peter," I whispered, finally pulling him in to a hug, while letting my own tears escape. "It's so awful. I'm so, so sorry."

He clung to me tightly, his body shaking with sobs. "You have to do something," he begged, his voice muffled against my shoulder. "You have to find out who did this. You have to make them pay."

I pulled back slightly, holding his shoulders and looking him in the eye. "I will, Peter. I promise you I will find out who did this. I won't stop until I do. I promise you this."

He nodded, wiping at his eyes with the back of his hand. "Thank you. This is so hard. I mean why? He was just a boy. He had his whole life ahead of him. Why? Why would anyone... Why?"

I nodded in agreement, knowing that nothing I could say

would ease his pain. "I know it's hard, Peter. I know," I repeated, placing a comforting hand on his shoulder. "But we'll get through this together. I promise."

He hid his face in his hands, shoulders slumped. He was carrying a burden that no parent should ever have to bear.

"Angela," he said with a sniffle as he looked up at me again. "She's... they showed him to us. She broke down completely. I don't know how she will ever survive this. I don't know how I will."

I wrapped my arms around him again, feeling his body tremble with grief. I had promised him I'd help, but I knew deep down that it wouldn't be that easy. The road ahead of us was long and uncertain, and we would have to be careful not to lose ourselves in the midst of it all.

"We'll take it one day at a time," I murmured, rubbing soothing circles on his back. "We'll get through this together."

Peter nodded; his eyes were still wet with tears. "Thank you, Billie Ann. Thank you for being here."

I squeezed him tightly before stepping back.

My heart ached for Peter and Angela. I had to put all our differences aside and not remember the fight that had made us not speak for years. This was more important. I wanted to be there for him. I wanted desperately to help him. Losing a child was one of the worst things that could happen to a parent, and I couldn't imagine what they were going through. I had dealt with many distraught mothers and fathers over the years in the force, and I knew something like this had the potential to tear even the most stable families apart.

"Let's go and find Angela, Peter," I said, squeezing his shoulder gently. "I'll see if there's anything I can do to help her."

Peter nodded. "Thank you."

I managed a small smile, feeling both grateful and burdened by his words. I hadn't been close with either of my brothers for years. "Just doing what any sister would do," I said with a shrug.

We headed toward the crowd. I saw Angela huddled in a corner with a police officer, her face buried in her hands. My heart broke all over again as I approached her, not knowing what to say or how to comfort her.

"Angela," I said softly, placing a hand on her shoulder. She looked up at me, her eyes red and puffy from crying. "I'm so sorry. I can't even imagine what you're going through right now."

She let out a strangled sob and buried her face in her hands again. I glanced at the police officer, who gave me a nod before stepping back to give us some space. I crouched down next to Angela, placing a hand on her back and rubbing soothing circles.

"We're here for you," I said gently, my heart breaking for her. "We'll get through this together, I promise."

She looked up at me, her eyes filled with pain and sorrow. "I don't know how," she said, her voice barely above a whisper. "I don't know how to live without him. He was my everything."

"I know," I said softly, feeling my own tears welling up. "But you're strong, Angela. You've been through so much in your life, and you've always come out the other side. You can do this. I will help you. Both of you."

She nodded, her body racked with sobs. "I just want him back," she cried out, her voice breaking. "I want my son back."

"I know," I said. "I know. And we'll do everything we can to make sure whoever did this pays for what they've done. I promise."

Her body was shaking with grief. "Thank you," she whispered, her voice hoarse. "Thank you for being here."

Peter's herculean frame was shaking with sobs, while Angela's soft body trembled. Peter was a big guy, but he seemed smaller somehow, frailer than I remembered him. I thought briefly about the last time I had seen the two of them. The things they had said to me, the things I had said back. I had honestly never thought I would see either of them again. I had told them I never wanted to. Not after what they did.

"Despite our differences, we're still family and we'll get through this," I said again firmly, looking from one to the other with conviction. It was all I could do in this moment. "We'll make sure justice is served."

Peter and Angela stared at me with eyes that were awash with pain and sorrow but held a tiny spark of hope.

My promise wasn't much, but it was all I had to give them.

TEN

BILLIE ANN

I made my way back to where I had left Tommy. He sat hunched on the park bench between his parents, who I had been told had arrived to pick him and Charlie up when they heard what had happened. Tears were still falling from his eyes and his face was white with shock. His mother had one arm wrapped around her son's shoulders while her other hand grasped tightly at his small one; his father glanced up at me from beneath furrowed brows, a storm of emotions building in his expression. Taking a deep breath to steady myself, I stepped forward into their circle.

"I know this is difficult, but I need to talk to Tommy about what he saw in the maze," I said, trying to sound as gentle as possible. Tommy had taken a liking to me, and now said he would only talk to me.

The father hesitated, his tired eyes scanning my face. He ran a hand through his disheveled hair and sighed.

"He's still in shock," he said finally. "Can it really not wait?"

I shook my head and tried to explain the importance of getting Tommy's testimony while it was still fresh in his memory. "I promise to be as quick as possible," I said.

Tommy's mother gave a subtle nod of permission, and I dropped to one knee so that I was level with the young boy.

"Hey, Tommy," I said. "I know this is really scary, but I need to ask you some questions about what happened in the maze. Can you tell me what you saw? I know you have probably told this before, but I want to hear it again, in case you remember something else. I need to know about everything you saw or heard because that might help us find out who did this."

Tommy sniffled and wiped his eyes with his sleeve. His eyes were red and puffy. In this moment I thought he was the bravest little boy I had ever met.

"M-my friend... Charlie... he was dead," he choked out. "On the ground. There was blood."

"And you walked into the maze together, right?"

"Y-yes. He was right behind me."

"Did anyone else walk in there with you? Did you see anyone following you?"

He shook his head and wiped his nose with his hand. "I don't think so. There were other people there, both in front of us and behind us, like groups of them. I couldn't see them, but I could hear them scream... you know for fun. Because of all the scares."

"So, no one was with you, like close to you when you were in the maze?"

"No, but when we went down the wrong direction, a group came toward us, yelling it was the wrong one, that it was a dead end, and we turned around. Charlie was right behind me then. That was the last time... the last time I..."

"That you saw him?" I asked.

He nodded, fresh tears spilling down his cheeks. "I took a turn and I think he went another way, I don't know, but I made it outside, and thought he would come out right after, but he didn't."

"So, you went back inside to look for him?"

"Y-yes. And that's where I found him. On the ground. People were stepping over him, like he was just a doll."

I closed my eyes briefly, thinking that had to be beyond traumatizing. I knew Tommy's life would never be the same again, and it made me so angry. "And then you carried him out?" I asked.

"Yes. I dragged him some of the way, across the ground because he was so heavy."

"I see. Did you see anyone in there who was acting suspicious?"

"What do you mean?"

"Like anyone who seemed weird or strange to you? Who was looking at you in an odd way? Anyone that scared you?"

"I was supposed to be scared."

"Yes, of course," I said. "But anyone that was different in any way?"

He looked at his fingers and shook his head. They still had blood on them from carrying Charlie. My heart broke for them both, and for my brother and his wife. I felt awful. This had to be the worst case I had ever been on. I feared it might destroy me.

"Okay, I think that's enough," his dad said. "He can't take any more of this."

"I understand," I said. "I'm so sorry, Tommy. I will do my best to get justice for Charlie, Okay?"

He lifted his gaze and his eyes met mine. "I made fun of him, you know?"

"What do you mean?"

"I told him he was a wimp, because he was so scared of going inside of the maze."

"I see," I said. "That must be really hard for you to think about now."

Tommy nodded sadly. "I didn't mean it. I didn't know he was going to... to—"

"It's not your fault," I said quickly, not wanting him to blame himself for something that definitely wasn't his fault. "You didn't know what was going to happen. No one did."

"But I could have been nicer to him," he said, tears welling up in his eyes again.

I patted his shoulder. "You're a good kid, Tommy. Don't blame yourself for something you couldn't have known."

Tommy nodded, still crying. I stood up and turned to his parents. "Thank you for letting me talk to him. I will make sure to keep you updated on the case."

The parents nodded, still looking at their son with heartache in their eyes. I walked away, feeling like I had just witnessed something too heartbreaking to put into words. The image of Tommy's tear-streaked face stayed with me long after I left the scene.

When I got home, I walked to my son Zack's room and stared at him for a long time in his sleep, beyond grateful that I had my son still here with me.

ELEVEN

Then

Betty woke up to the sound of the birds outside her window. She stretched her arms and legs and realized that she was not alone. Her husband was sleeping soundly beside her, his arm draped over her waist. She smiled, feeling incredibly happy and content.

She turned toward him and placed a soft kiss on his lips, causing him to stir awake.

He opened his eyes and smiled at her, "Good morning, my beautiful wife."

Betty felt her heart flutter at the sound of those words. She couldn't believe that she was finally married to the man of her dreams. She snuggled closer to him, "Good morning, my handsome husband."

He got up from the bed and disappeared into the kitchen. Betty heard the sound of sizzling bacon, and the aroma of freshly brewed coffee hit her nostrils. She smiled, knowing that he was making her breakfast in bed.

He came back to the bedroom carrying a tray full of food,

placing it carefully on the bed. She sat up and thanked him, taking in the sight of the delicious feast he had prepared for her. As she ate, he sat beside her, watching her enjoy every bite. They talked about their plans for the day, but Betty couldn't help but feel distracted by the way her husband looked at her. She knew that he wanted her, and the feeling was mutual.

After they finished eating, he leaned in for a kiss. It started off soft and sweet, but quickly turned into a passionate embrace. Betty felt her body responding to his touch, and soon they were making love on the bed.

As they lay there, spent and breathless, Betty felt tears of joy welling up. She couldn't believe that she was so lucky to have found someone who loved and cherished her so much. She knew that their love was meant to last a lifetime, and she was grateful for every moment they spent together.

They stayed in bed, wrapped in each other's arms, and Betty knew that she had found her forever home in her husband's love. The way he looked at her, the way he touched her, and the way he made her feel—it was all that she had ever wanted in life. She knew that nothing could ever compare to the love that they shared.

They lay there in silence, and Betty couldn't help but think about the future. She knew that there would be challenges and struggles, but she was ready to face them all with her husband by her side. She knew that they would conquer every obstacle together and come out stronger on the other side.

Finally, her husband broke the silence, "I love you, Betty. You make me the happiest man in the world."

Tears welled in Betty's eyes as she replied, "I love you too, more than anything in this world."

They held each other tightly, savoring the moment. Betty felt her heart fill with happiness, love, and contentment. She knew that this was just the beginning, but if the rest of it was half as good as right now, she was a lucky girl.

"What do you want to do today?" she asked. "It's the first day of our lives together."

He smiled and parted his lips to answer, when there was a knock on the door.

"Who can that be?" she asked, puzzled.

"I'll make them go away, whoever they are," he said and got dressed fast then rushed downstairs.

It is probably someone trying to sell us something or maybe Jehovah's Witnesses or something, she thought contentedly. She closed her eyes and lay back on the pillow, while hearing Travis opening the door downstairs. Voices emerged up the stairs, but she couldn't hear what was being said. It sounded for a minute like it was her sister, but it couldn't be. Her sister knew they were spending this time to themselves before they left for their honeymoon later tonight, and her mother came back home. Plus, she would have called first. No, it had to just be someone who sounded like her.

The voices rose in strength and it puzzled Betty. Was Travis yelling at whoever it was? They had to have been awful people then, because Travis never yelled. At least she hadn't heard him do so. The yelling grew louder, and at some point she was certain she heard her name being mentioned. Betty sat up in bed, feeling anxious. She wondered who could be at the door and why they were yelling her name. She quickly got dressed and made her way down the stairs.

As she reached the bottom of the stairs, Travis slammed the door shut and walked toward her. He looked at her startled, his nostrils still flaring.

"What are you doing up? Get back to bed. I wasn't done with you."

"Who was that? Who was at the door?"

He shook his head. "Oh, that? It was no one. Just someone trying to sell me a vacuum cleaner. I didn't pay attention."

Betty frowned.

"That didn't sound like a salesperson. What did they want?" she pressed, feeling a sense of unease.

Travis shrugged. "I don't know, it was just some crazy person, I guess. Don't worry about it, everything's okay now."

But Betty couldn't shake off the feeling that something was wrong. She felt a knot forming in her stomach and the hairs on her arms standing. "Why were you yelling?"

Travis sighed, his face contorting in anger. "It doesn't matter. Let's just forget about it and enjoy our day together."

But Betty couldn't shake off the feeling of unease. Something was off, and she knew it deep down in her gut. Yet she decided to forget it for now. This was, after all, their honeymoon and she wouldn't let something this silly ruin it.

TWELVE

BILLIE ANN

After leaving my son's room, I made my way down the stairs, my heart heavy with sorrow. I had called my parents from the scene, telling them what had happened to their grandchild. The news I had to deliver to my parents was not something any parent or grandparent should ever have to hear. I could hear in my mother's voice that she was crushed. They were still awake when I came home even if it was the early hours of the morning. As I stepped down into the living room, I saw my mother and father sitting on the couch, holding each other tightly. My mother's eyes were red and puffy, and tears streamed down her face. I tried to speak, but my voice failed.

I cleared my throat and tried again, barely able to whisper, "Mom? Dad?"

In their eyes was an expression of shared agony and grief that seemed to pass between them silently. Dad stood slowly and shuffled over to me with heavy steps. He drew me into a tight embrace, his shoulders shaking as he wept softly.

"What happened, sweetie?" he asked, his voice low and soothing. I had always been able to count on my dad in times of need. He was the rock of our family, and I was his only daughter. Seeing him this broken, made the realization sink in of what had happened, and I felt the shock rush through my body.

My nephew. Peter's son. Gone.

I inhaled deeply to steady myself before I spoke. The words left my lips in a quivering whisper. "So far, all we know is that they found him inside the tangled maze of the haunted trail by the jail."

My mother's sobs grew louder, and my dad tightened his grip on me, his own eyes welling up with tears.

"Why? How did it happen?" he asked, his voice choked with emotion.

I shook my head, feeling helpless. "I really don't know, Dad," I replied, my voice trembling. "The investigation is still ongoing, the forensic team was still working the scene when I left, and we're still interviewing everyone who was there and waiting to look at the evidence found. There were hundreds of people there, participating in the event, so it's quite the job. We're still hoping and praying we'll find the murder weapon, if the killer didn't take it with him." I paused, realizing by the look on my parents' faces that I had spoken too much. They didn't need details like that.

My mother wiped her tears away, her voice wavering as she spoke. "Was he alone? Did he suffer?"

My heart ached as I heard the pain in her voice. I had to protect her from the truth, but on the other hand I worried she might hear it later on. Maybe from a neighbor, a friend, or even on the news. Still, I couldn't get myself to tell her that the boy's throat was slit. I simply couldn't.

"We don't know for sure, Mom," I said softly. Then added, "But the paramedics said that he probably died instantly. He wouldn't have felt any pain."

My mother let out a sob, burying her face in her hands. My dad pulled me into another hug, and we sat there in silence, holding each other tightly. The weight of the tragedy was heavy on our shoulders, and the silence was thick with sorrow. It was a moment that I would never forget, and one that we would never be able to fully recover from.

I could tell that my parents were in shock, still trying to process the news. I reached out and took my mother's small hand, holding it tightly. It was important that we leaned on each other during this difficult time.

My voice wavered as I spoke, and salt-tinged tears rolled down my cheeks. I felt helpless as I looked at my mom and dad sitting next to me, their faces etched with worry and pain.

"I'm so sorry," I said again, wishing there was something more that I could do to make the situation better. I knew I shouldn't, but I felt guilty. Like I could have done more, like I could somehow have prevented this tragedy.

"God is punishing us," my mother said, shaking her head. "We have let our sheep stray."

She paused and gazed on me. My heart dropped. Did she mean me? Was she making this about me and my life?

"What are you talking about, Mom?"

She shook her head again, but the look in her eyes was still there. She continued. "But we must remember that he never puts more on us than he knows we can bear. We must be strong. For when I am weak, he is strong."

My dad rose to his feet, then walked to the window and looked out into the darkness. He rubbed his forehead, then turned to look at me, his eyes filled with deep pain. "Your mother is right. This is a test of our faith. We cannot let this break us and cause us to doubt him. God is with us in our pain. But we must act. Billie Ann, you can make this right. You have to do everything you can, do you hear me? For your brother's sake. We will look after the children as much as needed."

My mom stood. "I'm gonna call our prayer circle. Ask them to pray for us—and for you, Billie Ann."

A wrinkle grew between my eyes. "Why me?"

"For you to find your way back to us," she said. "And to God. We need to think of your children too and what kind of example you're setting for them."

I sighed. I knew they were upset, but I had to defend myself. "God and I are perfectly fine. And so are my children," I said.

My dad took over, trying to smooth things out. "We will ask them to pray for you to solve this for us, for Peter."

I nodded, feeling the weight of the task. I had promised them I would find out who murdered my nephew, and I was going to live up to that promise, no matter how I felt about my parents and my family right now.

As we sat there, for a long time in silence, I couldn't help but think about Peter and Angela. They had lost a child, and nothing would ever be the same for them. My heart felt heavy with sorrow for them.

We would never forget the tragedy that had struck us, but we would find the strength to move forward one day at a time. We simply had to. And I would have to step up my game and be the one to bring them closure. It was a lot that rested on my shoulders, and I just hoped that I could live up to it.

THIRTEEN

ANDY

Andy lay in the dirty alley, his body convulsing with withdrawal symptoms. He had been on a bender for days and now he had no money left to buy his next hit. His mind raced as he thought of all the ways he could get his hands on some drugs. He could feel the cold pavement beneath him. His head was spinning and his body ached. He couldn't remember the last time he'd slept or eaten properly. All he could think about was the burning desire for his next hit. He tried to get up, but his limbs were heavy and uncooperative. Yet somehow, he managed to stand up. He stumbled forward, his feet tripping over each other as he looked for anyone who could give him what he needed. His mind was hazy, and his vision was blurry, his eyes bloodshot and his movements unsteady. He desperately needed his fix, and he knew that his only chance was to beg on the street. He spotted a group of people huddled together in an alleyway and he stumbled toward them.

"Hey, you guys got anything?" he slurred, his voice barely audible. He swayed on his feet as he moved toward them, his mouth dry and his voice hoarse as he begged them. "Help a fellow out? Please?"

The group looked at him with disgust and one of them stepped forward. "We don't have anything for you, junkie," he spat, kicking Andy to the ground.

Andy groaned in pain, clutching his stomach as another guy stepped forward, and he kicked him again. More kicks fell on him as they all joined in, laughing and calling him names, and Andy cried out in agony. He curled up in a ball, trying to protect himself as best he could. But the blows kept raining down on him, leaving him bruised and battered. He begged them to stop, but they paid no heed. Andy couldn't get up; he just took the beating, feeling helpless and alone. He didn't know how much longer he could take this. The pain was too much to bear, and the constant rejection was taking its toll. He wanted to scream out, to let everyone know how much they were hurting him, but his voice couldn't find the strength to do so.

Finally, they grew bored of torturing him and left him lying there in the dirt. Andy stayed on the ground, writhing in pain, his body racked with withdrawal symptoms. He lay there for what seemed like an eternity, the searing pain in his body making it hard to move. He knew he needed help, but he was too ashamed to ask for it. He couldn't bear the thought of anyone seeing him like this.

As the sun began to set and the alleyway grew darker, Andy's mind began to play tricks on him. He saw things that weren't there, heard voices that were just a figment of his imagination. He was losing his grip on reality and there was nothing he could do to stop it.

He crawled along the ground, his hands and knees leaving a dusty trail in their wake. He reached the dumpster, peering into its dark depths. His eyes were desperate and hungry as they swept over the contents: broken glass, rotting food scraps, empty beer cans... and there! A small corner of a plastic bag sticking out from underneath an old piece of cardboard. Andy grabbed it with trembling fingers, hoping against hope that it contained what he was searching for. But all that filled his palm were a few used cigarette butts. His jaw clenched in anguish, and he hurled the bag away from him, screaming out his frustration at the sky.

As he sat there, defeated, a woman approached him. She had long, dark hair and wore a tight dress that hugged her curves. Andy looked up at her with bleary eyes, his mind cloudy from withdrawal.

"You look like you could use a little help," she said, a sly smile on her face.

Andy didn't trust her, but his body craved the drugs too much to care. "What kind of help?" he asked, his voice barely audible.

"I have what you need," the woman replied, pulling out a small plastic baggie filled with white powder. "But it's not free."

Andy searched his pockets frantically, but he knew he had no money. "I don't have anything," he said, his voice desperate.

The woman leaned down, her face inches from his. "I'm sure we can come up with a way for you to pay me back," she whispered, her hand trailing down his chest.

Andy knew what she was suggesting, but he was too weak to resist. He took the baggie of drugs from her, his hands shaking with anticipation as he emptied the contents onto his hand. He snorted the powder quickly, feeling the high wash over him like a wave.

The woman watched him with a satisfied smirk on her face. "There's more of it if you follow me."

Andy stumbled to his feet, his mind already hazy from the drugs. He followed the woman down the alleyway, his steps unsteady and his heart racing with excitement. The woman opened a door to a dingy apartment, and Andy followed her inside.

The room was dimly lit, and Andy could barely make out the furniture. He saw a couch in the corner and a mattress on the floor. The woman sat on the couch and patted the space next to her. Andy stumbled over and sat down, feeling the drugs taking over his body.

The woman leaned in close, running her fingers through Andy's hair. "You're a good boy," she whispered, her lips brushing against his ear. "And you're going to make me a lot of money."

Andy's heart sank as he wondered what she meant. Just then the door opened and a dark figure entered. The woman got up, and she approached the figure, who was holding a bundle of hundred-dollar bills, and she grabbed it.

"He's all yours," she said, then blew him a kiss. "Bye, handsome."

FOURTEEN

BILLIE ANN

As I walked through the doors of the police station, the weight of the world was on my shoulders. I paused at the entrance of the conference room for a brief second, before walking in. The team was seated at the long table, all eyes on Chief Becky Harold as she paced the length of the room, her voice like a bell ringing through the air. Big Tom and Scott made space for me to sit between them. The conference room buzzed with an air of anticipation, as if each person present held their breath, waiting for the crucial moment to strike. Big Tom, Scott, and I sat at the forefront. Their eyes were sharp and focused. They were both dressed in impeccable suit jackets and jeans, exuding authority; they commanded respect from everyone in the room. But this investigation was too complex for just two detectives; other experts had been summoned to lend their expertise.

A forensic scientist that I had worked with before, named Dr. Martinez, stood beside a whiteboard covered in intricate diagrams and formulas. With an intense gaze hidden behind wire-rimmed glasses, she had meticulously analyzed every piece of evidence collected from the crime scene by the jail; she had fixed pictures up on the board for us to look at. Her attention to detail was unparalleled, and I felt good that she was on the case with us.

Next to her stood a profiler named Agent Thompson. Clad in a tailored black suit, he exuded a calm confidence that matched his reputation as one of the best in the field. He surveyed the room, studying each person's reaction and body language, as was his annoying habit. You always felt like he was analyzing you, and for that reason I always refrained from talking about my personal life to him. He was, however, a good addition to our team, and I was pleased to see that Harold had created a strong group.

"The victim was a ten-year-old boy," Chief Harold said, her voice laced with sadness. "He had his throat slit, and that was the cause of death. We found no DNA on him, which means that we have no leads as of yet."

My stomach dropped like a stone, but I needed to focus on finding answers, not succumbing to emotions. I refused to. I simply refused to.

Chief Harold turned to me. "I'm sorry for your loss," she said, her voice softening. "Your nephew didn't deserve this."

I nodded, feeling tears prick at the corners of my eyes. "Thank you, Chief. I appreciate your sympathy."

"But this also means you're off the case," she added, making sure the other officers in the room could hear her. "I'm placing Tom in charge."

I sighed, annoyed, even if I knew it was coming.

She gave me a small smile before continuing. She was letting me in the room, at least. I was allowed access to the case, if not control of it, and I was grateful to the Chief for that.

"We've been combing through the area where your nephew was found, but there's no sign of any other physical evidence. Hundreds of people walked through the trail just last night, and so far, no one has any account of seeing Charlie or anything suspicious happening to him or in the lead-up to his death. Most of the maze-goers were children—there's no one with a connection to Charlie either."

I furrowed my brow. I knew I wasn't supposed to take part in the investigation anymore, but how was I supposed to just stay away? I knew I wouldn't be able to and was going to help out in any way I could, even if it was from the sidelines.

"There has to be something," I said. "If there were hundreds of people going through that maze, then someone must have seen something. Anything."

Tom nodded. "They did find some fiber evidence underneath Charlie's fingernails. It's a small lead, but it's something. The lab is analyzing it and hopefully we'll get the results soon. It might give us something."

"Now the media is all over this story," the Chief continued. "They're already calling from everywhere to get statements. I will hold a press conference later today, hopefully with news. But don't say anything to anyone. I will handle the press. We need to make sure this doesn't get out of hand. It's reaching national headlines as we speak. A young boy brutally murdered in a haunted trail by the jail, in front of the entire sheriff's department. It's not good, people. This doesn't make us look good."

I nodded solemnly in agreement at the Chief's words, aware of how serious it was. I had seen firsthand how quickly news like this could spread and cause chaos.

The meeting continued on, but my mind was spinning with questions. Who could have done something so heinous to an innocent child? Was the attack random, or was this someone Charlie knew? Suddenly I felt guilty that I didn't know more about my own nephew.

Chief Harold gave me a nod of approval before dismissing the meeting. I lingered behind, lost in thought as I tried to piece together the fragments of information I had. I couldn't let my nephew's killer get away with this. I needed to find them, for my family's sake. I had promised them this.

Big Tom came and sat by me, then placed a warm hand on my shoulder. "I know this can't be easy for you, Billie Ann. But there's something I need to show you. You're not gonna like it."

I looked up at him. "What is it?"

Big Tom opened the file and pulled out a glossy photograph of a long, curved blade. He placed it on the table in front of me and said, "We just heard from the lab. This is the murder weapon. The knife that was found at the scene with your nephew's blood on it."

"Okay? I already know this. I saw it on the board when Martinez went through it. What about it?"

He sighed. "We believe it belongs to your brother. Peter Wilde."

My eyes grew wide. "How do you know?"

"We found fingerprints on the handle of the knife. And some belonged to your brother," he said, his voice heavy with sadness. "I'm sorry."

I felt as if the air had been knocked out of me. A chill ran through my body, and I had to say it out loud. "My brother?" My voice was barely a whisper as I looked around the room, trying to deny what I had just heard. My own brother was now our lead suspect?

Big Tom put a comforting arm around my shoulders. "We'll get to the bottom of this, Billie Ann. We'll find out what happened. For now, we need to bring your brother in for questioning."

I nodded, feeling numb and in shock. "Okay," was all I could manage to say as we made our way out of the conference room. They needed to interview Charlie's parents anyway, to find out more about Charlie: whom he hung out with and what he was doing in the days leading up to his death, but now this.

I didn't know what to believe anymore. My world had been

turned upside down, and I didn't know how to make sense of it all. My brother wasn't a very nice person and I had never liked him much. We had our differences and always had. And he wasn't going to take kindly to the questions they were going to have to ask.

FIFTEEN

Then

Betty hummed a cheerful tune as she knelt on the bedroom floor, sorting through the rumpled pile of laundry from her honeymoon with Travis. She ran her fingers over the soft fabric of his Hawaiian shirt and smiled dreamily at the memories it evoked: gentle waves lapping against white sandy beaches, crystal-clear water glimmering in the bright sunshine, romantic strolls along moonlit pathways. It had been absolutely perfect.

She lifted a pair of Travis' shorts, held them to her face, and breathed deeply. Saltwater and sunscreen from their beach days still clung to the fabric. She smiled at the memories: the way his tan lines contrasted against her pale skin, the sound of waves crashing as they sipped fruity cocktails in plastic cups, the way he laughed when she tried on ridiculous hats in a tourist shop. For that week, they were free from deadlines and bills and responsibilities. It had been the perfect escape from reality.

Betty's gaze focused out the window, her thoughts drifting across the small town to where Travis was now. At the police station. She remembered his excitement when he got promoted to detective right before they married, and how proud she was of him. But of course, it also brought her worries. It wasn't a very safe job. Every day was a possibility that something might happen to him. Something awful. She had to get used to that. She wished there was a way for her to see what he was doing and know that he was still okay. The sound of his keys jangling in the door at the end of the day would be like a beacon of light, telling her that he had made it through another shift safe and sound.

"You'll get used to it," he had told her with a kiss when she had voiced her concerns over breakfast. But she failed to see how you could ever get used to anything like that. It didn't seem possible. Was she always going to have this gnawing sensation of fear in the bottom of her stomach? Would it ever go away?

She didn't like to think of him out there chasing criminals, risking his life for people's safety. Instead, she preferred to go back to thinking of their honeymoon.

Betty felt a warmth spread throughout her body as the memories of their honeymoon flooded back. She remembered how Travis had held her hand tightly, not wanting to let go even when they were strolling along the beach. And the kisses they had shared in secluded spots while nightfall blanketed them with soft starlight—those moments would be forever engrained in Betty's heart. Tears of joy sprang from her eyes as she realized what immense love and kindness she had found in Travis.

As she continued to fold laundry, Betty couldn't help but hum a tune. She felt so content and happy and couldn't wait to start their lives together as a married couple. She knew there would be ups and downs, but she was ready to face them all, as long as she had Travis by her side.

Suddenly, there was a knock on the door. Could it be Travis? Betty ran to the door and opened it. But of course, it wasn't Travis. It was her younger sister, Laura.

"Oh, Laura, I'm so glad to see you!" Betty exclaimed,

welcoming her in. "Travis is at work, but he'll be home soon. Would you like to come in for some iced tea?"

Laura paused on the front stoop of the house, and she took a deep breath before entering.

Betty watched her worriedly and closed the door behind her. As soon as they entered the cozy kitchen, Betty filled two glasses with iced tea and gestured for Laura to sit down at the table. Taking a seat beside her, Betty studied Laura's face and said softly, "What is it, sweetheart? I can tell something is wrong."

Laura methodically stirred her tea, her spoon clinking against the sides of the glass. She met Betty's eyes and sighed. They hadn't seen or spoken to each other since the wedding, which was almost a month ago. It was highly unusual for them to not speak for this long. They would at least check in once or twice a week. But Betty had been busy, so she didn't think much of it.

"Betty, I need to talk to you," she said softly.

Betty's heart sank as a feeling of dread came over her. She pushed a strand of hair behind her ear and quietly asked, "What's going on, Laura? Is it Mom?"

It was natural for her to think about her right away, since she had been sick with cancer in the throat a few years ago, but the doctors said they had removed it all. There was still the chance it could come back.

She clamped her lips tight, shook her head slowly, and the movement seemed to be weighed down by such a heavy silence that Betty felt her chest tighten.

"No," Laura said softly. "She's okay."

Betty's eyes widened as a lump formed in her throat. "What is it then?"

Laura's eyes were brimming with tears, her lower lip trembling. She reached for Betty's hand and gave it a gentle squeeze before shaking her head again.

The look of worry and fear in her eyes caused Betty's heart to sink like a stone. Betty tilted her head, brow furrowed in confusion. "Just tell me. What's wrong?" she asked, her voice barely above a whisper.

Laura's gaze fixed on the floor as she drew in a deep breath.

"It's about Travis," she said quietly.

Betty's hands trembled and her heart pounded in her chest as she waited for Laura's answer. She could barely force the words out of her mouth.

"What about Travis?" she asked, her voice quavering.

Laura hesitated for a moment, not wanting to tell her sister the news. She took a deep breath before finally speaking. "Betty, I don't know how to say this."

"Just say it," Betty pleaded, fear coursing through her veins. "Please. Just tell me what happened."

SIXTEEN

BILLIE ANN

I watched on as my colleagues Tom and Scott questioned my brother on the other side of the glass. The Chief had told me I could follow the investigation from a distance, and she would make sure to keep me updated ad hoc, but I couldn't interfere and definitely not interview my own brother. I had naturally complained and told her I knew my brother better than anyone and would know if he was lying and could make him talk, but she wouldn't hear of it. So, instead I watched while Tom and Scott did the job. It made me feel frustrated, overwhelmingly so. My brother looked tired and defeated, with sweat beading on his forehead from his thick dark hair, so much like Charlie's. His son had become his spitting image over the years. I could tell the interrogation was taking a toll on him. At least I could hear what was going on. I couldn't intervene, but I'd trained Tom and Scott myself.

The room was small and plain, with a single table in the center and four chairs surrounding it. My brother sat in one of the chairs, while the detectives sat across from him, their eyes fixed on him.

"Can you explain to us why your fingerprints were found on this knife?" Tom asked, his voice stern.

My brother looked at the photo, recognition flickering in his eyes. "That's mine," he confirmed.

"It's the weapon that was used to kill Charlie," Tom replied, hoping to get a reaction.

My brother looked alarmed.

"When did you last see it?"

"I don't know," he said, his voice barely a whisper. "I just don't know how it ended up there in the haunted trail."

"Are you suggesting that someone else may have used the knife?" Tom pressed.

"I don't know," my brother repeated. "All I know is that my son is gone. Dead."

"Where did you keep the knife? Did your son, or anyone else, have access to it?"

"In a drawer at home... It's not something we have out. He wouldn't have used it."

"And when was the last time you saw it?" Tom and Scott exchanged a knowing look, their suspicions clearly not dispelled.

"I don't know," my brother pleaded. He seemed panicked. Chief Harold was with me and stood close to me while we watched them.

I shook my head. "I should be in there."

"It's a conflict of interest," she said.

"I don't care," I shot back.

Tom and Scott both leaned forward, their eyes locked on my brother's face. "What do you mean, you don't know?" Tom snapped. "Your fingerprints were on the knife that killed your son. You're lying to us."

"I'm not lying!" my brother shouted suddenly, his voice echoing in the small room.

"Come on, man," Tom said, his voice low and urgent. "You gotta tell us the truth."

Then he placed a photo of Charlie from the murder scene, bloody, and his throat slit open.

That broke my brother. He clasped his mouth and started sobbing. A small shriek left his mouth as he stared at the picture of his dead son.

"They shouldn't do that," I said to the Chief. "It will break him. It would be impossible for anyone in that situation to think rationally."

My brother's eyes darted back and forth between the two detectives, the sweat on his forehead increasing. He seemed to be struggling with something deep inside him.

"He sometimes made you mad, didn't he?" Tom suggested.

My brother looked up, and I could see Tom notice he'd hit a nerve.

"Kids can be difficult, and it's your right as a parent to discipline him."

My brother nodded.

"Have you ever punished Charlie for his behavior?" Tom said.

"Yes... In the past. When he's done something wrong," my brother admitted. "He's always acted out."

"We found old bruises on Charlie's left arm. Marks. The remains of a good beating. Was that you, or your wife?"

"Me... don't bring her into this," my brother exclaimed. He was fiercely protective of his wife, I knew that. But I was shocked to hear him confess to beating Charlie.

"And this time you took it too far—"

"No," my brother interrupted.

But Tom kept going. "I put it to you that you followed him that night. Looked for the chance to really teach him a lesson."

My brother looked uncomfortable shifting in his seat.

"Or again, your wife—"

"I did it!" he suddenly screamed, breaking Tom's speech. His voice echoed off the walls of the small room. "I killed my own son!"

Then as if he thought they hadn't heard him the first time, he repeated it over and over again.

"I did it, okay? I killed him! I killed my own son."

Tom and Scott looked shocked, as did I and Chief Harold. I couldn't believe my brother would say something like that. And I most certainly didn't believe him. It was just not possible. I wanted to run to him, to tell him to stop, but I was powerless to move. I wondered what he had been through in the last few years. I didn't know much about my brother's life now. Was he well? Was he struggling? Was his mind clear? My head kept spinning with this new development. I didn't know what to think all of a sudden. All I knew was that something was wrong about this.

"Why?" Scott asked, his voice full of incredulity.

"I don't know," Peter replied, his voice shaking. "I just... I lost control. He was always so difficult, always pushing my buttons. And that day... I don't know, I just snapped."

Tom and Scott exchanged a look. I wondered if they believed him. They seemed just as shocked by his proclamation.

I couldn't bear to watch anymore and turned away from the glass. Chief Harold followed me, her hand resting on my shoulder.

"I'm sorry," she said softly. "I know this is hard for you."

I shook my head, tears stinging my eyes. "I can't believe it," I whispered. "I can't believe my own brother could do something like that."

"I know," she replied. "But we will have to arrest him now. That's a confession with a motive."

There was a moment of stunned silence, broken only by the

sound of my brother's ragged breathing. Tom and Scott exchanged a look, then Tom reached forward to switch off the recording device.

"You're under arrest," he said quietly. "You have the right to remain silent and to an attorney. Anything you say can and will be used against you in a court of law."

Peter didn't react, didn't move as they handcuffed him and led him out of the room.

I felt numb, as if my mind had shut down completely. I wanted to scream. I wanted to yell. But most of all, I wanted to find out the truth. I refused to accept this as being it. Had my brother done this? To his own son? I couldn't believe it. I couldn't just stand there and watch as Peter was taken away. I couldn't get this confession to add up with how he had acted at the Haunted Jail Trail the night before. Why had he been so adamant about me finding the killer? That was not the behavior of someone about to confess. Had he spoken to someone since? What had he realized in the time since I last saw him?

I turned to Chief Harold, my eyes pleading with her. "I need to talk to him," I said, my voice hoarse. "Please, let me talk to him."

She hesitated for a moment, looking deep into my eyes, then nodded. Something in her eyes made me think she wasn't so sure about this confession either. "Okay," she said. "But you have to promise me that you won't interfere with the investigation. We need to follow the proper procedures, and anything you say might compromise the case."

"I understand," I replied, my heart racing. "I just need to talk to him. Please."

She sighed heavily, then nodded again. "All right," she said. "I'll arrange for you to visit him in the holding cell, but you have to stay within the guidelines. No leading questions, no coercion, no tampering with the evidence. It's reason for firing you if I catch you. Agreed?"

"Agreed," I said, nodding eagerly.

Chief Harold left to make arrangements, and I stood alone in the small room, my mind racing with questions and doubts. A sense of dread was washing over me, along with the feeling that time was running out.

SEVENTEEN

ANDY

Andy's eyes fluttered open, but he couldn't see a thing. Panic set in and his heart raced as he tried to remember the events leading up to this moment. The last thing he remembered was the woman he met and the drugs she gave him. But there was a man, and then everything went black.

He groaned as he sat up. He tried to feel for anything in the darkness. His hands touched cold, rough walls, and he tried to follow them to find a door, but his movements were restricted, his legs weak and he had to fall to his knees. He sat in silence for a moment, taking deep breaths to steady himself.

"How did I get here?" he muttered to himself before he scrambled to his feet and stumbled forward till he hit the door. He tried to pull it, but there was no handle. Then he pounded on it with all his might. His fists ached, and his voice grew hoarse as he screamed for help, but still there was no response.

The longer he stood there in the darkness, the more his mind raced with possibilities. Was he kidnapped? Was he going to be held hostage? Was this some kind of sick game? The thought led him to pound on the door once more in panic.

"Is anyone out there? Help me!"

He screamed but no one answered. As Andy pounded on the door, the sound reverberated through the small, dark room, filling it with a deafening echo. He stopped, listening closely for any sign of life beyond the door, but there was only silence.

He tried to calm himself down, taking a deep breath and focusing on his surroundings. The air was thick and musty, like it hadn't been ventilated in weeks. He could barely see anything, but he could make out the form of a small worn-out mattress on the floor in the corner of the room. Clearly, whoever had put him here had no intention of making him comfortable.

Andy shook his head, trying to clear the fog that clouded his thoughts. He needed to remember what had happened, how he had ended up in this nightmare. He remembered the woman, her seductive smile, and the way she had slipped him the bag of drugs. She had taken him somewhere, he recalled. Then there was a man, a shadowy figure who had appeared out of nowhere and led him away. At least he thought it was a man. He didn't remember a face. Andy slumped back against the wall, feeling defeated and helpless. He was trapped in this dark room with no idea where he was or who had put him here.

As his eyes slowly adjusted to the darkness, Andy realized that there was a faint light coming from underneath the door. He crawled toward it and pressed his ear against the rough surface. He could hear muffled sounds of people talking and laughing, but he couldn't make out any words. But someone was out there. Or was it a TV? There had to be someone out there. Someone who had to know he was in here? Who must have heard him pound on the door? And done nothing?

"HELP!" he tried again, even if he knew it was in vain. If someone wanted to help him, they would have done so by now. Crying, he slumped to the cold floor, landing on his knees.

He closed his eyes and tried to recall anything else that could be of use. But no matter how hard he tried, he couldn't remember anything more. It was as if a part of his memory was wiped out, leaving him with only fragments of the night's events.

The darkness was suffocating, and Andy felt like the walls were closing in on him. He needed to get out of there, to escape this hellhole before it was too late. He pounded on the door again, but his fists were weak now, and the pounding sounded more like a soft tapping.

Suddenly, he heard footsteps outside the door, and his heart began to race. Was someone finally coming to rescue him? The footsteps grew louder, and he heard the sound of keys jingling. A bolt was unlocked, and the door creaked open.

Blinding light flooded the room, and Andy had to squint his eyes to adjust to the sudden change, and once he did, he saw someone standing there, the figure nothing but a shadow due to the strong lights behind him.

"W-who are you?" he said, squinting his eyes.

The shadow didn't answer, and instead, pulled out a pack of cigarettes and lit one up, taking a long drag before they finally spoke.

"You don't need to know who I am," he said, his voice low and gravelly. "All you need to know is that you're here and I am holding your life in my hands."

"What does that mean?"

The man bent forward and put his head close to Andy's ear, his breath hot against his skin. He was wearing a white distorted mask, Andy now realized, so he couldn't see his face.

"It means," he whispered, "that you do what I say, and maybe you'll get to live another day."

Fear gripped Andy's heart.

"Please... let me go," he pleaded. "I don't know what you want from me, but I swear, I'll do anything you ask."

The masked person chuckled, taking another drag from his cigarette before blowing out a cloud of smoke.

"Anything, huh? Well, we'll see about that."

EIGHTEEN

BILLIE ANN

Chief Harold's quick footsteps echoed down the corridor, and I followed a few steps behind. As we approached the holding cell area, I could see Peter through the bars of the small cell. His head rested in his hands, but our eyes locked for a moment before he quickly averted them.

I squared my shoulders. "Can I talk to him alone?"

After a moment's hesitation, Chief Harold nodded reluctantly. I knew she had a brother who was in prison for sexual assault, which he claimed to not have committed. I think she understood my situation better than most in this moment.

"All right. But remember what I said. Don't do anything that could compromise the investigation. If anyone asks, I will deny that I let you do this, understood?"

I nodded and stepped forward into the cell. I glared up at the camera in the corner, knowing this would be recorded. But I had nothing to hide.

"Why did you do it?" I asked, standing in front of him.

He bowed his head and a single tear rolled down his cheek. In a low whisper he said, "I can't explain it. An uncontrollable urge filled me, like something else was in control."

My heart sank and I sat down next to him on the bench, struggling to keep my own emotions at bay. I shook my head. "That's not what I meant."

He looked up with confusion. "What did you mean?"

I leaned forward, pushing my face close to his. "Why did you confess?"

His slumped shoulders barely moved as he spoke, voice quivering with emotion. "What does it matter? My son is gone."

I shook my head. "I'm not buying it."

"Face it, Billie Ann. The knife is mine. It used to hang on the wall of my living room. My wife will tell you so. My fingerprints were on it. I'm guilty."

He sighed deeply, rubbing the lines on his forehead as if he was trying to wipe away the memories, but nothing could do that. He looked me in the eye and pleaded. "I did it. Just live with it."

My brow furrowed as I studied him, my confusion becoming concern.

"This isn't like you," I said softly. "I might not agree with you on a lot of things."

I paused, remembering the arguments we used to have about politics, the things he used to say and the way I knew that would have shaped who he was as a father. "But one thing I do know about you is that you're always looking out for everyone else, shouldering the burden of responsibility—especially when it comes to your wife. She's counting on you right now."

He sighed, his shoulders slumping even farther, and he ran a hand through his hair before looking away. His gaze seemed unfocused, distant.

"Are you protecting her?"

"No," he said quickly. "I don't know what to do," he admitted in a worn voice. "It's like everything just feels... wrong somehow."

I reached out and my fingers brushed his cold, clammy

hand. He pulled back at first, but then allowed me to take hold. I searched his face for some hint of innocence, but all I could see was guilt and shame.

"I know you didn't do this," I said, trying to convince him as much as reassure him. "I'll find out the truth. Somehow."

He looked up at me then, and in his eyes, I saw a pool of despair.

"I'm sorry," he said, his voice thick with emotion. "But I am guilty, and there's nothing you can do about it. This is how it has to be. I lived a full life."

My grip on his clammy hand tightened as tears pooled in my eyes. I stared into his sullen face, trying to muster some hope that the man sitting before me was still my brother—the one who had taught me how to ride a bike, to shoot a gun, and to stand up for myself in the face of bullies. The gravity of this situation felt like a boulder pressing down on my chest. With a determined voice, I said, "I won't give up on you. I don't care what anyone else says. Just tell me the truth, and I promise I'll do everything in my power to help you."

He stayed silent for a long moment, his eyes flickering warily between mine. His thick chest rose and fell as he released a heavy sigh. "But you don't even like me. We haven't talked in years, Billie Ann."

I pushed away the heaviness that had settled over me and looked him straight in the eye. "That doesn't mean I don't care about you, or Charlie. I might not agree with the way you discipline your children, but that doesn't mean you're a killer."

He rolled his eyes and shook his head, disbelief written all over his face. "You're being ridiculous," he scoffed, his lips forming a tight line as his brow furrowed together in annoyance. "Just let it go, okay?"

"That's not an option. Not for me," I said firmly, my jaw set with determination.

He laughed dryly, crossing his arms over his chest. "What's the point?" he asked, the sarcasm evident in his voice.

"You are the point. Your family. You have another son, remember? I know Jimmy's been estranged for some time, and you never did tell me why, but he is still your child, even if he is an adult. Mom and Dad will be crushed over this as well. Did you think about that?"

He scoffed again. "Mom and Dad. They never talk to me either."

"But they talk to Jimmy. I know that much. And they loved Charlie."

He hid his face in his hands. "I don't care anymore. Just leave me alone. Please."

I could see the pain and guilt in his eyes. "Please, just tell me the truth," I pleaded with him. I looked at him, deep worry in my eyes. I was trying so hard to find my brother in there, behind all this nonsense. But I couldn't see him. "I want to help you," I said gently. "But you have to tell me what happened. No more lies, no more secrets."

His body tensed and his hands balled into fists as he glared at me. He growled through gritted teeth, "Just leave me alone, Billie Ann!"

I took a deep breath and placed my hand on his shoulder, squeezing it tightly. "If you don't want to tell me, then that's okay. But know that I'll never give up on you. You're my brother, and I love you. And I know deep down that you love me too."

He let out a small whimper before standing up and walking to the back of the cell, his face twisted in pain. "Go home, Billie Ann," he muttered, his voice barely audible. "Just go home."

I watched as he disappeared into the shadows, wondering if I had lost him for good. Then I turned around and left, pressing back my tears.

NINETEEN

Then

"What happened to Travis? Tell me what happened, Laura."

Betty stared at her sister sitting across the table from her. She was still stirring the iced tea, the sound of the spoon hitting the sides, annoying Betty immensely.

"Laura!"

She cleared her throat and looked at her fingers. "It... it happened on the night you were married."

Betty looked at her, puzzled. "On our wedding night? What are you talking about?"

"I was in the bathroom, inside of the house, and he... Travis and one of his friends, or colleagues, I don't know, they stood outside of the door as I opened it. They had been drinking, it was obvious, but..."

She paused and looked briefly at her sister, then back down at her fingers.

"But what, Laura?" Betty asked. "Why were they outside the door? Did they make fun of you? They can be a rowdy bunch from time to time."

She shook her head, a tear escaping her eye. "N-no, that's not what happened."

"Then what did? Tell me, Laura."

"They... they forced themselves on me, Betty. Both of them." Laura's voice quivered as she spoke, and the spoon in her hand clattered against the side of the glass. She closed her eyes for a brief moment taking in a deep breath to steady herself. A tear escaped the corner of her eyes, and her face cracked as she gave in to the rest of them. Tears rolling down her cheeks, she continued, without looking directly at her sister. "I-I tried so hard... to fight them off, but they were too strong. I told them to stop, but they didn't listen."

Betty sat frozen, her mind struggling to process what she had just heard.

Laura looked up at her, her eyes filled with tears. "I was scared, Betty. I didn't know what to do. And then Travis told me not to tell anyone. He said it would destroy you and he would deny it. No one would believe my word over two cops," she said, her voice barely above a whisper. "I came here the next day, to talk to you, but he wouldn't let me in."

Betty's heart sank as she realized the magnitude of what her sister was saying. But then she thought about her husband. His kind face, his soft hands, his smile. She thought about all of the people he had helped over the years. The people they passed who thanked him for his protection. He could never do something like this. But Laura. Perhaps Laura was struggling. Perhaps she was jealous.

"Oh, Laura. You always had such a good imagination. Tell me, had you been drinking, huh?"

Laura's face fell. "What? No, I wasn't drunk. Betty, I'm serious. This really happened."

Betty waved her hand dismissively. "Travis would never do something like that."

"What? Betty, I'm not lying. Please, believe me."

But Betty wasn't listening. She looked at Laura for a moment with sadness in her eyes, and then her face changed. "You always were the drama queen, Laura. Making up stories to get attention. And now, on my wedding night no less? Who do you think you are, trying to ruin everything like this?"

Laura's eyes welled up. "I wasn't imagining anything, Betty. I didn't make it up. It really happened. I thought about simply not telling you, but how could I live with myself if I didn't?"

Betty's expression turned from one of disbelief to anger. "How dare you accuse my husband of something like that? He would never do anything like that. You're just jealous because I have a happy marriage and you don't."

Laura shook her head, standing up from the table. "I knew you wouldn't believe me. But it happened, Betty. And I can't keep it inside anymore."

Betty stood up as well, towering over her sister. "You need to leave, Laura. I never want to see you again."

Laura nodded, a tear falling down her face. "If that's how you wish it to be, then I can't stop you."

"And don't you dare tell anyone else those lies of yours; do you hear me?"

"They're not lies!"

Laura tried to protest, but Betty cut her off. "I don't want to hear it. Get out of my house, and don't you dare come back until you can tell me the truth."

As Laura stumbled out of the house, Betty's mind was made up. She would never believe such a ridiculous story, especially not one about the happiest night of her life. She couldn't let anything ruin that. And as for Laura, well, she didn't need her anymore.

TWENTY

BILLIE ANN

As I sat on the porch, staring out into the dark abyss, I couldn't help but feel a wave of sadness wash over me. The day had been long and tiresome, and all I wanted was to cuddle up with my kids and pretend that none of this had even happened. Instead, I settled for a glass of chardonnay as I tried to figure out how to convince Tom and Scott to let me into the case. I took a sip of the chilled wine, watching the amber liquid swirl around in the glass. The warmth of the day lingered in the air, but the sun had finally set, bringing with it a cooler breeze. I sat alone on the porch, listening to the crickets chirp and the rustling of leaves in the palm trees.

The pizza box sat empty on the table beside me, the only remnants of dinner with my children. I had ordered a pizza for myself and the kids, but even their beautiful faces and uplifting voices couldn't lift my spirits. The kids had gone off to their rooms hours ago, and I needed to figure out my next steps.

I took another sip of my wine, feeling the coolness of the glass against my lips. The bitterness of the chardonnay hit my tongue and I savored the taste. But even the wine couldn't ease the pain that twisted my heart. It had been a rough day at work, to say the least, and I couldn't shake off my concerns for my brother.

As I took another sip of wine, a car pulled up in the driveway. I sighed, hoping it wasn't another problem I had to deal with. However, my worries faded away as I saw Danni get out and walk toward me. She strode up to the porch with a confident grace, her long dark hair trailing behind her. She was wearing tight-fitting jeans and a low-cut top that accentuated her beautiful body.

"Hey there," she said, flashing me a brilliant smile. "Mind if I join you?"

I shook my head, feeling grateful for the distraction. Danni took a seat beside me on the porch swing, crossing her legs and leaning back. Her scent wafted over to me, a heady mix of perfume and lotion.

"Are you okay?" Danni asked, her eyes softening with concern.

I hesitated for a moment. I didn't want to burden her with my problems.

"It's just been a long day," I said, taking another sip of wine. She grabbed the glass from between my fingers and took a sip.

"Do you want to talk about it?" she asked.

I looked at her beautiful lips that I wanted to kiss so badly. "I'm not sure."

She shrugged. "It might help?"

"I don't know."

She placed a warm hand on my arm and looked me deep in the eyes. My heart melted and I felt so drawn to her. I wanted to kiss her, but I also wanted to cry at the same time. I had called her earlier and told her about my nephew in a moment when I needed to talk to someone about it.

"Billie Ann," she said. "Your nephew was murdered. This

has to be hard on you. Please do yourself a favor and talk to me. You can't keep bottling everything up. It's not healthy."

I looked away, unsure of what to say. The pain was still too raw, too fresh, and I didn't know if I could handle reliving it all over again.

"It's just... hard," I said, my voice barely above a whisper. "I can't believe Charlie is gone. I barely knew him, but he was still family. It's like everything is falling apart."

Danni nodded understandingly, her hand still on my arm. "I can only imagine what you're going through."

"I don't want you to," I admitted, biting back the tears that were welling up in my eyes. I couldn't let her see me like this. I took in a deep breath and regained my composure. "I don't want you to worry about me. I will be okay."

Danni leaned in closer, her face inches from mine. "You don't have to go through this alone," she whispered, her breath hot against my skin. "I'm here."

"I'll be fine," I said. "I don't need your help."

Danni's hand slid down my arm and on to my hand, her touch sending a jolt of electricity through my body. Then she let go of me and turned away.

"I get it," she said softly. "You don't want to talk to me about it. I just wish you would. I know things aren't easy with your family, but you never told me why. What happened between you and Peter?"

Her eyes locked on to mine, searching for answers that I wasn't ready to give. I tried to swallow down the turmoil raging within me, pushing it further into the depths of my soul.

"It's such a long time ago," I said.

I stared at her and could feel the worry etched into my face. Had I pushed her away? I loved her, but I didn't want to depend on her or her support. For all I knew she could leave me tomorrow.

"So," I added. "How was your day?"

"Why do you shut me out like this?" she asked. She got up from the swing and stood in front of me. "You do it all the time. Whenever I bring up your family and especially your brothers, you don't want to talk to me."

"What are you talking about?"

"Why haven't you spoken to your brothers for years? Any of them?" she asked, throwing out her arms. I could tell by the skin on her throat that she was getting agitated. It was flushed in red spots. I stared at her, wondering if I could tell her, but then decided against it.

"It's just how it has always been."

"It's how it has always been?" she repeated angrily. "That's not an answer, Billie Ann. If you love me, then you have to let me in. You can't just keep saying weird things to make me shut up or change the subject whenever it gets uncomfortable."

And that's when it hit me.

"This is how it has to be."

"What?" she asked. "What are you talking about now?"

"'This is how it has to be. I lived a full life.' It was something Peter said when I talked to him. After he confessed. I didn't think much of it in the moment, but now I do. Thank you, Danni. Thank you!"

I grabbed her face in my hands, and our eyes met. I leaned in closer, my lips hovering just inches from hers. Her lips met mine halfway, soft and warm. I melted into the kiss, feeling the heat of her body against mine and the sweetness of her lips. But as we pulled apart, she pushed me away and her expression turned angry.

"What the heck is going on, Billie Ann? Are you trying to shut me up by kissing me? Is that it?"

"No, no, you're not understanding, I just..." My words trailed off as she cut me off with a dismissive wave of her hand.

"Never mind. This was a mistake," she said, turning to walk away.

"Danni, please, let me explain," I pleaded, reaching out to grab her arm, but she shrugged me off.

"Please, Danni..."

It was too late. She had already left without looking back. My heart sank as I watched her disappear into the night.

TWENTY-ONE

JEREMY

Fourteen-year-old Jeremy and his sister Alexandra bounded toward the entrance of the Boo at the Zoo haunted trail, nearly bursting out of their skins with excitement. The smell of popcorn and cotton candy was strong as they passed by the ticket booth. As they stepped onto the path, set in between animal cages at the zoo, Jeremy felt a rush of excitement pulse through him. With his best friend and twin sister, Alex, by his side, he was certain this night was going to be unforgettable. They plunged into the darkness, weaving in between spooky creatures and animatronic monsters and real-life animals. At every turn, they jumped and screamed, doubling over in laughter until tears streamed down their faces. Nothing could stop them from having the time of their lives. As they made their way through the winding path, Jeremy felt like a young child again. He laughed, screamed, and jumped upon every scare hiding behind every corner.

When they walked down a narrow path, next to the lion's cage, he could hear them as they moved behind the fence, but all he could see was the glowing of their eyes. Jeremy noticed a patch of tall grass just off to the side. After deciding that this was the perfect spot for a surprise attack, he slowly stepped into the shadows and knelt down. When Alex drew close enough, Jeremy jumped out with overexaggerated facial expressions and wild gestures. His sister managed to let out a loud gasp before erupting into fits of laughter. The look of joy on Alex's face was all Jeremy needed as proof of his success. They had always both enjoyed a good scare.

Jeremy and his sister had been running through the dark, foggy woods, laughing in between shrieks of terror. But as they rounded a bend in the path, they heard a rustling sound behind them. Jeremy felt a cold hand on his shoulder. When he slowly turned around, he saw a tall figure dressed in a white mask standing just inches away from him, an ominously large kitchen knife glinting in their hand.

Jeremy's feet seemed to be glued to the floor. He was unable to move or process what was happening until it was too late. The figure lunged forward, brandishing the blade. Jeremy opened his mouth to scream, but before any sound escaped his lips, he was gone.

TWENTY-TWO

BILLIE ANN

I pulled up outside my brother's house in St. Cloud and parked the car. As I got out, I was overwhelmed by the sheer magnitude of the scene before me. Hundreds of white and yellow candles flickered eerily in the wind, holding vigil as if to protect the breathtaking array of flowers that blanketed the entire front lawn like a royal purple carpet. It was a beautiful display, but it was also heart-wrenchingly sad, reminding me of each and every person who had met and loved Charlie.

My steps faltered as I approached the display, and my throat tightened painfully when I saw the photos of Charlie that had been placed around it. In each one his bright smile shone out from behind dark brown eyes that now would never open again. Tears started to blur my vision, and I swallowed hard against the lump in my throat as I stared at the pictures, a wave of sorrow washing over me.

I stood there for a moment, lost in my thoughts, the sound of the breeze rustling through the flowers the only thing breaking the silence. I couldn't help but think about how unfair it all seemed, how much pain my brother and his family had been through. It was a heavy burden to bear, and one that no number of condolences or well wishes could ease. Still, I was going to try and show Angela my support.

Slowly, I reached out and touched one of the candles, feeling the warmth of the flame against my fingertips. It was a small comfort, but it was something. I closed my eyes and whispered a silent prayer, hoping that somehow, someway, my nephew could feel the love and warmth that surrounded him.

As I slowly blinked away the fog of tears, a gentle hand settled on my shoulder. I turned to see Angela standing there, her eyes swollen and glassy from hours of tears. We stayed like that for what felt like an eternity, standing together in complete silence and paying respect to the life that was no longer with us.

We stepped into the foyer, the door closing ominously behind us. Angela's body was racked with sobs as we made our way to the living room. She stumbled to the couch and collapsed into its softness, her face hidden in her hands. I knelt before her and drew her tearstained face to my chest. Her cries reverberated off the walls, and it seemed like an eternity until they finally quieted.

"I can't seem to stop," she said, wiping the tears away with a trembling hand.

"It's okay," I said softly, giving her shoulders a gentle squeeze. Angela and Peter had met in high school, and I had known her since before then. "It's a lot right now. It's only natural."

She hugged herself tightly, like she could protect herself from the pain. "It's just so hard... to comprehend, you know? I lost both my son and husband in less than twenty-four hours."

"I know," I said, my voice soft with empathy. I looked at the woman in front of me, wondering if she believed her husband could actually have done this. "It's unimaginable. But you're not alone, we're all here for you."

Angela's gaze met mine, her eyes like two small pools of anguish. Her shoulders were hunched in on themselves, and a tremble shook her entire body. I wished I could say something to ease her pain, but all I could do was reach out and hold her hand.

"It's just not fair," she whispered, her voice cracking. "He was so young, he had so much ahead of him."

I took her hand in mine and squeezed it gently. "I know it's not fair. It's not fair at all. But he'll always be with us, in our thoughts, in our memories."

Angela nodded, her eyes still damp with tears. "Thank you," she said, her voice low. "Thank you for being here."

I embraced her tightly, feeling the full force of her grief in the pressure of her body against mine. I was shocked that she was trusting me with her pain. I wanted to take all of it away, but instead just held her close and silently offered my support. When she finally pulled away, I looked into her eyes and saw a deep sadness. Although it was as if an unbearable weight had settled between us, I gently squeezed her hand and said, "We need to talk about Peter. I have some questions I need answers to. Can you do that?"

She sighed heavily and shook her head. I stayed with her while she cried, rubbing circles on her back with my free hand until she regained enough composure to speak.

"Okay," she said and nodded.

"I'll make us some coffee," I said and made my way to the kitchen. "Then we can talk."

TWENTY-THREE

Then

Betty sat in her cozy living room, basking in the warm glow of the fireplace. She sipped on her hot cocoa and watched the flames dance, feeling content. Travis was sitting next to her reading a book. They had been married for four years now and were happier than ever. Betty didn't think about her sister and all her nonsense anymore. She hadn't seen her since the day she came to the house, and that was just fine with her.

Betty and Travis had built a beautiful life together. They had a spacious house, he had an amazing career, and best of all, they had each other. They had been through some tough times, but they had always supported each other. Betty was grateful to have Travis in her life. He was her rock, her partner in crime, and her soulmate.

As she sat there, Betty's phone rang. She let it go to voicemail and when she listened to it, she realized it was her sister. "Call me," she simply said. It happened from time to time, but more rarely now after years had passed. Betty rolled her eyes and deleted the message. She had no interest in the drama that her sister always seemed to bring with her. Betty was happy with her life and didn't want anything or anyone to ruin that.

Travis looked up from his book and noticed the expression on Betty's face. He knew that look all too well. "Problem with your sister again?" he asked, his voice calm and reassuring.

Betty shook her head and smiled at him. "No, just a message. But I don't care. I have you and our life together. That's all I need."

Travis put his book down and wrapped his arms around Betty. "I love you, Betty. I'm glad we're in this together."

Betty leaned into him, feeling safe and loved. "I love you too, Travis. I couldn't imagine my life without you."

They sat there for a while longer, enjoying the warmth of the fire and each other's company. Betty knew that no matter what happened in life, everything would be okay, as long as she had him.

He glanced at her, then exhaled a heavy sigh. She narrowed her eyes and squinted, studying him. "I know that sound. What's going on?"

"How do you feel about moving to Florida, more precisely north of Orlando?" he asked, his voice tinged with apprehension.

She gave him an astonished look. "Orlando? But that's so far away?"

He shrugged, avoiding eye contact. "Yeah, I was thinking we could get a house down there."

"What? Travis, why this sudden change of plans?"

"Nothing major," he said, trying to remain nonchalant. "Just thinking of getting transferred. Try something new."

"Hmm," she murmured as she considered his words. She had to admit a move to Florida wasn't a bad idea; after all it was always warm down there. "Well, come to think of it, then maybe it wouldn't be too bad. It's nice and sunny down there," she finally said with a small smile.

That made him grin in relief. "That's a deal then. I will ask for the transferal tomorrow when I get into the station."

He leaned over and kissed her lips tenderly, and she felt nothing but pure bliss radiating from their embrace.

TWENTY-FOUR

BILLIE ANN

The smell of freshly brewed coffee filled the air as I grabbed the two mugs and padded softly into the living room. Angela was seated in an armchair, her face pale and drawn, fingers tapping anxiously against her lips. When she noticed me hovering near her, she looked up with glassy eyes that were void of emotion. Her eyes met mine for just a moment before turning away again. Taking care not to startle her, I slowly lowered myself onto the chair next to her.

I looked at Angela, my voice soft and gentle. Her eyes were wet and rimmed with red, her lips trembling. She blinked, nodded slowly, but still couldn't speak.

"Angela," I said, placing a comforting hand on her shoulder. "I know this is probably one of the most difficult things you've ever had to go through, but I need to ask you some questions about your son and husband. Peter confessed to the murder of Charlie, as I told you on the phone. I am however struggling to believe he would do such a thing. But again, I haven't spoken to him in years. I need to get a picture of the whole thing in order for me to understand it. What was Peter's relationship like with Charlie?"

Angela took a deep breath and squeezed her eyes shut. She clenched her jaw and exhaled, her shoulders shaking as she struggled to find the courage to speak. Her mouth opened and closed a few times.

"Was he good with him?" I added. "Were they close?"

As I sat across from Angela in her quaint living room, a heaviness hung in the air. Sunlight filtered through the delicate lace curtains, casting ethereal patterns on the worn-out armchair she nervously occupied. Her eyes, clouded with anguish and fear, darted around the room as if searching for an escape.

"Angela," I tried again, gently, leaning forward to show her that I was there to listen and understand. Not to judge her. I knew I was probably the last person she trusted right now, as we had never gotten along well. "I know this is difficult for you, but it's crucial for us to uncover the truth. Please, tell me about their relationship. They found marks on Charlie's arms, as if someone was beating him."

Her voice trembled as she finally whispered, "I closed my eyes to it. You do what you need to do, to get by, to survive but... my husband, he-he hurt him."

Her words hung heavily in the air, like a dark cloud threatening to unleash a storm of despair. I reached out, placing a hand gently on hers, offering what little comfort I could muster.

"He hurt Charlie? Peter did?" I asked.

She gave me a look, then shook her head. "You're just here to stir up trouble, aren't you? You want your brother to be guilty, don't you? And there you have it. He admitted to it. Are you happy? You got your way. You managed to prove that we are bad people, just like you wanted to. You never liked us."

"That has nothing to do with it," I said, pulling back. "I'm actually here because I can't believe Peter would do such a thing. I want to understand, Angela. Please?"

She exhaled and hid her face in her hands again. "I don't

understand, why would God allow such a thing to happen? We have been faithful, we have been so faithful to him, to the church. I spoke to Pastor Stan earlier and he said"

I knew Angela was about to go down a path I didn't want to follow. "I'm gonna stop you right there," I said. "I have absolutely no interest in hearing what Pastor Stan has to say about anything, or anyone else from the church for that matter. I want you to tell me what's been going on. I need you to, please, Angela."

With tears streaming down her face, she took a deep breath and began to unravel the horrifying truth that had been hidden behind closed doors for far too long.

"It started with small things," she whispered, her voice barely audible. "Harsh words, raised voices... Then one day, he lost control. He lashed out at our son in a fit of rage. The beatings became more frequent, more brutal..."

I listened intently to every word that escaped Angela's trembling lips. The depth of her pain and despair was palpable, filling the room like a suffocating fog. Yet, her courage in sharing this unimaginable horror showed a flicker of strength buried beneath her anguish.

As she recounted the details, her voice grew stronger, fueled by a growing determination to expose the truth. She described the bruises and welts that marred her son's innocent body, the fear that haunted his eyes whenever his father entered the room. Each word pierced my soul, igniting a fire within me. I couldn't believe he had become this kind of man. Perhaps he was a killer.

"Did he ever hurt Jimmy, Charlie's older brother?"

She scoffed. "What do you think? Of course, he did. He was never good enough. Nothing ever is for him. But he didn't hurt him as bad as Charlie, though."

"What do you mean?" I asked in hushed tones, unable to look her in the eye.

Angela sighed heavily and slowly nodded her head.

"He was savage sometimes," she said, her voice trembling with emotion. "Especially these past months. Peter was under an immense amount of pressure at work, and he took it out on us here at home. When Charlie didn't behave the way Peter wanted him to, he would lash out and hit him. Not long ago, Charlie came home late from a friend's house and your brother... he beat him with a belt mercilessly. I could see the bruises and marks on his skin. He-he wasn't doing well. His grades were slipping, and Peter believed that if he disciplined him harshly, it would eventually get better. I tried telling him that nothing good can ever come out of violence, but he never listened. He wasn't the best husband or father, Billie Ann," Angela finished sadly, "I'm sorry to say so because he's your brother. I'd always thought it would be me who suffered the most when he snapped one day—not Charlie."

I felt as if I'd been punched in the gut. How could this be? My brother, whom I had grown up with and thought I knew, was he capable of hurting his own child? I knew he was strict with his children and kept them on a tight leash, but violence? Beatings? My throat tightened as I fought to keep my voice steady.

"And how was he around him in the days leading up to Charlie's death?" I asked.

Angela shook her head and tears started to stream down her face. "It was bad, really bad. They were yelling at each other constantly and he was so violent toward him. I knew something was going to happen, I just never thought..." she trailed off, unable to finish her sentence.

I stayed with Angela for a few more minutes, rubbing her back and offering faint words of comfort as she sobbed. After several moments of silence, I asked the question that weighed heavily on my mind. "Do you really think he's capable of having done this?"

The room was silent except for the ticking of a nearby clock.

Angela hesitated for a moment before nodding slowly. "Yes," she said, her voice barely audible. "I didn't want to believe it, but everything... the way he acted, the things he said... it all points to..."

My heart ached for Angela. She had already suffered unimaginable heartache after losing her son, and now to consider that her own husband may have been responsible in his death was shattering. Tears filled her eyes and spilled down her cheeks.

"And he wasn't with you at the time Charlie was killed?" I asked.

"No. He had left in his truck."

"Where did he say he went?"

She sighed. "He didn't say. We had another fight and he just took off. I tried to call him but he left his phone here. Our fight was so ridiculous, I wanted him to come home so we could talk it out. It frustrated me that I couldn't get ahold of him. But I guess he did that on purpose, huh? So he couldn't be traced. He didn't come back till around nine thirty. That's when he told me he was sorry for everything, that he was in trouble at work, and that's why he had been so angry. He cried and said he knew he had been a terrible husband and father. I forgave him. How could I have known what he had done?"

"You couldn't," I said. "There is no way, Angela. Did he seem different? Like out of sorts?"

She nodded. "Very. It was like I barely recognized him anymore. He hasn't been himself for these past months."

I placed a gentle hand on her arm as I asked, "Did he have a laptop?"

She nodded with a sniffle and gestured for me to follow her. We took slow steps down the hallway, our feet whispering against the carpet. She stopped at the third door on the left, steeling herself before she opened it.

"It's in his office," she said in a breathy whisper. "Do with it what you want. I don't care anymore."

I nodded and entered. It hadn't changed much in the many years since I had been there last.

"Thank you, Angela. I'm so sorry you have to go through all of this."

Angela didn't say anything in response. She just stared blankly ahead, lost in her own thoughts and grief.

As I made my way toward Peter's desk, I couldn't help but feel a sense of dread wash over me. I didn't want to believe that my brother was capable of something so heinous, but everything Angela had said pointed toward his guilt.

As I approached his desk, I noticed that it was immaculately clean. Everything was organized and in its place. It was strange to see such a pristine workspace amidst all the chaos that had ensued.

I opened the lid of the laptop sitting on Peter's desk and powered it on. It required a password, but it wasn't difficult to guess. Peter had always been terrible at choosing secure passwords.

As I scrolled through his files, going through his emails and search history, I stumbled upon something that made my blood run cold. I closed the lid again, then grabbed the laptop in my hand. As I was about to leave, I spotted a small Fitbit band on the desk as well, then grabbed it and left. I made Angela sign the paperwork allowing me to take it, then left their home.

TWENTY-FIVE

ANDY

Andy was lying on the cold concrete floor, his body shaking with withdrawal symptoms. Sweat was dripping down his forehead and his eyes were bloodshot. He was craving for a fix, any kind of drug that would help him forget about his captivity.

Suddenly, the door to his room creaked open and a tall, muscular man walked in. He was still wearing the white mask. Andy's heart skipped a beat; he was relieved to see someone, anyone, after days of being alone in the dark.

"Please, man," Andy begged, crawling toward him. "Please, give me something. Anything. I'll do anything you want."

The man sneered at him. "You're pathetic," he spat.

He was going to die; he could feel it. And all he could do was wonder what he had done to deserve this. Did he owe this person money? Was it some of the people he had borrowed money from who were behind this? Who wanted him dead? It had to be.

"Please," he stuttered. "Tell them I will get them the money. Please."

That made the man laugh out loud. "Money? You think this is about money?"

"Then what is it? What do you want?"

And then the man brought out a claw hammer, his fingers caressing the worn, wooden handle. And Andy felt everything go black.

TWENTY-SIX

BILLIE ANN

I trudged up the steps of the police station the next morning, my brother's laptop was weighing heavily in my grasp. I felt like I was carrying a piece of him with me, and dread tickled at my spine as I thought about what secrets might be found inside the small device. I knew Scott intended to search Peter's home for evidence later this afternoon, but somehow I felt that the laptop was important and we needed to act fast.

Scott sat at his desk, his hands behind his neck and a mischievous smirk on his face. As I lowered the computer onto the desk, he leaned forward eagerly, almost as if he was expecting something incredible.

He ran a hand smugly through his disheveled hair. "Have you ever cracked a case this fast?" he asked, unable to contain his excitement.

I shook my head, a little bit frustrated. I knew Scott was trying to do his job, that getting a confession was the best a detective could hope for. But something was wrong, and I wish he felt it too. I felt like there was something missing from the puzzle and glanced at Peter's laptop where it sat on the desk.

"It's not over yet," I said with an air of determination. "We need to go through this as soon as possible. Let's get cracking."

Scott leaned forward in his chair; eyes fixed on the illuminated screen. His fingers tapped out a frenzied rhythm on the keyboard as he opened folders and scanned through their contents. I stared in amazement at the way Scott worked, trying to make sense of my brother's digital life. Scott's proficiency in hacking had not come easily; it was a journey that had begun years ago. As a fresh-faced recruit at the police academy, Scott had been captivated by the sheer potential of technology in solving crimes. While his peers focused on traditional investigation techniques, he had delved into the uncharted territory of cyberspace.

In those early days, Scott immersed himself in books, online forums, and countless hours of trial and error. He admired the vigilante hackers who walked the thin line between justice and chaos. But unlike them, he yearned to use his skills for the greater good, to bring criminals to justice and protect the innocent.

Scott sought out mentors within the law enforcement community who could guide him in his quest for knowledge. With their guidance, he refined his techniques and developed an innate understanding of how criminals operated in the digital realm. He learned to follow the breadcrumbs left behind by cybercriminals, tracing their virtual footprints through countless layers of encryption and obfuscation.

But it was his insatiable curiosity that truly set Detective Scott apart from his peers. While others saw technology as a tool, Scott saw it as an extension of himself—a sixth sense that allowed him to see beyond what met the eye.

Fear crept up my spine as I watched him, uncertain what we would find or how it might turn out. I had checked the forensic files and realized Jimmy, Peter's eldest son's fingerprints were also on the knife. Scott had told me they didn't think it was important, since they had Peter's confession, but I wasn't so sure of that.

Scott was hunched over the computer, typing away at a furious pace. I looked down to the table and saw the Fitbit I had unearthed from my brother's office. It was an unassuming black band with a small display in the center that held mysterious secrets. I offered it to Tom, who stood nearby with watchful eyes. "Do you know anything about these things?" I asked as he took it into his hands.

Tom examined the Fitbit closely. "Yeah, I used to have one," he said. "Let me show you."

He plugged the Fitbit into the computer, and Scott began navigating through the device's settings. I watched as he worked, amazed at how effortlessly he seemed to move through the technology. It was a skill I wished I had, but I just didn't have it in me. Not enough.

As he worked, Scott chatted about the case. He talked about how the team had worked well together and how proud he was of their work. I nodded along, barely listening. My mind was focused on the Fitbit, on the potential clues it might hold.

Finally, Scott let out a small sound of triumph. He had found what he was looking for.

"Check this out," he said, turning the computer screen toward me. "This is the Fitbit's data. It tracks your steps, heart rate, and even your sleep patterns."

I leaned in to examine the screen. It showed a graph of my brother's heart rate, and I felt a pang of sadness looking at it. It was a strange thing, to see a visual representation of someone's life, even if it was just their heart rate.

But as Scott continued to scroll through the data, my sadness turned to shock. There was definitely a spike in my brother's heart rate on the night of the murder. But there was also something else.

"Look at this," Scott said, pointing to the graph.

I stared at it, then pointed. "This is around the time Charlie was murdered. Around eight thirty-three p.m. Is this really accurate?"

"It is," Scott said. "It shows every step you take."

"I'll be... that son of a gun..."

I trailed off, unable to finish my sentence. The realization hit me like a ton of bricks. Something about this wasn't right.

TWENTY-SEVEN

Then

Betty and Travis stood in the middle of their new living room, surrounded by a sea of open boxes. They had just finished unpacking and were admiring the cozy little house they now called home. The sun streamed through the windows, glinting off the hardwood floors and cream-colored walls with dark wood accents. The pair couldn't help but smile—Travis was thrilled to be working as a detective, and Betty was ecstatic about starting a brand-new life here.

"I think we will be very happy here," Betty said, serving him a cup of steaming hot coffee. She also handed him a cookie, and they took a small break.

Travis was starting his new job tomorrow, so this was their last chance to get everything settled. From the next day on, she was on her own in this place, all day long while he worked. It was a very small town outside of Orlando, and Betty wondered if she would like it here. She had a feeling she might, but it was very different than what she was used to. She didn't let Travis know her doubts though as she didn't want him to feel bad. He had received a promotion, he said, and was so excited about it. Betty only wished she could get pregnant so she could start her part of the life they had dreamed of together. But so far, it hadn't happened, and she was getting more and more nervous as the months passed by. What if she couldn't conceive?

You can't think like that. It will happen. When the time is right.

Betty tugged at a box, her muscles straining under the weight. She shaded her eyes with one hand and smiled. The sun felt like an oven baking her back as it shone down on their new home, producing a spectacular view of the small town. "I think this is going to be our best adventure yet," she said, looking to Travis.

Travis grinned back at her, "I couldn't agree more."

Betty and Travis moved in silence as they continued unpacking the boxes. Suddenly, a sharp rap at the door disrupted their trance-like state. Betty opened it to find a mail carrier on the threshold, with a single letter in their hands.

"Who is it from?" she asked, looking at it, turning it in the sunlight. "There's no sender?"

The mail carrier answered her question with a clueless shrug, then tipped their cap and left. Betty stared at them for a moment before closing the door gently. She turned back to Travis, eyebrows furrowed in confusion.

She opened the envelope and pulled out the contents. It was an article, and the headline terrified her to the core. Her face went pale, and she stumbled backward. Travis quickly caught her.

"What is going on? Who was that?"

She stared at the article, its glossy paper reflecting off her glassy eyes. She read it quickly then returned it to its envelope before shaking her head in confusion.

"Nothing," she said softly. "Just the mail carrier."

He took a step closer and squinted his eyes at what remained in her hand. "What is that?" he asked.

She shook her head then leaned over and pecked his cheek. "It's nothing, really," she said, trying her best to push the article to the back of her mind. She didn't want to ruin their happy moment. "Just a reminder to pay the utilities bill."

The expression on Travis' face shifted between confusion and resignation. He huffed, "All right," and adjusted his baseball cap.

Betty turned away to hide the fear in her eyes.

For hours they unpacked boxes and arranged furniture. By sundown, both of their backs were sore from stooping, and they had to practically crawl into bed in exhaustion. As she curled up under a blanket, Betty's arm muscles ached, along with every other muscle in her body. Yet she couldn't fall asleep. She kept thinking about the envelope that she had hidden downstairs, trying to forget its existence. But the more she tried to, the more she couldn't let it go. Who in their right mind had sent her this? It was too scary to even think about.

She waited until Travis' heavy breathing indicated he was deep asleep before slipping out of bed. She tiptoed to the living room, retrieved the crumpled, cream-colored envelope from underneath the book where she had hidden it, and unfolded the wrinkled newspaper article. Her heart raced as she read every word, her eyes widening with each sentence.

TWENTY-EIGHT

BILLIE ANN

As I made my way to the visiting room of the jail that my brother had been taken to, my mind drifted back to the tragedy that had brought me here. It was just over there, in the swampy forest next to the jail, that my nephew had been brutally murdered. The haunted trail that wound through the woods had been closed down and blocked off by police tape, making it seem even scarier.

I pushed the thought from my mind as I spotted my brother, dressed in a standard-issue orange jumpsuit, sitting at a table. He looked up and our eyes met, and I could see the fear and sadness etched on his face.

I took a deep breath and sat down across from him. "How are you holding up?" I asked softly.

My brother let out a shaky breath before answering. "I didn't know you cared so much."

"Stop it, Peter. Of course I care. We're family. No matter what."

He shrugged. "It's tough in here, but I'm managing. It's just hard to be away from everyone and everything I know."

I nodded, understanding his pain all too well. "I know it's

not much, but I brought you something," I said, sliding a small package across the table.

He opened it carefully, revealing a few photos of our family and a letter from our mother. His face lit up as he looked at them, and I could see a glimmer of hope in his eyes.

"Thank you," he said, his voice choked with emotion. "You didn't have to do that."

"Now I don't know how long you're going to be here, but I have a feeling it won't be much longer," I said.

His eyes grew wide with surprise. "What do you mean? I told you I am guilty. I am waiting for trial and expect to get the chair for this. I'm prepared to take the consequences of my actions."

I scoffed. "That's all fine and dandy, brother, but I don't believe you did it. In fact, I think I can prove you didn't do it."

He snarled at me and shook his head. "You're out of your mind."

"Am I?" I said. "Let me put this in a way you can understand it. This is my theory."

"Oh, can't wait to hear this," he said, lifting his hands, resigned.

"Your little Fitbit that you wear often seems to be the witness I needed."

"And how so?" he asked.

"It shows that you only took twenty-four steps between eight p.m. and nine thirty p.m. Twelve to get to your truck, and twelve to get back inside of the house. The rest of the time you were in your truck. If you had been at the haunted trail, you would have walked several miles to get to the maze at the end of it."

He shrugged. "So what? I could have taken it off."

I shook my head. "That's what I thought too at first. But if you had left it at home, then it wouldn't show any motion at all. It did count twenty-four steps, which is approximately what it takes from your driveway and into the house, where you later took it off in your office."

"I could have left it in my truck when I entered the haunted trail," he said, panicking.

"That's another possibility, but see the thing is it also recorded your heartrate. And at no point in the hour and a half where you are gone, does it stop recording your heartbeat. Which tells me you were wearing it all the time while driving around in your truck. There are several spikes in it, probably because you were angry and fighting with Angela."

My brother sent me a look, and I could tell I was right in my conclusions. Still, he wasn't ready to admit it.

"Okay," he said. "If you're so darn smart, sis, then tell me why on earth would I admit to having murdered my own son, if I didn't do it?"

"I asked myself that very question too, and that's where your search history on your computer plays a big part."

A frown grew between his eyes. "What search history?"

I took in a deep breath. This was the ugly part. "You have been researching pancreatic cancer. A lot. So, I went through your phone records and noticed you have been talking to your doctor several times recently. I called him up and he confirmed it to me."

Peter grew pale. "Confirmed what?"

"That you are sick. He gave you six months, because it was metastatic and by your research you knew it was going to be six very painful months. You'd rather be executed than commit suicide, am I right? Or at least die in prison, where no one would mourn you, where your family didn't have to sit by your side, crying. Your youngest son was gone, there was no reason for you to stick around. And here comes the last part of my theory. I think you believe your other son might have killed him. You wanted to protect Jimmy. He still has a full life ahead of him, and you wanted to give him that, as a goodbye present. So, tell me why did you think Jimmy killed his brother?"

Peter's face went white as a sheet, and he looked like he was about to pass out.

My brother took a deep breath and looked away. Silence lingered for a few minutes, before he spoke.

"Why would Jimmy do something like this?" I asked.

My brother hesitated for a moment.

"We have his fingerprints on the knife, Peter."

He rubbed his face, then sighed. "Look, I don't think he's thinking straight. He's been very angry lately, and during a visit to his place recently, I found a list in his bedroom, he'd titled it 'Hitlist.' His brother's name was on top of that list. I tried to ask him about it, ask him what it was, and why he had it, but he ended up throwing me out in a fit of rage. I thought that maybe it was just a joke, or a way for him to get his rage out, so I didn't think more of it. But when Charlie died, and the knife turned up as the murder weapon, I knew it was Jimmy. I gave him the knife a few years ago. Angela doesn't know about the list. I can never tell her, and I don't want you to either. If he did hurt Charlie, he can't have done it with a sound mind. Please protect him, Billie."

I felt a lump form in my throat as my brother spoke. So much pain and heartache had been bubbling below the surface, hidden from everyone. But now, it had all come crashing down, and I could feel the weight of it all crushing me.

"Listen," I said, taking a deep breath. "I understand you wanting to protect your son. But no matter what, the truth needs to come out. If Jimmy isn't thinking straight, and he did kill Charlie, they'll take that into consideration in his sentencing."

My brother shook his head, his eyes glistening with tears. "This is all my fault. You must hate me."

I wondered if Peter knew I'd seen the bruises on Charlie's

arms. Even though I knew he wasn't a killer, his confession had brought to light the way he had treated his two sons.

"I don't hate you, Peter. I never have," I said.

With that, I turned and headed out of the visitation room, my mind whirling with thoughts and emotions. It was going to be a long road ahead, but I was determined to see it through to the end. No matter what it took.

TWENTY-NINE

ANDY

Andy lay on the cold, hard ground. He was in excruciating pain, his body racked with sobs that came out as guttural moans. Everything hurt, from his head down to his toes. He could feel the dull throb of his broken bones and the sharp sting of his open wounds from the damage inflicted by the hammer. The room was pitch-black, and he couldn't see a thing. He could hear the sound of his own labored breathing and the drip of blood hitting the cold concrete floor.

His tongue felt like sandpaper in his mouth. His stomach had been churning for hours, and he was lightheaded from the emptiness. The darkness pressed in on him, and it felt as if he had been stuck in that room for an eternity. He had no idea how long he'd been there or when this nightmare would end.

He blinked back tears and a single droplet escaped down his stubbly chin. His body shook as a low wail escaped from his throat, and he curled up in a ball on the cold stone floor. The smell of urine and dampness filled the air, and each sob echoed off the bleak walls. He wished for someone to burst through the door and save him, but instead he was left alone in the darkness. For hours and hours with no end.

Till suddenly the door to the room swung open slowly, letting out a shrill creak as it did so. A ray of light streamed in from the hallway, illuminating the dark and dreary chamber. Andy's eyes widened in surprise as he blinked away spots in his vision, struggling to adjust his gaze to the room's newfound brightness.

The man with the white mask entered, a phone clutched in his hand, and made his way over to where Andy lay. His right leg was twisted at an impossible angle and a pool of blood had gathered around him. He looked up pleadingly as the intruder drew closer, one outstretched hand trembling with fear. "Help me," he whimpered, desperation choking his voice. "Please, help me."

The man towered over him, his face hidden behind the mask. Then he lifted the phone. He snapped a few pictures with it, the flash illuminating Andy's battered and broken body.

"Please... someone... help..." he cried.

The man didn't flinch. He raised his phone to his eye, snapping off a few more pictures as Andy's desperate pleas echoed in the silence.

"Please! Help me!" he screamed.

The man exhaled a deep, slow breath and then a sharp cracking noise reverberated through the room. Andy felt a sudden pain in his lower back and realized he'd been struck with a hammer again. The man's laughter echoed off the walls as Andy winced in agony.

The man tucked his phone into his pocket and slowly made his way to the door. He turned back for one last look at Andy's body.

"Have fun with the rats," he said, then disappeared behind the door.

Andy was left alone in the dark room, only the dull thumping of his heart echoing off the walls.

THIRTY

BILLIE ANN

The door to the Chief's office creaked as I entered. She was standing by her desk, clutching a phone in one hand while the other hand pressed so hard against her forehead that her skin blanched. Her gaze darted about the room, and an expression of tightness took over her usually composed face. She motioned for me to take a seat, then mouthed "one moment" before continuing her conversation.

I sank into the rich, buttery leather of the chair and surveyed the office: diplomas, awards, photos with dignitaries hung on the walls, a bronze bust of an unknown person stared at me from one corner, while shelves filled with books lined another. I felt my stomach twist as I wondered what had the Chief so agitated.

She slammed down the phone and turned around to face me. Her eyes were like lasers, drilling into mine as she spoke in a low rumble. "Make it fast," she said, urgency ringing in her voice.

My voice was shaking as I explained. "My brother didn't kill Charlie. I just went to see him and"

But before I could finish the sentence, she cut me off with a raised hand. Her expression softened and she said firmly, "I'm gonna stop you right there. I already know your brother didn't do it."

My mouth dropped open in shock and my eyes widened as I looked at her. "You do?" I asked, barely making a sound.

"Yes," she replied. Her voice was grave and heavy with sorrow as she continued. "The call I just received here told me there's been another one, last night, a double homicide. Or attempt. One died, the other is in critical condition."

Chief Harold wearily settled into the chair and rubbed her tired eyes. "Two teenagers, twins, were attacked at the zoo. Both with their throats slit on the haunted trail. The incident hasn't been reported beyond Melbourne jurisdiction, that's why it was kept quiet for so long. Witnesses saw someone wearing a plastic mask leaving the scene." My phone vibrated and I looked at the display. It was my mother. I decided not to pick it up. I would have to call her later.

My chest was tight and my lungs burned. I could barely breathe. Another brutal attack, this time two teenagers. Was it really possible?

Her eyebrows furrowed as she leaned forward. "So, you talked to your brother?" she asked, her voice low and serious.

"I got him to admit that he was covering up for someone else," I said, my jaw tightening.

"Who?" she pressed, her eyes narrowing.

"His older son Jimmy, I'm afraid. He decided to take the fall for him."

The Chief's eyes widened in alarm as she processed what I had said. Her mouth opened, and the single word "Jesus" spilled out without her realizing it. She shook her head, snapped back to attention, and spoke with urgency. "Okay, we need to get this Jimmy—and fast."

I nodded in agreement; my brother had already told me where to look. "I know where he is," I said.

THIRTY-ONE

Then

Betty lay motionless in her bed, eyes fixed on the door. Silence hung in the air as Travis quietly gathered his things and stood to leave for work. With each step he took toward the door, a wave of worry washed over her. She felt like she was suffocating but couldn't make her mouth move or her limbs respond. As soon as the click of the front door sounded, Betty shot up from where she lay, and grabbed the phone from the nightstand.

She wiped her eyes with the back of her hand and called her mother's number, trembling so much she had to try twice before it went through. When her mother answered, the tears broke forth anew, her throat tightening as if a fist were squeezing it shut.

"Mom," she sobbed. "I don't know what to do."

"What's wrong, child?" her mother asked, concern evident in her voice.

Betty's hands trembled as she forced a gulp of air into her lungs. Her gaze flitted around the room, searching for the correct words. "Travis... Travis," she managed to say, but her voice was weak and uncertain.

"What about him?" asked her mother, confusion in her voice.

"He... someone sent me an article," she finally managed to say. "I didn't know what to do, so I just stayed up all night."

Betty's mother scoffed, her voice rising in frustration. "What article? Betty, you're not making much sense. What was it about?"

Betty's breath hitched as tears rolled down her cheeks. She clutched the phone tightly, her body shaking. "It was about a detective at our old police station, where Travis used to work," she said softly. "I think it was about him. It didn't say a name."

Her mother sighed and softened her tone. "And what did the article say?"

Betty's voice was shaky and barely audible through her sobs as she talked to her mother on the phone.

"That he... that he was accused of raping a suspect while she was in custody," Betty said between choked breaths. Her throat felt like it had been deprived of air, and she couldn't keep her hands steady no matter how hard she tried. She felt frozen in place, unable to move or breathe. "It couldn't be proven, so he wasn't charged with anything," she whispered, "but they decided to transfer him to another precinct in another state."

Her mother sneered. "And Travis is supposed to be involved in this? This is ridiculous. Can't you see that?"

Betty's tears flowed again. "Who'd send me something like this? Why?" she said, her voice quivering with emotion.

"Listen," her mother said. "It might just be someone trying to hurt you. People can do the meanest things. It doesn't have to be about him. In fact, I don't think that it is."

"But what if it is? Mom, what do I do?"

Her mom went quiet for a few heartbeats, then said, "You do nothing. This is not worth losing your marriage over. You have a good life. Travis is good to you, and you don't have to work. You're lucky, do you hear me? Don't ruin it. I would throw that article far away, burn it if you have to."

Betty's tears started to blur the words on the news article in her hands. She wiped them away with the back of her hand and studied it closely, wondering what secrets Travis was hiding from her. Her heart pounded as she thought about the possibility that this was about him. Sniffling through her tears, she muttered, "I don't want to ruin anything, but I can't stop thinking about it."

Her mother's voice was gentle as she spoke, the same way it had been when she tucked her in at night.

"I know how hard this is for you, honey. But you have to believe that Travis loves you—he has never given you cause not to. This isn't easy, but look at your father and me—before he died, we had been together for more than thirty years. We had our ups and downs but remained together. It's worth making the effort for something so special. Trust me."

Betty wiped her face with the back of her hand, feeling a glimmer of hope. Her breath was slowing to a steady rhythm. "Okay, Mom. Thank you."

"Anytime, sweetheart. Just remember, trust is the foundation of any good relationship. Don't let anyone or anything undermine that. Just forget about it. You go take a shower, have some breakfast, and start your day like it's any other day. You'll see, everything will be fine."

Betty nodded, feeling slightly calmer. "Okay, okay. Thank you, Mom."

"Anytime, sweetheart. You know I'm always here for you."

Betty hung up the phone, feeling like her lungs had been punched. She bit her lip and looked in the mirror; panic stared back at her from wide brown eyes. Her mother's words echoed in her mind. "This isn't the end of your world!"

But there was a hollow ache inside that said otherwise.

With slow steps, Betty entered the bathroom, her feet heavy on the tile. She stayed rooted to the spot, fighting against a wave of despair that threatened to engulf her as she thought of Travis. No—she wouldn't let this be the end.

Summoning her courage, Betty inhaled deeply, refusing to give in to her fears.

THIRTY-TWO

BILLIE ANN

As I approached Jimmy's small house, I couldn't shake the feeling that something was off. The neighborhood was dingy, with graffiti scrawled on the walls and stray dogs barking in the distance. My team and I were on high alert, our hands resting on the guns holstered at our hips. I had convinced Tom to let me come with them. I knew he risked getting in trouble later for this, if the Chief found out, and that worried me.

We reached the front door and knocked, but before we could even announce ourselves, a barrage of gunfire erupted from inside the house. My heart raced as I lunged for cover behind one of the police cars parked on the street.

My team scattered, seeking refuge behind nearby buildings and vehicles as we returned fire. The sound of bullets ricocheting off metal filled the air, and my ears rang with the deafening roar of the guns.

"Police!" I yelled. "Put down your weapon!"

I peered over the car hood, scanning the windows of Jimmy's house for any sign of movement. But all I could see was the shattered glass and bullet holes peppering the walls.

My pulse quickened as I realized this wasn't going to end

well. We needed to get closer. I needed to make sure my nephew survived this. Somehow. I thought about my brother alone in his cell, about Angela's tear-stricken face. I was the only one with the power to help them get their son back. I couldn't let something terrible happen to him.

"Cover me!" I yelled to my team, before sprinting toward the house. As I approached the front door, more shots were fired. I stumbled but managed to keep my footing and keep moving. I knew I had to get inside that house. If it was Jimmy shooting at us, then he could be certain that my team would shoot first and ask later, when going in. I couldn't let that happen. I wanted him alive.

I kicked down the door and charged inside, gun raised. The room was empty, but I could hear movement coming from upstairs. I took the stairs two at a time, my heart pounding in my chest.

As I reached the top of the stairs, I saw him. Jimmy. He was holding a gun, and he looked scared. We locked eyes for a moment, and I could see the fear in his.

"Stop," he yelled. "Don't come any closer!"

I stopped, then looked at him, puzzled. I hadn't seen him in many years, but this wasn't the Jimmy I remembered. He was skinnier, and his eyes were darting around the room.

"Jimmy, it's me."

"Who are you?" he asked, pointing the gun at me. It was shaking in his hand.

I frowned.

"It's Billie Ann, your aunt," I said.

Jimmy's eyes widened as he looked at me, confusion etched on his face. "Billie Ann? Is it really you?" he asked, his voice strained. He tilted his head slightly, like he wasn't sure he believed me.

I nodded, keeping my gun trained on him in case he tried

anything. The way he looked at me made me nervous. Sweat sprang to my forehead.

"Yes, it's me. I have come to talk to you, please put the gun down."

But Jimmy just shook his head, his eyes darting manically around the room. "I can't."

"What do you mean you can't? I'm your aunt, remember? I used to take you to the zoo? We would feed the giraffes? You loved the giraffes?"

That put a small smile on his face, but it disappeared fast, and he shook his head. "No, no. You're not her. They're trying to trick me. I'm not falling for it. I'm not."

"What are you talking about? How about we put down the guns—both of us—and we go outside and take a little drive in my car. How about that?"

"NO!" he yelled so loud it startled me. "I can't leave. I have to stay here."

"Why?"

"They told me not to leave the house. They're always watching," he muttered to himself, his voice barely audible.

I took a step closer to him, trying to keep my voice calm and reassuring. "Jimmy, there's no one here but us. But you're not safe here. The police are outside trying to get to you. If you go with me then I assure you nothing will happen to you. I can protect you. We need to go."

But Jimmy just looked at me with a haunted expression. "You don't understand. They're always watching, always listening. They won't let me leave," he repeated.

My heart sank as I realized what was going on. Peter was right. He was sick. Very sick. He had no idea what was going on around him and obviously heard voices in his mind. Voices telling him what to do. This was bad. I felt scared, terrified of him getting shot. I had to get him to calm down and put the gun away before my team burst in here and shot him. He had opened fire on us, so it was bound to happen any minute now, if I didn't take him outside, unarmed.

Jimmy's eyes kept darting around the room, as if trying to locate the source of the voices he was hearing. His breathing was labored, and his hands shook as he clutched the gun.

"Who are they?" he whispered, looking at me with a mixture of fear and confusion.

"There's no one here, Jimmy," I said, trying to keep my voice calm and steady. "It's just me. And I want to help you."

But he didn't seem to hear me. He continued to mutter to himself, his gaze shooting rapidly around the room, as if trying to locate invisible threats.

I took a step closer, and he raised the gun, pointing it at my chest.

"Stay back!" he shouted, his voice hoarse.

I froze, my heart racing. I could feel the weight of the gun in his hand, and I knew that one wrong move could mean the end for both of us.

"Jimmy," I said, my voice barely above a whisper. "I'm your family. You can trust me."

But he just shook his head, his eyes wild with fear. "No one can be trusted," he muttered. "No one."

I took a deep breath, trying to think of something to say that would calm him down. "Jimmy, do you remember when we used to go fishing together? Sometimes we took the boat out on the ocean for some offshore fishing. Just you, me, and your dad? I think you were no more than eight or nine years old the time that I caught that bull shark, and you helped me reel it in. We fought her for about an hour before she finally gave up, remember that?"

For a moment, his eyes softened, and I could see the faintest glimmer of recognition. "Yeah," he said. "I think I remember."

"That's who I am, Jimmy," I said, taking a step closer. "I'm your family. And I want to help you."

For a moment, he seemed to consider my words. His grip on the gun loosened slightly, and I felt a glimmer of hope.

But then, just as suddenly, his eyes widened with fear again. "No!" he shouted, raising the gun once more. "You're lying! They told me you're not really my aunt! They told me you're one of them!"

I took a step back, raising my hands in surrender. "Jimmy, please, listen to me. I'm not one of them. I'm your family. You can trust me."

But Jimmy just shook his head, his eyes darting around the room as if looking for a way out. "No," he muttered. "No one can be trusted. Not even family."

I could feel my heart pounding in my chest, my adrenaline pumping as I tried to think of a way to get through to him. But before I could say anything else, I could hear my team arriving inside. They had realized I wasn't coming out and now they were coming to my aid. But they would shoot him, if they saw him point the gun at me. I couldn't let that happen. The boy was sick, he wasn't evil. But they didn't know that.

"Police!" a voice shouted.

I breathed a sigh of worry. They would take one look at him holding the gun and then it would be over for him. I had to act fast. Things were about to get a lot more dangerous.

"Jimmy, we need to go," I said. "I need to take you some-place safe."

He raised the gun once more. "You're lying! You're one of them!"

My heart sank as I realized that logic wasn't going to work with him in this state. I had to act fast before he did something that he would regret.

I took a deep breath and lunged forward, tackling him to the ground. The gun clattered to the floor, and for a moment, we grappled on the ground.

But I had training on my side. I pinned him down with ease,

holding his arms behind his back as he struggled and thrashed beneath me.

"It's okay, Jimmy," I said, trying to soothe him. "It's going to be okay."

But he just kept struggling, his eyes wide with fear and confusion.

I felt a hand on my shoulder, and I looked up to see one of my team members standing over me.

"We need to get him out of here," he said, his voice low and urgent. "Now."

I nodded, knowing it was time to get Jimmy out of danger. I released my hold on him, and my team member helped me lift him to his feet.

Jimmy was still struggling and screaming, and it made my heart ache. The little boy I had known was gone. It terrified me to see him like this. It broke my heart. He looked up at me with tear-filled eyes, and I could see the fear and confusion still etched on his face.

"We're going to get you help, Jimmy," I said, trying to comfort him. "We're going to make sure you're safe."

As we stepped out of the house, I could see the police officers outside, weapons drawn and ready. But my team had already explained the situation, and they held their fire as we moved toward them.

THIRTY-THREE

BILLIE ANN

I was stirring the pot of pasta sauce on the stove, the aroma of simmering tomatoes filling the cozy kitchen. The soft glow of twilight peeked through the window, casting a warm hue over the room. From where I stood, I could catch glimpses of the boats going by slowly in the canal. The wind had picked up and the water looked choppy, while the thick mangroves by the water were swaying, and the leaves on the palm trees rustling.

As I stirred the pot of pasta sauce, my mind wandered to thoughts of Jimmy. I was worried about him, but glad that we got him in without any harm. He had been taken to the psychiatric emergency room, for evaluation, but there was no doubt in my mind that he was very sick. He had rambled on in the car while going there, about how he believed he was related to the Clinton family, and that's why the FBI was monitoring him. I worried that he really had killed his own brother, and that was heartbreaking to me. I had a feeling that he didn't even know what he had done. It was such a tragedy.

Lost in my thoughts, I hardly noticed the sound of approaching footsteps until they grew louder and more distinct. They belonged to my daughter, Charlene.

"Mom, there's someone I want you to meet," she said; her voice sounded nervous.

I turned around to face her, wiping my hands on my apron. My daughter had recently grown to be taller than me, and as she stood in front of me now, I could have sworn she had grown again. Her long blonde hair flowed across her shoulders. "Okay, who is it?"

She stepped aside to reveal a man standing behind her, his hands pushed deep into his pockets. My heart sank as I took in his appearance. Whoever he was, he looked to be in his late twenties, at least ten years older than my daughter.

"Mom, this is Tyler."

I tried to keep my expression neutral as I greeted him. "Hello, nice to meet you."

He smiled and extended his hand. "Likewise. I've heard so much about you."

I couldn't help but feel uneasy about the situation. My daughter had never mentioned this man before, and I had no idea how they had met. She was only seventeen.

"I have invited Tyler to stay for dinner," she said. "I hope it's okay."

I smiled, awkwardly, taken aback by this sudden turn of events. "Yes, yes, of course. You're more than welcome."

As we settled into our seats at the dinner table, I observed their interactions with keen interest. Charlene's new beau, a towering figure with long limbs and a rugged beard, reached across the table for the pasta bowl. Charlene's musical laughter filled the room as she responded to something he said. My youngest son Zack erupted into giggles, while William rolled his eyes in mock exasperation. They all moved and spoke with such familiarity and comfort, as if they had been a family for years. Meanwhile, I felt like an awkward outsider, unsure of how to join in on their easy banter. Their casual familial bond only heightened my feelings of isolation and disconnection. Was I the only one who found this bond strange?

"Mom, Tyler and I met when I was with Dad at the golf course a few days ago," my daughter said, twirling her fork in her spaghetti.

I raised an eyebrow. "And how old are you, Tyler?"

"Twenty-eight," he replied, taking a sip of his wine. "But age is just a number, right?"

I gritted my teeth, trying to remain calm. This was the first time Charlene had brought home a guy, and I worried this meant it was serious. But how could it be? They had just met.

"No, it's not. You're an adult, and my daughter is still in high school."

My daughter's face fell. "Mom, please don't ruin this for me. Tyler is different from all the other guys I've dated. He understands me."

I sighed, but I was intent on protecting my daughter.

"I'm sorry, sweetie, but I can't condone this," I said firmly, looking at her and then back at Tyler. "I don't think it's appropriate for you to be dating a man almost ten years older than you."

Tyler leaned forward, his face serious. "I understand your concerns, ma'am, but I would never do anything to harm your daughter. I care about her deeply, and I promise to always treat her with respect."

I couldn't help but soften a bit at his sincere words, but my maternal instincts wouldn't let me let this go so easily. "I'm sorry, but I still don't think it's right. I can't have you seeing each other. Not till Charlene at least turns eighteen."

My daughter scowled, pushing her plate away. "You never let me do anything! I hate you!"

She stormed out of the kitchen, leaving Tyler and me sitting there in awkward silence. I didn't know what to say, and I could tell he was uncomfortable as well. After a few moments, he cleared his throat.

"I should go," he said, standing up from the table. "I don't want to cause any more trouble."

I nodded, feeling guilty for ruining my daughter's happiness. But I knew deep down that this was the right decision.

"I'm sorry, Tyler," I said softly. "I hope you understand."

William and Zack cleared their plates fast and disappeared up the stairs without a word.

Tyler headed toward the door. "I do understand. Thank you for dinner, ma'am."

As soon as he left, I walked over to the sink and rested my head against the cool metal. I knew I'd have to follow Charlene up the stairs and explain things to her. I couldn't believe she'd think the age gap was okay; we'd always had open and honest conversations about dating. But it had been a tough year, with everything that had happened in our family. The divorce, my sexuality. Perhaps this was just Charlene's way of acting out.

I was hunched over my computer, my eyes bleary and my mind reeling with thoughts from dinner, when I heard the soft knock on the front door. I knew it was Danni. She always had a way of showing up just when I needed her most. Seeing her was a sight for sore eyes. I feared she was still mad at me after our fight, but she was smiling now.

She came in, a bottle of wine in one hand and two glasses in the other. "Hey," she said softly, heading straight over to the living room, perching on the edge of the couch and pouring us both a glass. "You need to take a break, come sit with me for a minute."

I followed her, feeling the weight of the day dragging me down. She wrapped her arm around me as I took a sip of the wine. It was warm and comforting but didn't do much to take away the pain of what had happened. I decided to let her in, just a little, and tell her what was going on.

"I had to arrest Jimmy today. For Charlie's murder," I blurted out, feeling the tears welling up in my eyes. "He's only twenty-three. You should have seen him, screaming and completely out of it. Something wasn't right with him."

Danni clasped her mouth. "I'm sorry," she whispered. "That must have been really tough."

I pulled away, wiping my tears with the back of my hand. I didn't like her seeing me like this. I sighed. "We took him to the psychiatric emergency room. They're keeping him there for three days to evaluate him, but they're pretty certain he is having some sort of manic episode."

Danni nodded, taking a sip of her wine. "I'm sure that's for the best," she said. "It's not your fault, you know. You did what you had to do."

I shook my head. "But what if we never find out if he killed his brother?"

Danni looked at me with a seriousness that made me uneasy. "You can't blame yourself for something that's out of your control," she said firmly. "But you can take care of yourself."

I sighed heavily, leaning back into the couch. "I just feel so helpless," I admitted. "I'm supposed to be the one in charge, the one who can fix things. But I can't fix this."

Danni took my hand, her touch gentle and reassuring. "You don't have to fix everything," she said softly. "Sometimes all you can do is be there for the people you care about. And I'm here for you."

I looked at her, feeling a sense of gratitude wash over me. Her presence was a balm to my wounded soul, and I knew I could count on her to be there for me no matter what. Even if I wasn't always the easiest person to love.

"I don't know what I would do without you," I said.

Danni smiled at me, a warmth in her eyes that made my heart skip a beat. "You don't have to worry about that," she said. "I'm not going anywhere."

We sat there in silence for a while, the only sound the faint hum of the air conditioner. Danni's presence was a comfort to me, and I knew that I could get through anything as long as she was by my side.

"I'm just so tired," I admitted. "Like everything is just too much."

Danni reached out and took my hand, giving it a gentle squeeze. "I know," she said softly. "But you need to take breaks. You can't keep pushing yourself like this."

I looked at her, feeling a sense of gratitude for having her in my life. "Thank you," I said.

Danni smiled at me, her eyes filled with warmth and affection. "Anytime," she said, leaning in to give me a soft kiss.

I leaned into her, letting her wrap her arms around me once more. It didn't solve all my problems, but in that moment, it was enough to know that I wasn't alone. I had her, and that was everything.

"So, I'm gonna go see Mike tomorrow," she said casually. "Probably have dinner with him and the kids."

I sat up, feeling a twinge of surprise and jealousy. "Mike?" I repeated. "Your ex?"

Danni nodded, taking a sip of her wine. "Yeah," she said. "Just to talk about the kids, you know."

I tried to hide my jealousy, but I was uncomfortable. "Of course," I said, trying to keep my voice steady. "That makes sense."

Danni looked at me for a moment, as if sensing my hesitation. "Is everything okay?" she asked, her tone gentle.

I tried to shrug it off. "Yeah, everything's fine," I said, forcing a smile. "It's just... I don't know. It's weird, I guess."

Danni put her wine glass down and leaned in closer to me.

"What's weird?" she asked, concern etched in her features. "You see your ex all the time."

"Not all the time. We barely talk. We text and email and see each other briefly when dropping off Zack. William and Charlene are too old to be told to go to their dad's every other weekend, so they take care of that themselves. Admittedly they barely ever see him, but nothing is stopping them from going over there. Joe hates my guts after I broke his heart and since I'm fighting him on the house that he wants so badly."

Danni sighed. "Yeah, but remember that my twins are younger, only five years old. They need both their parents, and they need us more than teenagers do. I have to get along with him, for the children's sake."

I took a deep breath, trying to steady my nerves. "It's just... I guess I didn't expect you to see him so often after what he did, you know? You go over there several times a week. You have to remember that he cheated on you many times over the years. I know you have children together, but I worry that you'll forgive him or forget how much he hurt you," I said, feeling the words tumble out of my mouth. "And I can't help but feel a little jealous."

Danni's expression softened and she reached out to take my hand. "Hey, it's just to talk about the kids," she said. "You're being silly. There's no reason to be jealous."

I nodded, feeling foolish for letting my emotions get the best of me. "I know, I know," I said, feeling my cheeks flush with embarrassment. "I'm sorry, I just..." I paused, unable to keep calm. This was stirring me up inside. I couldn't pretend like it wasn't.

"No, this worries me," I said. "Why do you have to have dinner with him?"

She shrugged. "Because he asked me to go to dinner with him."

I gave her a look. "Couldn't you meet under less romantic circumstances?"

"What do you mean?"

"A dinner is kind of intimate, don't you think? Does he know you're seeing me? Have you told him?" I asked.

She sighed and clasped her hands together. "I think it is time for me to go. You're obviously upset, and I can't talk to you when you get like this."

"Like what? Asking you a simple question? Have you even told him? You haven't, have you?"

She exhaled. "If you must know, then no, I didn't see any reason to break his heart."

"What do you mean? Does he want you back? Does he think there's still a chance? After all he did to you? Why are you concerned about breaking his heart?"

She rose to her feet, leaned over, and kissed my forehead. I felt like a child. "I need to go. We can talk later, okay?"

"No, that's not okay, Danni. I want to talk about this now."

"Yeah, well, I don't. This is all a little much. I have to think of my children. They're my priority right now. We have just started to date. I can't make a big commitment right now. I told you this from the beginning. It's too early for me. We're moving too fast. I asked you to take it slow, remember?"

I swallowed hard, trying to push down my anger and frustration. Didn't she understand how much this scared me? She had been married to this guy for years. And now they were going out to dinner? Like a couple?

It hurt like crazy.

"I'll see you later," she said and began to walk away.

I tried to stop her, but my phone rang and as I pulled it out of my pocket, I was glad of the distraction.

THIRTY-FOUR

Then

Betty sat rigidly on the couch, her gaze fixed on a static-filled TV screen. Travis was next to her but she couldn't bring herself to break the suffocating silence that had settled between them. His presence felt oppressive, like a heavy fog rolling in.

It had been five years since they started trying for a child. Five years of failed attempts and heartbreak. Betty had been to countless doctors, tried every fertility treatment in the book, but nothing seemed to work. It was a constant reminder of her own failure as a woman.

"Betty, are you mad?" Travis finally spoke up. He held his empty beer can up in the air.

"No," Betty said. She went to the kitchen and fetched him another beer, then handed it to him without a word.

He grabbed her arm. "Betty, talk to me, what's the matter?"

"What is there to talk about?" Betty responded, her voice flat and eyes focused on the crumbs scattered on the kitchen counter. This morning she had woken up late, her stomach queasy with anticipation, only to find that she had gotten her period—again. Her disappointment was a lead weight in her chest.

"I know this is hard, but it will come," he said. "You just gotta give it more time."

"I don't need you to remind me how hard this is, Travis. I live it every day."

"I'm not trying to remind you of anything. I just want to support you."

"Support me? How can you support me when you're the reason we can't have a child?"

Travis' face changed drastically as Betty spoke, his eyes widening with hurt before shifting to anger. He threw his hands up in frustration, pointing an accusing finger at her. "What the heck, Betty? It's not like I'm deliberately doing this to you!"

Betty shook her head sadly. "I know that. But it still doesn't change the fact that I can't have a baby. Every time I see pregnant women or babies, it feels like a knife in my heart. We barely even make love anymore," she said softly, her voice breaking with emotion.

"Well, excuse me for not being in the mood to do something that just reminds us how we can't have a child!" Travis snapped back, his words echoing around the room as his rage intensified.

Betty's face reddened, and her fists were clenched as she rose to her feet. "Don't you think I know that?" she said, taking a step closer, her anger palpable. "Don't you think I feel the same way? But at least you don't have people asking you when we're going to have kids every time we turn around or telling us to just relax and it will happen one day. It's not that simple."

Travis' back was stiff and his mouth was pursed, his gaze chilling as it pierced Betty. It was almost like he was accusing her of something she hadn't done. Tears stung the corners of her eyes as she realized that he may have been blaming their infertility on her. Deep down, she knew it wasn't fair, yet in that moment it felt like the truth.

"I'm sorry," she whispered, tears streaming down her face. "I just don't know what to do anymore."

Travis slowly crumpled the beer can in his hand and dropped it into an overflowing trash can. He wiped a sleeve across his lips and flashed her an easy smile. "Go get me another beer, and come keep me company while I watch some TV?" His voice was low and inviting.

"Come watch TV? That's your answer? That's all you have to say to me?"

Betty slammed the door behind her as she stormed out of the house. She couldn't believe how Travis was acting. How could he be so insensitive? She needed a break from him. She needed to clear her head.

As she sat on the porch steps, she saw a small child sitting on the pavement outside of the neighbor's house across the street. It was dark out, and she wondered what he was doing here alone. Where were his parents?

She walked over to the child and knelt down in front of him. "Hey, are you okay?" she asked gently.

The boy looked up at her with big brown eyes and nodded his head shyly. "I'm waiting for my mommy," he said softly.

Betty's heart broke. She couldn't imagine leaving a child alone outside at night. "Do you happen to know where your mommy is?" she asked him.

He shook his head. "No, she said she'd be right back but she's been gone a long time."

Betty's maternal instincts kicked in and she couldn't just leave the child alone outside.

"Come on, let's go knock on your door and see if your mommy is home now," she said to him, holding out her hand.

The boy took her hand and they walked to the neighbor's door. Betty knocked, but there was no answer. She tried a few more times, but still no answer.

Now she was getting worried. She didn't know this child or

his mother. What if something had happened to her? She made a decision.

"Okay, we're going to go to my house and wait for your mommy there," she said to the child.

The boy nodded, and Betty led him by the hand back to her house. Travis had fallen asleep in front of the TV and was snoring heavily. She took the boy to the kitchen and sat him down.

Betty's eyes scanned the young boy before her, taking in his sunken cheeks and hollowed eyes.

"When is the last time you ate?" she asked, concern laced in her voice.

The boy shrugged nonchalantly, but as soon as he spotted the bread on her counter, a primal hunger overtook him. Betty quickly made him a ham sandwich with thick slices of meat and slathered-on mayonnaise. She poured him a glass of ice-cold milk, hoping it would soothe his parched throat.

As he ate, Betty couldn't help but study the boy's disheveled appearance. His clothes were tattered and dirty, and there was a deep scar across his cheek. She wondered where he had come from and why he seemed so lost and alone.

The thought crossed her mind to call the local police station and report him missing, but for some reason, she couldn't bring herself to do it. Instead, she decided to wait with him until his mother returned, offering him a warm place to rest and a comforting meal to ease his worries. As she sat next to him, she couldn't shake off the feeling that there was more to this boy's story than met the eye.

THIRTY-FIVE

BILLIE ANN

The bright blue light of my phone illuminated the darkness, and I squinted at the caller ID. A wave of panic swept over me as I saw my mother's name, like an unwelcome omen. My chest tightened, and dread engulfed me, and I furrowed my eyebrows in confusion. My heart thumped against my ribs as if it was trying to escape.

"My mom is never up this late," I said, my voice a whisper. "Why is she calling me at this hour?"

Taking a deep breath, I rubbed my temples; the phone call from my mother had come in out of the blue at this late hour.

I answered the call, hearing a brief silence before my mother began speaking in a thin, raspy voice that sounded like it had been wrung dry.

"Honey. Sorry to call you this late."

"Hey, Mom," I said, trying to keep my voice steady. My chest tightened as I heard my mother's voice crack and choke up. She struggled for air between her sobs, and a chill ran down my spine. It was like someone had stabbed me with a needle of guilt. I had never heard my mother sound so broken.

I heard my mother's sobs coming through the phone. I could feel the anxiety rising in my chest.

"Mom, what's wrong?" I asked, dreading her response.

She couldn't form a complete sentence, but managed to choke out, "It's your cousins..." Her despair seemed to envelope me from afar.

"My cousins?" I repeated, bewildered. "Auntie Tessa's twins?"

"Yes," my mother sobbed. "They were attacked."

My stomach turned and a coldness crept up my spine as I processed the news. I felt my heart sink, like a stone in my chest. I opened my mouth to ask what had happened, but I already knew. The teenagers that had been attacked the night before in Melbourne. It had to be them.

"What? How? Are they okay?" The panic was rising within me, and I could feel my hands trembling as I tried to keep my voice steady.

"Jeremy is dead, Alex is in the ICU, in the hospital," my mother said, her breaths coming in ragged gasps. "It was brutal, honey. They don't know if she is going to make it."

I felt a lump form in my throat as I tried to process the gravity of what my mother was saying. My cousins, whom I had watched grow up along with my own children, and whom I loved, had been in a tragedy. And worst of all, I knew exactly what had happened to them. They were the ones my Chief had talked about earlier, when she told me about the attack at the zoo. I wondered if the detectives on that case had connected Jeremy and Alex to me yet—if Chief Harold knew. It was a different town; not our jurisdiction, but the murders were so clearly linked. To me. I knew I had to get to the hospital right away to be there for my family.

"I'm coming, Mom," I said firmly, already starting to grab my car keys and wallet. "I'll be there as soon as I can."

"Thank you, sweetie," my mother said, her voice shaking with emotion. "We need you here."

I ended the call and stared blankly ahead, my mind racing in confusion.

My heart was tightening at the thought of what my aunt must be going through. She was younger than my father by ten years and had been late when having children. Our kids were close in age, but she was another family member I rarely saw. We had been close when I was younger, she always had a calming presence, and we used to paint together in the sunroom at the back of her house, but I assumed my mother had kept her from me in the last few years. Scared for people to find out that my marriage had broken down. And why.

As I started driving toward the hospital, I couldn't shake off the feeling of dread gnawing at me. Who could have done this to my cousins? Was it really Jimmy? I knew the answers to those questions would be hard to find, but I would do everything in my power to discover the truth.

THIRTY-SIX

BILLIE ANN

I arrived at the hospital, and a sterile smell filled my nostrils, making me feel even more uneasy. As I walked into the room, my mom and dad were there waiting for me. My mom's eyes were red-rimmed, and my dad looked like he hadn't slept in days, which I was sure he hadn't.

"Aunt Tessie is here too," my mom said, nodding toward my aunt who was sitting in a chair by the window.

She looked at me when she heard her name, tears streaming down her face.

"How is Alexandra doing?" I asked, my voice barely above a whisper.

My mom shook her head. "Not good. They haven't told us much, but she is on life support. She was in surgery for two hours, but they might have to do more."

"And Aunt Tessie? How's she holding up?"

"Not good," my mom said. "She had to go identify Jeremy at the morgue, and she's been broken ever since. The doctor gave her a sedative, and now she's just sitting there."

I felt a knot form in my stomach. Poor Aunt Tessie. She had lost her husband three years ago to cancer and had been heartbroken ever since. She was finally getting back on her feet, and now this?

I walked over to my aunt and took her hand. She looked up at me with a pained expression.

"I'm so sorry," I said, trying to hold back my own tears. "Is there anything I can do to help?"

Aunt Tessie looked up at me, her eyes red and puffy. She just shook her head and buried her face in her hands. I could see her whole body shaking with sobs. Finally, she looked up at me again, and petted my arm. "No, honey," she said, her voice barely audible. "There's nothing anyone can do. It's just too much to bear."

I sat with Aunt Tessie for a while, holding her hand and trying to comfort her as best I could. My parents sat on the other side of the room, looking just as devastated as Aunt Tessie. It was hard to believe that just a few days ago, everything had been normal. Now, our entire world had been turned upside down.

As I sat there, I couldn't help but think about Jeremy. He had been such a good guy—always smiling, always making everyone laugh. It was hard to imagine that he was gone. And Alexandra...

I couldn't bear to think of what Alexandra was going through. She had always been so full of life, so full of energy. It was hard to imagine her hooked up to machines, fighting for her life. I felt a knot of anger form in the pit of my stomach. She was just a kid—fourteen years old. How could something like this happen to her? It wasn't fair. None of it was fair. I felt a lump form in my throat as tears threatened to spill down my cheeks. I leaned over to Aunt Tessie and whispered in her ear. "We're gonna get through this," I said. "We have to be strong for them."

Aunt Tessie nodded, looking up at me with tears in her eyes. "I know," she said. "But it's just so hard. So damn hard."

I squeezed her hand, feeling helpless and lost. There was

nothing I could do to make things better, no magic cure that could bring Jeremy and Charlie back or make Alexandra better.

Suddenly, the door to the room burst open and a doctor rushed in. "I'm sorry to interrupt," he said, "but we need to speak with you about Alexandra's condition."

My mom, dad, and I all stood up, our hearts racing. Aunt Tessie was still too upset to be hearing this but she had given her consent for the staff to talk with my parents. The doctor led us out into the hallway and began to explain what was going on. The surgery had been successful in stopping the bleeding, but the damage to Alexandra's brain was severe. She was in a coma, and they weren't sure if she would ever wake up. The next twenty-four hours would be critical for her future.

My mom burst into tears, and my dad put his arm around her shoulders. I felt numb. This couldn't be happening. The doctor continued to explain the procedure they had done and what they were doing to monitor Alexandra's condition. But my mind was elsewhere. I couldn't believe what was happening. My cousin was fighting for her life and my family was falling apart.

As the doctor finished speaking, my mom and dad went back into the room to be with Aunt Tessie. I stayed in the hallway, needing a moment to process everything. I couldn't believe that Alexandra might never wake up. It was a nightmare. My heart felt heavy as I watched my parents try to console each other. Aunt Tessie was still sitting in the room, lost in her own grief. I felt so helpless that I didn't know what to do.

As the doctor left, I walked back into the room. Aunt Tessie looked up at me, and I could see the pain in her eyes.

"What did he say?" she asked, her voice shaking.

I took a deep breath and sat down beside her. "She's in a coma," I said, my voice low and hoarse. "They don't know if she's going to wake up."

Aunt Tessie let out a cry of pain, and I put my arms around

her. We sat there in silence, both lost in our own grief. If this was all Jimmy's work, then it would just about kill my parents and rip apart our family. Tom had told me the twins' names were also on the list found at Jimmy's. It didn't look too good. I wasn't ready to let our family be torn apart. I needed to get to the bottom of this, and I had a feeling my work was far from done yet.

THIRTY-SEVEN

Then

Betty watched the young boy in front of her. His tousled blond hair was matted with dirt, and his cheeks were smudged from the day's play. He had a small frame, and his thin, grubby clothes hung loosely off his body. She saw that his fingernails were blackened with soil and offered him some paper and crayons to pass the time while waiting for his mother to return. He smiled at her gratefully and introduced himself as John, revealing he was only five years old.

Betty smiled at John and asked, "So, John, do you have any siblings?"

His gaze dropped to the ground, and he bit his lip. With a slight shake of his head, he said in a low voice, "No. It's just me and my mom." A profound sadness seemed to fill the room.

Betty's gaze softened as she looked into the little boy's eyes. Her heart ached for someone so young to already feel such loneliness. She leaned in and placed a gentle hand on his shoulder.

"Where is your mommy?" she asked again. The boy averted his gaze and stared at the ground, and Betty knew he had been asked this many times before without giving an answer. Because he didn't have one.

John's shoulders rose and fell in a single, defeated shrug. Betty felt her heart drop into her stomach. She couldn't comprehend the anguish he must be feeling. Reaching out, she placed her hand onto his forearm and gave it an affectionate pat, hoping to bring some kind of solace.

"Hey, don't worry," she said in a soft voice that nevertheless carried a note of determination. "We'll figure it out. Together."

Betty watched as the boy stifled a yawn and rubbed his eyes. She hesitated for a moment before suggesting, "I know it's getting late. How about spending the night? We have an extra bedroom all ready—complete with fresh sheets and a fluffy pillow."

The boy's gaze was distant and his shoulders slumped in exhaustion. She guided him to the bathroom and began running lukewarm water into the tub. She glanced at the little boy in the mirror, watching his reflection as she lathered his hair with shampoo. Using her fingertips, she created a spiky wave, careful not to get any soap in his eyes as he peered up at her. He smiled timidly and met her gaze in the mirror, their laughter echoing off the tile.

As she cradled the shivering child in a warm towel, she could hear Travis snoring from the living room. His beer can was still clutched in one hand; he was passed out on the sofa as usual at this time. She quietly hurried down the stairs to the kitchen and set about warming some milk for the boy. He drank it with great satisfaction, and she felt such deep love for him.

Betty's heart sank as she and John slowly trudged up the stairs. The silence between them seemed to speak volumes, with Betty's mind racing with a mix of emotions; anger at his mother for leaving him alone, yet also an overwhelming sense of compassion for the small boy who had no control over the circumstances he'd been dealt. He was small and fragile, his feet barely making a sound on the carpeted hallway. He didn't deserve this life he had been given.

Betty stepped into the bedroom and showed him to a single bed, neatly made with freshly laundered cotton sheets. She stooped over him and tucked him in, smoothing out the wrinkles in the blankets. Her heart filled with an overwhelming sense of protectiveness. She placed a glass of cold water on the bedside table and brushed his forehead with a gentle kiss before whispering a soft good night.

But as she stood up to leave, she felt a small hand cling to hers.

"Please don't go," John said, his voice barely above a whisper.

Betty's eyes filled with tears at the sight of the small boy, curled up in a fetal position, alone and shaking from fear. She could feel his despair and without hesitation, she crawled into bed beside him, enveloping him in a tight embrace as the warm blankets cocooned them.

"It's okay, John," she said softly. "I'm here."

Betty felt her chest tighten as she listened to the rhythmic rise and fall of the small boy's breathing, lying next to her in the darkness. She reached over to stroke his face tenderly and a wave of protectiveness washed over her. How could any parent just abandon their child out on the street like this? Tears pricked at the corners of her eyes.

Maybe he didn't even have a mother?

Maybe I can be his mother?

THIRTY-EIGHT

BILLIE ANN

My hands shook on the steering wheel as I drove to Jimmy's house. Tears blurred my vision, and despair hung like a heavy fog in the car. The hospital had been filled with grim faces as we all waited for any news on Alexandra's condition. But waiting felt unacceptable—I needed to do something, find some answers, and break out of this nightmare. I had checked in with the team, and since the connection had been made between the teenagers, the case was now ours to solve. They were all working hard on interviewing witnesses at the scene in Melbourne and taking statements, but so far, there had been no good clues to follow just yet. I couldn't stop thinking of my nephew.

Jimmy had always been part of our family, but at that moment he was a suspect, accused of murdering someone close to us. How could someone who shared our blood do such a thing? I clenched the steering wheel as I thought back on all that I knew of him—he had been obsessed with dinosaurs and LEGO when he was younger, he was nerdy and detail-oriented, a quiet boy as far as I knew. The idea of him committing such

violence seemed impossible. Could he really have killed Charlie
and Jeremy and hurt Alexandra?

When I arrived at the house, yellow and black crime scene
tape fluttered in the night breeze. I knew the team had already
searched most of the building and found nothing of interest.
Most of the street had been cordoned off for the investigation
and police cars clogged the side streets. Whispers of what
happened hummed through the hushed crowd that lingered by
outside. I walked up to an officer that guarded the scene and
was pointed to a forensic tech who stood on the porch taking
photographs. The flash played over her protective gloves as she
supervised other technicians that searched inside for crucial
evidence.

I cleared my throat and asked, "What do we have so far?"
My voice wavered and I tried to make it firmer. I hoped no one
would realize I shouldn't be there.

The tech officer scanned the room with her thoughtful gaze.
She pointed to a few spots on the floor. "We've found some
blood splatters here on the kitchen tile," she said. "Plus, there is
evidence of the gunshots that blasted through the place when
we arrested him."

My head bobbed ever so slightly as I remembered the events
of the last few days.

I nervously ran a hand through my hair, my eyes narrowed
in anticipation. "Anything else?" I asked. "I was told there was a
list of names somewhere. Did you find it?" I held my breath as I
waited for the answer.

"As a matter of fact, we did," she said as she took me to the
back room. I could see the shelves lined with stacked white
evidence bags, labeled and numbered in black marker. She
pulled one out from the box and showed it to me.

My hands trembled as she reached into the bag and pulled
out a crumpled sheet of paper. It was covered in Jimmy's blocky
scrawl. A chill ran down my spine as I read through the Hitlist

—there were names I recognized—including my cousins Jeremy and Alexandra. The cold knot in my stomach tightened as I stared at the page, unable to process that my nephew had made this list.

He is sick, Billie Ann. He's very sick.

The tech officer pointed to a long black box on the table. She opened it and pulled out something that made my heart sink. It was a grotesque mask, with a wide, open mouth and white eyes filled with terror. A shiver ran down my spine when I remembered the report from Charlie's murder: the murderer had been seen wearing a costume featuring a white mask just like this one.

"Are you okay?" the tech officer asked.

The room spun around me and my knees buckled. I gasped for breath as the truth sank in; my nephew had used his own hands to brutally take the lives of two people he shared a family with. I staggered backward, my stomach roiling, feeling like I might faint.

I need to get out of here. Now!

As I made my way back to my car, I couldn't help but feel a deep sadness and pain. My whole body felt weighed down with grief as images of Jeremy and Charlie flashed before my eyes. Jimmy was connected to both crimes, what more could I do to save him?

THIRTY-NINE

BILLIE ANN

I had been up all night, combing through the evidence my team had collected. As I stared out the kitchen window, watching the sun break through a dazzling display of orange and pink hues that bounced off the glass-like surface of the canal below, I felt as if I was in some kind of trance; yet even this serene beauty could not soothe my troubled soul. I wasn't supposed to be working either of the cases, and Chief Harold had already called me to ensure I kept away from the station. But Tom had sent me emails with copies of the main case files. He knew I could help. He was a good friend.

William's and Zack's incessant arguing over the last bowl of cereal only added to my distress, their words sounding like nails against an old chalkboard. I hadn't told them about their cousins yet and what had happened to them. Not yet. I felt it was too early, and I didn't want to scare them. But right now they were getting on my last nerve.

"Can't you two just settle down and eat your breakfast quietly for once?" I barked, my voice carrying a sharpness that I immediately regretted. I threw my hands in the air, exasperated. My shout echoed through the kitchen and caused my children to abruptly freeze, their eyes wide with shock as they stared at me. As soon as I could see the hurt on their faces, I regretted my sharply spoken words.

I swallowed back the heat of my frustration, and it trickled down my spine in a weary wave. I sighed, "I'm sorry. I didn't mean to yell. Just... please. Finish up." I gestured at the scattered papers and textbooks on the table. "It's almost time for school."

As they retreated upstairs to get dressed, I sipped my coffee and tried to shake off the fog of fatigue. I had no idea how to get through this day. I had called my mom earlier and asked for news on Alexandra, but there was still nothing to report. Mom and Dad had gone home to get a few hours of sleep, and were about to return to the hospital when I called.

"Okay, keep me updated," I had said with heavy heart.

I was going to call the psychiatric hospital later today and ask them how far they were in evaluating Jimmy and when he would be ready to be interviewed. The team needed to try to interrogate him, if they were allowed to.

A boat sailed past my backyard, and I couldn't help but feel a pang of envy. The passengers onboard were laughing and chatting, completely unaware of the storm that had recently battered my life for days on end. They looked so happy and content, not knowing the kind of heartache I had been through. I suddenly wished to be in their shoes, living a worry-free existence.

The weight of the world seemed to be bearing down on me, and every breath was a reminder that the situation was real, not some distant nightmare. I had to stay composed for myself and my family, as well as for Alexandra and her battle to stay alive.

With a deep breath, I gathered myself and headed upstairs to check on the boys. They were arguing again, this time about who got to use the bathroom first.

"Will has been in there for half an hour," Zack said,

hammering on the door. "I need to brush my teeth and pee before we go."

"When I'm done," William yelled from behind the closed door.

"But I really have to go. Now," Zack said and looked up at me for help. "Badly."

Zack banged his fist on the bathroom door, furrowing his brow. "Will, I'm gonna burst if you don't let me in! Like right now!" His hand flew to his crotch as he groaned with desperation.

"Just a second," William yelled from within.

Zack stood outside, crossing and uncrossing his legs, dreading the thought of wetting himself.

"You'll just have to wait like everyone else," William yelled. "Till I have done my hair."

"You're so mean!" Zack cried.

Charlene came out of her room, holding the keys to her truck. "Guys, we're leaving now. I want to go early today so I can have time with my friends before school starts."

"Don't you mean your boyfriend?" William yelled.

I stared at her. "You're not still seeing him, are you?"

She rolled her eyes. "Just get the kids ready or I will leave without them," she said, then walked down the stairs.

"But, mo-om, I really have to..." Zack whined.

"Guys, enough!" I said firmly, but not with the same sharpness as before. "We all need to get ready for the day. Let's work together and get it done."

William emerged from the bathroom, zipping up his jeans. Zack rushed in and slammed the door shut behind him.

Once downstairs, the boys exchanged a glance, their eyes wide with resentment for each other. They snatched up their backpacks and headed for the door, not looking back.

I stepped forward and shouted after them. "Zack, don't forget your dad is picking you up today." His hand shot up in a wave before he disappeared out the door. When they were gone, I was left standing alone, feeling relieved but also frustrated.

Sighing, I headed back into the kitchen and grabbed my coffee cup from the counter. As I took my first sip, my phone vibrated on the countertop. Feeling a sudden chill in the room, I glanced at the display. An unknown number stared back at me. My hands started to tremble as I unlocked my phone and read the message; my mouth went dry and I felt like I couldn't breathe. Suddenly, my phone slipped from my fingers and clattered against the tile floor.

FORTY

Then

Betty's stomach ached as she stood on the wooden porch of John's house, across the street from her own. The sun was shining down through the leaves of the palm tree. Her hand trembled as she reached for the doorbell. Going over there had become her daily ritual in hopes that John's mother had come home.

A week had passed now since she found him in the street, and so far, the house remained quiet, as if it had been abandoned for years. The curtains were drawn tight in every window. The driveway was empty, and aside from the creaking of tree branches in the breeze, all was still. Betty had kept a close eye on it for many days, and seen no sign of life, no one coming and going. Betty was starting to worry. What if the boy had been abandoned? What if he was all alone in the world? The poor kid. She couldn't leave him like that. She had grown fond of him over the past week. She enjoyed taking care of him and the thought of leaving him to fend for himself was unbearable. She knew that if she contacted the Department of Children and Families, then he would end up in the foster system. She couldn't do that to the poor boy.

Travis was annoyed with her and kept telling her to report it, but she told him to wait. His mother was going to return.

"We can't just keep a child, you know," he grunted this same morning over breakfast.

"Why not? Has anyone reported him missing?" she asked. "You're a cop, you should know."

Travis shook his head in disbelief, his brow creased and emotion playing across his face.

"No, there has been no missing person report on any child around town." He paused for a beat, steeling himself to say the sentence that he felt needed to be repeated. "But still. You can't just keep him."

Betty met his gaze without wavering, her posture rigid with determination. "I'm not. I'm taking him to his mother as soon as she returns," she said firmly, willing him to understand. She softened her voice, but there was an unmistakable finality in her tone. The conversation was over. There was no more to be said.

Now, John's house loomed before her, a giant beast with its crooked paint job and lopsided roof. She stood on the front porch for a few seconds, gathering her courage. With a deep breath, she pressed the doorbell and waited. When no one answered, she knocked on the door in rapid succession and called out, "Hello?" Anxiety coursed through her veins as she waited.

Betty's finger hovered over the doorbell, uncertainty gnawing at her gut. The wind whistled through the nearby palm trees, and she felt the hot breeze hit her face. She tried to suppress a sigh as she pressed down on the button again, only to hear an echo of silence. She pondered the possibility of turning around and going back home, like she had done so many times before. But then something stirred inside of her; something that told her to try something else this time.

Betty's hand shook as she reached for the door handle. She expected it to be locked tight, but it turned easily in her grasp. She let out a quiet gasp and stepped inside hesitantly. The air was still and heavy with anticipation; she could hear her heart thudding in her chest as she took careful steps deeper into the old house.

Betty stepped into the living room, cringing from the layer of dust that coated the furniture and shelves. Her eyes followed a trail of debris to the kitchen, where she gagged at the smell of rotting food. Gritting her teeth, she waded carefully past piles of dishes in the sink, feeling squelchy footsteps on the sticky-sweet floor as she made her way to the back hall. With each step, Betty's stomach churned with a growing sense of dread, yet she pressed forward, desperately hoping for any clues that would lead her to John's missing mother.

How had a child been living in this?

Just as she was about to give up, she heard a faint noise coming from upstairs. Betty's heart raced as she tiptoed up the creaky staircase, her mind racing with possibilities of what she might find. When she finally reached the top of the stairs, she was met with a closed door at the end of the hallway. Betty took a deep breath before turning the handle and pushing the door open.

Betty stepped cautiously into the bedroom to find John's mother, pale and still, on the bed. Her eyes snapped to the syringe lying discarded on the nightstand next to her. Betty's mouth twisted in revulsion before she rushed toward the phone, her fingers frantically pressing 911.

As she waited for help to arrive, Betty stood over the woman, her gaze hard with anger. What kind of a mother would do this?

Betty couldn't bear the thought of John coming back to this nightmare. She made a decision right then and there that she was going to take care of him. She was going to be his new family.

As the ambulance arrived and paramedics rushed past her, Betty promised herself that she was going to give John the life he deserved. A life filled with love and happiness. Betty was going to be his mother now. And no one would ever hurt him again.

FORTY-ONE

BILLIE ANN

Chief Harold burst through the front door with a ferocity that filled the room. Her eyes darted around as she took inventory of the situation, the tension palpable in the air. She turned to me, her gaze piercing and intense, and I could feel my hands shaking even more. Nestled on the cool tile floor of my kitchen, fixated on my phone, I'd never felt so helpless.

The silence was unbearable until Chief Harold's voice boomed out.

"I came as fast as I could," she said, her tone reassuring. "What's going on?"

I looked up, feeling overwhelmed and at a loss. Tears pooled in my eyes as I struggled to find the words. "I didn't know who else to call," I said, desperation thick in my throat. "I'm completely... lost."

"Easy there, Billie Ann," she said in a gentle tone. "Take your time and just tell me what happened. You sounded really upset on the phone." She seated herself next to me on the floor, her long legs crossed at the ankles. The tips of her brown cowboy boots were decorated with silver stitching, and her jeans were tucked neatly inside them.

I felt my chest tighten, a heavy weight sinking to the pit of my stomach. I tried to steady my hands as I retrieved my phone from my pocket and showed her the image on the screen. Her usually lively eyes narrowed in confusion at the sight of the distorted figure in the picture.

"Who is this?" she asked with a worried voice.

My throat closed as I croaked out the words, "It's my brother."

I couldn't bring myself to look at the photograph of his crumpled body lying in a pool of blood. Chief Harold leaned closer, her face pale in horror as she took in the graphic details.

"Who sent you this?" she asked.

"Unknown number."

"Well, we need to trace it. Let me handle that."

I stared at the photo, tears springing to my eyes.

"He's hurt, but he looks to be alive still," the Chief said, her voice filled with a mix of frustration and worry. Harold's eyebrows knit together as she looked at the picture closer. The man—my brother Andrew—was on the floor in a strange position, his limbs twisted and broken in ways that made my stomach turn. The blood that pooled around him made my heart race.

Chief Harold took a deep breath as she studied the photo on my phone. Her face twisted in a grimace as she saw the broken limbs and the pool of blood surrounding him on the floor. Then she grabbed my hand in hers and pulled me into a hug.

"This is bad, Billie Ann," she said, when letting go of me. She was looking at me, her eyes worried. "I need to call this in and get the team over here ASAP."

I nodded, my heart racing with fear and worry for my brother. I hadn't seen him in years. He was a drug addict and we had lost contact with him after a Thanksgiving some years ago, when he showed up high and my mom had to throw him out. Since then, my parents hadn't wanted to talk about him, and he had been this shadowy figure of a family member that no one dared to mention. Over the years—before the fallout—my parents had tried everything to help him. Rehab after rehab, and he always fell back in. At some point I guess they just thought that they needed to cut ties with him. They simply couldn't deal with it anymore. I had always loved Andrew and been closer with him than Peter when growing up. Seeing him like this broke my heart. Who? Who would do this? To him? To my family? I watched as Chief Harold pulled out her phone and called a number, speaking quickly and urgently to whoever was on the other end of the line.

While waiting for the team to arrive, I paced back and forth, wringing my hands in anxiety. I couldn't believe this was happening to my family, and my mind was racing with questions and fears.

Finally, I heard the sound of sirens approaching, and I rushed to the door to let the team in. Big Tom and Scott rushed to me, eyes concerned. Big Tom pulled me into a deep hug.

"What's going on, Billie Ann? Someone is targeting your family..."

My hands trembled as I slowly brought my phone to them, displaying the image. They gasped in unison, eyes widening with shock and horror. Scott's forehead was creased in confusion and his skin ghostly pale. His voice was barely audible as he asked, "What sort of person could do this?"

"I don't know," I said, my voice shaky. "But I need you to find them. It's my brother. We need to find them. And him. Before they hurt him even more or kill him."

Big Tom nodded. "Don't worry, Billie Ann. Scott and I will find them."

"I need to call my parents," I said, feeling myself break down. "They deserve to know that he's hurt."

Big Tom nodded, and I pulled out my phone, calling my parents' number. My mother picked up almost immediately.

"Billie Ann?" she said, sounding worried.

"Mom..." I felt my voice choke up. "It's Andrew. Or at least I think it is. I got a picture of him. It's bad."

"What do you mean?" Her voice was shaking. "What... what's happened? Billie Ann, what's going on?"

"I don't know," I said, my voice choking up. "He's hurt. Bad. Someone has him. We don't know who did this or why. But we're going to find them and get him back."

There was a silence, and I could hear my mother crying on the other end of the line. It was a heartbreaking sound.

"I love him so much," she whispered. "I can't believe this is happening."

"I know, Mom," I said, my voice shaking. "We're going to figure this out. I promise."

There was another silence on the line, and after what felt like hours, she spoke again,

"We're on our way," my mother said. "We'll be there momentarily."

I nodded and put the phone down, and we all stood there in silence for a moment.

Looking over at Scott and Big Tom, I saw that their faces were hard, their jaws clenched. They were completely focused on the task at hand, and nothing was going to stop them from finding the one who hurt my brother. Immediately, they started assessing the situation. Looking at the photograph on my phone, they began to form an idea of what had happened.

"Look at this," Big Tom said, pointing to the placement of the body. "This wasn't just a random act of violence. Whoever did this had a sick plan. Look at the way his legs are twisted. Look at the way his head is turned around."

Scott nodded, "Any idea why?"

"Other than to cause the most pain possible, what else could it be?" Big Tom said. "He knows what he's doing. He did this to cause pain. Whoever this guy is, he wanted to hurt your brother. To cause him as much pain as possible."

I felt myself break down as the gravity of the situation hit me.

"It's like it's almost..." Scott said and trailed off.

"What?" I asked impatiently.

"Hmm," he added and zoomed in on the picture.

"I don't understand what you're saying," I said. "What is it?"

"A message," Scott said. "It's a message."

"I don't understand," I said. "What do you mean?"

"Look at it," Scott said. "It's like there's a message here. This wasn't just about causing pain to your brother. It's about sending a message to you. Look."

"Me?" I asked, furrowing my brow. "What do you mean by that?"

"Whoever did this wanted you to see it," Scott said. "Not just the photo, I mean. But they wanted you to notice this. This was a message for you."

I stared down at the photograph of my brother, his frail body bent awkwardly over a spot on the ground. I squinted, trying to make out what was hidden beneath him. An icy chill ran down my spine as I realized it was a message written in thick letters of drying blood.

I AM WILDE

FORTY-TWO

BILLIE ANN

As I stepped closer, the imposing brick building with its barred windows and heavy steel doors grew larger. I walked through the entrance to be met by a heavyset nurse with arms crossed over her chest. She narrowed her eyes as she spoke.

"Excuse me, ma'am," she said, from behind the glass wall. "Can I help you?"

"I need to talk to Dr. Jameson," I replied, flashing my badge. "It's urgent."

The nurse fidgeted, her eyes darting around as if she was trying to make an invisible decision. She finally sighed and stepped out of the way, gesturing for me to follow. We walked down a long hallway with beige walls and fluorescent lights flickering overhead. At the end of the hallway was a door labeled "Diagnosis Room"; the nurse opened it, and I stepped inside. The room was small and cluttered, with a lone desk in the center, piled high with patient files. A middle-age man in a white coat sat at the desk, his graying hair illuminated by the glaring computer monitor.

"Dr. Jameson?" I said, approaching him.

My voice wavered as I approached. He glanced up from his

work, a pair of glasses perched upon the end of his nose. "Yes, that's me," he replied.

I leaned forward and spoke with urgency in my voice, "I need to talk to Jimmy Wilde, as soon as possible."

Dr. Jameson sighed; the sound was heavy in the quiet office. He leaned back in his chair and pushed his glasses up the bridge of his nose with one finger.

"I'm afraid that's not possible," he said. "We're still evaluating him and he's not ready to see visitors."

I slammed my hand down on the desk in frustration, rattling the pen holder, papers, and pictures of Dr. Jameson's family.

"Sorry," I said, my voice low but firm. "I need to talk to him now. It's a matter of life and death. We have a missing person who is in great danger, and Jimmy may be the key to saving him."

Dr. Jameson looked at me skeptically, but his eyes flickered toward the badge in my hand. His eyebrows rose as he read my name.

"You need to be gentle with him," he said, standing up and leading me out of the office and down another hallway.

Was he letting me see Jimmy because I was related to him? Or was it my authority as an officer? I wasn't sure, but I wasn't going to question it either.

We walked silently, breathing in the antiseptic smell of the hospital. We passed by several rooms, each with its own patient, their faces full of despair and exhaustion. At last, we reached the room at the end of the hall where my nephew Jimmy Wilde was being held. Dr. Jameson paused before unlocking the door and gesturing for me to enter.

I stepped inside the room and found Jimmy sitting on his bed, eyes distant and expressionless. He looked up at me as I approached but his gaze seemed to drift farther away from me, like he had been somewhere else entirely. There was a tangible sense of sorrow that hung in the air.

"Jimmy," I said, my voice coming out in a hushed whisper. "Can you hear me?"

There was no response. I reached out and gently touched his arm, but he didn't react.

Dr. Jameson stepped in behind me and spoke up. "I warned you, he's in no state to talk right now."

I turned to him, frustration boiling inside me. "What did you give him?" I demanded. "He was different when I saw him last."

Dr. Jameson sighed and rubbed his forehead wearily. "We had to administer a sedative. He was becoming agitated and aggressive toward the staff. It was for his own safety as well as ours."

"I need him to answer my questions," I said. I still wasn't sure if Jimmy had taken Andy. I hoped I could take him off my suspect list to focus on other leads. Jimmy couldn't have used the phone and sent me the photo of Andy. We were tracing the call and trying to find something to identify Andy's location in the image, but we'd had no luck so far.

Dr. Jameson looked at me with a mix of pity and concern. "I'm sorry, but I don't think he's capable of answering any questions right now. He's heavily sedated and won't be able to give you any useful information."

I felt a wave of frustration and desperation wash over me. My brother's life was on the line and I needed answers. I turned back to Jimmy and tried again.

"Jimmy, please," I said, my voice cracking with emotion. "I know you're in there somewhere. I need you to fight this. I need you to tell me where Andrew is. Please. He's my brother."

The room was silent as the seconds ticked by and Jimmy stared blankly ahead. His pupils suddenly dilated and his eyes came into focus, looking at me with growing recognition. His throat gurgled as he spoke in a scratchy whisper.

"Your brother..."

Chills shot down my spine as I felt his intense gaze bore through me. He watched me intently, his expression eerie.

"Yes, Andrew. Uncle Andrew."

"He's dead," he said, then started laughing. "They're all dead."

I stared at him, my mouth agape and my fingers trembling. Jimmy's eyes were cold, his face pale and expressionless. I froze, feeling a chill run down my spine. "What do you mean, they're all dead?" I asked, my voice trembling.

Jimmy's laughter subsided, and he looked at me with a strange mix of pity and amusement. He leaned in close, his breath heavy with the smell of mint.

"You really don't know, do you?" he said, his voice low and husky. "Your brother, your uncle, they were just the beginning. There are more. So many more."

My heart sank as I realized what he was saying. "You're behind the killings, aren't you?" I asked, my voice barely above a whisper.

Jimmy smiled, a twisted, deranged grin that made my blood run cold. "Behind them? No. I am them."

I'm Wilde.

I backed away from him, my eyes wide with horror. Dr. Jameson stepped forward, looking at Jimmy with concern.

"That's enough, Jimmy," he said, his voice firm. "You need to rest now. And you need to leave, Detective Wilde. Now."

FORTY-THREE

Then

Betty watched as John ran around the backyard, his laughter filling the air. She leaned against the porch railing, a smile spreading across her face. It had been years since John had come into her life, and now he was officially her son. They had adopted him. She couldn't imagine her life without him.

Travis had been distant lately, but Betty didn't let it get to her. She knew he was out there trying to make a difference, catching bad people and keeping their community safe. It didn't matter to her that he spent less time at home, what mattered was that they were a family.

As she watched John play, she felt a sense of contentment wash over her. She had everything she ever wanted. A beautiful home, a loving son, and a husband who cared for her. Sure, they had their ups and downs, but they always managed to work through their problems.

She called out to John, who came running over to her. He looked up at her with his big, bright eyes and a toothy grin on his face. Betty knelt down and wrapped her arms around him, feeling his small body pressed against hers. She held him tightly, feeling his warmth and the beat of his heart against her chest.

"I love you, John," she whispered into his ear.

"I love you too, Mom!" he responded, hugging her tightly.

Betty felt like she could stay in that moment forever. She didn't need anything else but this moment with her son. She knew that life could be tough, but with John by her side, she could handle anything that came her way.

As she stood up, she saw Travis' car pull up in the driveway. She smiled, knowing that he was home. She watched as he walked toward her, a tired but happy expression on his face.

"Hey," he said, giving her a quick kiss on the lips.

"Hey," she responded, looking into his eyes. "How was work?"

"Busy, but good. We caught the guy who's been robbing the local convenience stores. He was dumb enough to brag about what he had been up to down at the local Irish pub. Can you imagine? Oh, yeah, and I'm getting a new partner soon, did I tell you that?"

"No. Who is he?"

"Apparently, it's some girl. Never been a detective in the field before, so I will have to take her under my wing. Teach her everything I know."

"I'm sure you will do a great job at it," Betty said. "If anyone knows his way around the job, it's you."

"Thanks, honey."

Betty felt a sense of pride in her husband's work. Even though he was away from home a lot, she knew he was out there making a difference. She leaned in and gave him a hug, feeling his strong arms wrap around her.

As they let go, John came running up to his dad, jumping up and down with excitement. Travis scooped him up, lifting him high into the air.

"Hey there, champ!" he said, smiling at his son. "You wanna throw some ball?"

Betty watched the two of them play, feeling a sense of joy wash over her. She had everything she ever wanted, and she felt grateful for it every day.

As the sun began to set and the day turned into night, Betty tucked John into bed and gave him a good night kiss. She walked out of the room, closing the door behind her.

Travis was sitting in the living room, a glass of whiskey in his hand. Betty walked over to him and sat down on the couch, leaning her head against his shoulder.

"Thank you for being such a great dad to John," she said quietly.

Travis put his arm around her, pulling her closer. "I couldn't imagine my life without him," he said, taking a sip of his whiskey. "And I couldn't imagine my life without you either."

Betty smiled, feeling a warmth spread through her body. She snuggled up closer to him, feeling safe and loved.

They sat there in silence for a while, enjoying each other's company. Betty knew that life could be tough, but with John and Travis by her side, she could handle anything that came her way. She was happy, truly happy, and she wouldn't have it any other way. She barely ever thought about her old life, back up north, or her family, that she never saw anymore. But sometimes she did miss her sister and knew she would have loved to get to know John. She hadn't heard from her in years. Not since she found out that it was her who had sent that awful letter with that disgusting article about a woman being raped, insinuating that it was Travis who had done it. She couldn't talk to her after that. She simply called her up, asked her if she had sent it, and when she admitted it, Betty told her to stay away from her and her family forever. It was the only right thing to do. Her sister thrived from drama, and Betty would have nothing of it.

As the night wore on, Betty and Travis finished their drinks and made their way to bed. They lay there in silence for a few moments, basking in the warmth of each other's bodies.

"Betty?" Travis said, breaking the silence.

"Yes?" she responded, turning toward him.

"I know I haven't been around as much lately, and I'm sorry. I just want you to know that I love you and John more than anything in this world."

Betty felt a lump form in her throat. She knew Travis wasn't always the most emotional person, but when he did show his love, it meant the world to her.

"I love you too, Travis," she said, reaching out to take his hand.

They lay there in silence for a little bit longer, before Travis spoke up again.

"I was thinking," he said. "How would you feel about going on a vacation? Just the three of us?"

Betty felt a smile spread across her face. She hadn't been on vacation in years, and the idea of a trip with her family sounded perfect.

"I think that would be amazing," she said, giving his hand a squeeze.

Travis grinned, looking happier than she had seen him in weeks. "Great! I'll start planning something."

Betty snuggled up closer to him, feeling grateful for the life they had built together. She knew that there would always be challenges and obstacles, but as long as they had each other, they could handle anything.

As they drifted off to sleep, Betty felt a sense of peace wash over her. She was happy, truly happy, and she knew that no matter what the future held, she had everything she ever wanted right here in her arms. Everything was perfect.

Until it wasn't.

FORTY-FOUR
BILLIE ANN

The once peaceful and serene atmosphere of my house had been turned into a chaotic war room. The comfortable furniture of my living room had been moved to lean against the wall, to make way for a bank of computers, laptops open with wires trailing away from the back, and desks piled high with documents and forensic evidence. Officers crowded around, faces illuminated by screens as they scrolled through data. Tom and Scott were talking to one of them, impatient expressions on their faces.

"How hard can it be to trace a darn cell phone?" I heard Tom yell.

The air was thick with tension as everyone waited for news; would there be a request for a ransom? Would there be more pictures? I still wasn't allowed to investigate, but I was now a lead, and I needed to stay close to my team in case the killer reached out again. Would they try to get to me another way? Would we be able to locate Andy in time? The text message with the picture of my brother haunted me. I was so worried about him. Police officers and detectives were scattered all around the house, each one of them performing a different task.

Some of them were setting up laptops in the living room, while someone was looking at the picture trying to decipher where it could have been taken. It was sent from a phone registered in my brother's name, but as I hadn't seen him in years, my phone didn't recognize the number, and tracing it took time. Time we didn't have.

They told me to not get involved. This was too personal. So, I stood in the corner of the room, watching as the officers worked tirelessly to find my brother. I felt horrible, I didn't like to be this inactive. Every inch of my body was itching to do something. I couldn't help but feel responsible for my brother's disappearance. I had always known that my brother had a tendency to get into trouble, but I never thought that it would lead to something like this.

As I stood there, lost in thought, the Chief walked over to me. "I'm so grateful for all you do," I said.

"You're one of ours. Your family is being targeted. Of course we will do everything we can. It's necessary. We will find him," she said. "But we need your help."

I nodded. Finally I was being involved. "What can I do?"

"We need you to write down everything you know about Andy," she said. "Anything that might help us find him."

I closed my eyes, trying to recall the last time I had seen my brother. It had been years, but I remembered it vividly. Andy and my parents had argued about something stupid, and he had stormed out of the house. I never knew what it was about but guessed it was about drugs. I shook my head as the memory flooded me and made me feel sick.

Chief Harold put her hand on my shoulder, "It's okay. Just take your time."

She walked away, leaving me alone with my thoughts once again.

I closed my eyes, trying to clear my mind. That's when it hit me—I knew my brother had struggled with drugs; I'd had sightings of him reported to me over the years. And drugs connected you to dangerous people. Maybe Andy had gotten himself into trouble with them again. Maybe this had nothing to do with what happened to Charlie and Jeremy and Alex? Maybe this wasn't Jimmy's work? I mean how would he send me the text if he was in the psychiatric hospital? I opened my eyes and walked over to Scott.

"Can you check if my brother had any connections with some gangs or people we know. Is he in the system?" I asked him. "He is a drug addict."

Scott nodded. "We already checked him out, but we didn't find anything. No arrests or anything on his record. Do you have any idea who these people could be?"

I shook my head, "No, I don't. But my brother was always involved with some shady characters."

Scott scribbled something down on his notepad. "I'll look into it again."

"Thank you," I said.

As I left Scott to do his work, I couldn't shake the feeling of dread that had settled in my stomach. My brother was in trouble, and I didn't know how to help him. I wished I had kept in contact with him, tried to help him before it was too late. But now, all I could do was wait and hope that we would find him soon. I knew Harold had sent a team out to Jimmy's house to search the area, and see if he could have kept Andrew somewhere around there, in a shed or a bunker or something like that, but so far, we had heard no news from them.

"I just don't understand it," I said to Harold as she approached me holding out a cup of coffee. She sipped hers and I took mine from her hand.

"There's a lot we don't understand," she said. "Can you be more specific?"

"I know Jimmy. I don't think he would do this."

She shrugged. "It's not unusual, I'm afraid."

"I know, but it's just..."

"What?"

"Why wasn't Andrew's name on the list?"

She narrowed her eyes. "The Hitlist?"

"Yes. His name wasn't on it. Charlie, Jeremy, and Alexandra's names were all on it, but not Andrew. Plus, when I spoke to Jimmy, he didn't mention Charlie or the twins at all. Only uncles and his dad. It seems odd, don't you think? Almost like he doesn't even realize what he is talking about. Like the list is so different than what he said. Does that make any sense?"

"A little," she said and sipped her coffee again.

I heard the door burst open and turned to see my ex, Joe, storming inside. He was red-faced and fuming, his eyes flashing around the room as he took in the chaos. But before he could take another step forward, Big Tom stepped in front of him.

"Easy now, Joe," Big Tom said, holding up a hand. "I'm gonna have to ask you to stand back."

"What's going on here?" he demanded, his voice loud and gruff.

"Police business."

Joe glared at him, "And no one alerted me?" he hissed. "I come here, bringing our son home to pack an overnight bag, and this is what I find?"

"This is police business," Big Tom repeated firmly. "I understand your frustration, but I'm afraid we can't let you in."

Joe's eyes narrowed, "What kind of police business? Tom? What's going on here? What's happened? This is my house, dang it."

"We're looking for someone," Big Tom said evasively. "It's sensitive."

"I have a right to know," Joe said, taking a step closer to Big Tom.

"I'm sorry, Joe, but we can't disclose any information at this time," Big Tom said firmly, blocking his path. People around town knew about the murder near the jail and possibly also about the one in Melbourne, but I had asked my colleagues to keep Andrew's kidnapping quiet for now. At least till we knew if he was dead or alive. If he was alive, we risked his life by letting the word get out. "It's best if you leave and let us do our job."

Joe hesitated for a moment before finally nodding, his anger dissipating slightly.

"Fine," he said, his voice thick with emotion. "But I want to know what's going on as soon as possible. My children live here. I deserve to know what's happening around them, what kind of environment they're growing up in."

"I understand," Big Tom said, his voice softening slightly. "We'll let you know as soon as we can. In the meantime, please give us some space to work."

"Just take Zack to your place for the night, please?" I said. "Charlene and William are fine upstairs."

He shook his head. "This is not over, Billie Ann. I refuse to let my children grow up under these circumstances."

Joe sent me a harsh look before turning and storming out of the house. I watched him go, my heart heavy with guilt. I knew that our relationship had grown toxic lately, but seeing him like this, so angry and hurt, made me realize just how much damage we had caused each other. I wondered if he was right. Maybe I couldn't provide for a safe environment for our children? The very thought made me want to cry.

"I think we have something," Scott said; he was looking at the photo on his computer. "The cell he is in appears to be recently built with cinder blocks. It appears to have been foam insulated, probably to make it soundproof. But that must have required a lot of foam at once? Maybe our local Home Depot or Lowe's noticed someone buying it in bulk or perhaps one of the local companies sold someone a lot of foam recently? Spray foam insulation can be an effective way to soundproof a room or building. It is made of a combination of polyol resin and isocyanate, and when the resulting polyurethane is applied, it expands to fill all the cracks, gaps, and crevices in the walls, ceiling, and floor. This creates an airtight barrier that can help to block out noise. It's a long shot and will require some footwork. But maybe worth a try?"

"I'm on it," Big Tom said and grabbed his phone. "If I have to call every Lowe's or Home Depot in the entire county, I will."

FORTY-FIVE

BILLIE ANN

Danni pushed open the door, and with her entrance, the room filled with warmth. Her hair was wild, her smile wide, and I felt my heart swell as she stepped closer and hugged me. She wore a soft pink cardigan that hung past her hips and an inviting smile on her face. A wave of security washed over me, and I basked in her comforting embrace.

"I came as soon as I could," she whispered, still holding me. "The twins are with Mike. How are you holding up? Where are the kids?"

"Charlene and William are upstairs, keeping to themselves; Zack is with Joe. I told the oldest ones what was going on, but not Zack. It's too much for him to understand."

"That's probably best," she said. "And you?"

I looked into her eyes, so full of concern and care, and felt the tears welling up. But I didn't want to burden her with my emotions, plus the living room was full of colleagues that I didn't want to see me break down, so I took a deep breath and forced a smile.

"I'm okay," I lied. "Just trying to take it one hour at a time. Trying my best not to break down."

Danni didn't buy it though, and I could see the worry etched on her face. She gently brushed my face and looked deep into my eyes.

"Don't lie to me," she said softly. "I know you're hurting. It's okay to feel sad and to cry. I'm here for you."

I felt my walls crumbling down at her words, and I couldn't hold back the tears any longer. Danni pulled me into her arms again, rubbing my back in soothing circles as I sobbed into her shoulder.

"Let's go in the back," she said and led me out to the patio. We sat on the porch swing, and we could still hear the murmuring of voices from inside.

"I just wished there was more I could do," I said. "To help my brother. To help my family. My parents are on their way here too. What do I tell them?"

"You tell them that you're a badass detective and you will solve this case and bring their son back home."

Danni's words were like a balm to my heart. She always knew how to put things into perspective. I wiped away my tears and gave her a small smile.

"Thanks, Danni. I don't know what I'd do without you."

"You'll never have to find out," she said, taking my hand in hers. "We'll get through this together."

I leaned my head on her shoulder, feeling her warmth and comfort. In that moment, I realized how much I loved her. Not just as a friend, but as something more.

"Danni?" I said, unsure if I should speak my thoughts out loud.

"Yes?" she asked, turning to face me.

"I know this might not be the right time, but I have to tell you. I love you. More than anything."

Danni's eyes widened, but then a smile spread across her face.

"I love you too, Billie Ann," she said, cupping my face in her hands. She was about to kiss me, when I spotted something—or rather someone—down by the boat lift in my backyard. I rose to my feet.

"Charlene!"

Danni looked up at me, confused. "What's going on, Billie Ann?"

I shook my head in anger. "That little... I told her to stop seeing him."

With determined steps I rushed toward the dock, each step angrier than the other. "Charlene! What do you think you're doing?"

Charlene and her boyfriend, Tyler, were leaning toward each other, about to kiss, but they jumped at the sound of my voice. They quickly pulled apart and Tyler held up his hands.

"We were just talking," he said, looking nervously at me.

"I know you don't approve, but we're in love," Charlene said. "You can't stop us from being together just because it doesn't fit into your mold of what you planned for your daughter."

"In love? You're seventeen years old, you don't know what love is," I spat, my anger boiling over. "Charlene, you know how I feel about this. I told you to never see him again. How could you disobey me?"

Charlene looked down at her feet, a guilty expression on her face. "I'm sorry, Mom. I just... he makes me happy. I didn't think you'd understand."

"Understand?" I shook my head in disbelief. "You're putting yourself in danger, Charlene. Tyler is ten years older than you. He's way too old for you."

Tyler stepped forward, his expression hardening. "Age is just a number, Billie Ann. We love each other and that's all that matters."

I glared at him, my temper flaring. "You stay away from my

daughter, Tyler. If I catch you near her again, I'll have you arrested."

Tyler sneered at me. "You can't do that. We haven't done anything illegal."

"Yet," I said, my eyes narrowing. "But I can make your life miserable if you don't stay away from my daughter. Do you understand me?"

Tyler's expression hardened, but he nodded his head. "Crystal clear," he growled, before turning on his heel and walking away.

I sighed and met my daughter's gaze. "Charlene, you're grounded. No phone, no computer, not even social media. You'll only be able to leave the house for school or if you go see your dad."

Charlene drew in a sharp breath, her eyes wide with shock. She waved her hands in the air, desperation on her face.

"Mom! That's not right! You can't do this!"

I straightened my spine and met her gaze resolutely. "I said I will and that will be the end of it. If you defy me and see Tyler again, he will come to regret it. This is no light matter, Charlene."

Her lips twisted in anger, and she blinked rapidly before finally spluttering out, "You are so... so... ugh!"

Charlene ran away, her shoulders shaking with sobs. I couldn't help but temporarily feel guilty for what I had just done, but I knew that it was for the best. As I trudged back toward the house, Danni jogged up to me and grabbed my arm.

"Are you okay?" she asked, concern etched on her face.

"I will be," I said, taking a deep breath. "I just can't believe she would disobey me like that."

Danni put her hand on my arm, giving me a sympathetic look. "Teenagers can be difficult to handle. You're doing the right thing by setting boundaries and protecting her. She'll see it one day when she is older."

I nodded, feeling grateful for her understanding. "Thanks, Danni. I just wish things weren't so complicated."

"I know," she said, wrapping her arms around me. "But we'll get through this."

I liked the *we* she put in there. It made me feel less alone. And frankly right now I needed that. I wanted to say something sweet, something to show her how grateful I was to have her in my life, but we were interrupted when Scott cautiously opened the creaky screen door and peered out into the night.

He smiled. "I think we have something. Someone had two hundred cinder blocks delivered from Home Depot four weeks ago to an address nearby. And ordered ten spray cans of foam spray insulation with it. It could be a long shot, but I think we should check it out."

FORTY-SIX

Then

Betty couldn't contain her excitement as the cab turned into the palm-tree lined driveway of the resort. It had been years since she and Travis had taken a trip together, and this time they had John with them. She couldn't wait to see the look on his face when he saw the crystal-clear waters and sandy beaches that Key West had to offer.

As they stepped out of the cab, Betty breathed in the salty air. She glanced over at Travis, who was grinning from ear to ear.

"We made it!" he exclaimed, slipping an arm around her waist. "We're here!"

John was beside himself with excitement, bouncing up and down on his toes. "Can we go swimming now?" he asked, his big eyes wide with anticipation.

Betty laughed and tousled his sandy blond hair. "Not just yet, buddy. First, we've got to check in."

Travis grabbed their suitcases from the trunk and led the way into the resort's lobby. The cool air conditioning was a welcome relief from the hot Florida sun. The lobby was spacious and airy, with tall windows that let in the sunlight and offered a view of the turquoise waters.

Betty couldn't help but feel a little starstruck by the opulence of the resort. She had never stayed in such a fancy place before. But she reminded herself that they deserved this vacation, after all the hard work they had put in over the years.

While Travis checked them in, Betty gazed around the lobby, taking in the luxurious furnishings and the impeccably dressed staff. She noticed a tall, dark-haired man walking toward her with a clipboard in his hand.

"Good afternoon, ma'am," he said with a smile. "I'm the resort's concierge. Is there anything I can assist you with during your stay?"

Betty couldn't help but feel a flutter in her stomach as the handsome man spoke to her. She felt foolish for feeling that way, but she was on vacation, after all.

"Actually, we were wondering if there are any family friendly activities around here? Our son is eight and loves to swim," she replied, trying to keep her voice steady.

The concierge's smile widened. "Of course! We have a children's program that includes swimming lessons, arts and crafts, and even a pirate treasure hunt on the beach. I can provide you with all the details at any time."

Betty's heart lifted at the thought of all the fun John would have. "That sounds perfect, thank you," she said, smiling back at the concierge.

Travis returned with their room keys, and they made their way to their suite. The moment they opened the door, they were met with a stunning view of the ocean. Betty couldn't help but let out a gasp of awe.

"This is amazing!" she exclaimed, rushing to the balcony to take it all in.

Travis chuckled at her excitement, setting their suitcases

down. "I'm glad you like it, honey. We deserve a little luxury, don't we?"

Betty turned to him with a grin. "Absolutely. And I can't wait to see the look on John's face when he sees this view."

As if on cue, John rushed past them and out onto the balcony. "Whoa!" he exclaimed, leaning on the railing and gazing out at the ocean. "This is awesome!"

Betty and Travis exchanged a smile, feeling happy to see their son so elated. They knew this vacation would be one they would never forget.

Betty couldn't help but feel a little self-conscious as they made their way to the resort's upscale restaurant for dinner. She had packed her best dress, but she couldn't help feeling under-dressed as she looked around the elegant dining hall.

Travis, on the other hand, seemed completely at ease in his shorts and T-shirt, his confidence evident in the way he carried himself.

But as they sat down at their table, Betty couldn't help but notice Travis' eyes lingering a little too long on their server, a young woman with long dark hair and a bright smile.

Betty tried to shake off the feeling of unease that was starting to settle in her chest, reminding herself that Travis loved her and that he would never do anything to hurt her. But as the night wore on, she couldn't help but feel a twinge of jealousy every time Travis' gaze wandered over to the server.

She tried to stay cheerful and engage in conversation with John, who was excitedly telling them about the pirate treasure hunt he had gone on earlier that day, but her mind kept wandering back to Travis and the server.

As the night drew to a close and they prepared to leave the restaurant, Travis handed the server a generous tip and exchanged a few words with her. Betty couldn't help but feel a pang of jealousy as he flashed her a charming smile.

As they walked back to their suite, Betty let go of the unease and pushed it aside. Travis had always been faithful to her, and she knew he loved her. Maybe she was just being paranoid.

But as they settled into bed that night, she couldn't find rest. She kept feeling like something was off. She tried to push it to the back of her mind and focus on the sound of the ocean outside, and sleep soon overcame her.

After a few hours, Betty stirred in the bed, feeling a strange sense of emptiness next to her. She opened her eyes groggily, and as her eyes adjusted to the darkness, she realized that Travis was not in the bed next to her.

Panic began to rise in her chest as she sat up, her heart pounding. She tried to call out his name, but her voice came out as a hoarse whisper. She looked around the room, but it was empty.

Her mind was racing as she tried to think of where he could have gone. Maybe he had gone out for a walk? Or to get a drink from the bar downstairs?

But as she got out of bed and made her way to the door, she heard a faint noise coming from the other side. A key card was swiped and the door opened. Not knowing what else to do, Betty froze in place. Travis' face appeared and she stared at him. "Where were you?" she asked.

But Travis answered with anger much to her surprise.

"What's it to you? Can't a guy go out for a drink without being interrogated by his wife?"

Betty felt her heart sink at his defensive tone. "I'm sorry, I didn't mean to come across that way. I just woke up and you weren't in bed"

Travis cut her off with a bitter laugh. "Of course, you didn't mean to come across that way. You never do. You're always so suspicious, always assuming the worst of me."

Betty felt tears prick at the corners of her eyes. "I'm not"

"Don't lie to me," Travis spat, taking a step closer to her. "I saw the way you were looking at me in the restaurant. You think I don't notice the way you're always watching me, always waiting for me to slip up?"

Betty felt like she had been slapped in the face. "Travis, I"

But he didn't let her finish.

"No, you know what? I'm sick of this. Sick of you always doubting me, always second-guessing my every move. I thought this vacation would be a chance for us to relax and enjoy ourselves, but all you've done is make me feel like a damn criminal."

Betty felt her heart shatter as Travis turned and walked away from her, leaving her standing alone in the dark hotel room. She wanted to call out to him, to tell him how much she loved him and how sorry she was for her insecurities. But she knew it was too late.

As she fell back onto the bed, tears streaming down her face, she realized that this vacation was not going to be the escape from reality that she had hoped for. Instead, it was going to be a painful reminder of all the cracks in their marriage that she had been trying so hard to ignore.

FORTY-SEVEN

BILLIE ANN

The car rumbled slowly over the gravel driveway as we arrived at the house in Merritt Island. The lot was completely overrun with vegetation—prickly vines and thick palms clung to the crumbling stucco walls and vibrant bromeliads tumbled down from the roof. Even Scott and Big Tom, two men who had seen it all, seemed wary as I stopped the car by the old gate. I felt as if we had stumbled upon a forgotten relic; a place that hadn't seen human life for far too long.

We stepped out of the car and approached the house. The gate was rusty and creaked against our weight as we pushed it open. The house looked long abandoned, with chipped paint around the windows and peeling boards covering what used to be glass. My voice came out as a whisper as I asked, "You sure this is the place?"

Scott nodded. "Yep. This is the address."

We all pulled out our guns and adjusted our stance, ready for anything. The air was heavy with humidity and the sweet scent of jasmine that had bloomed overnight. With my heart pounding in my chest, I couldn't shake the feeling that we were walking right into a trap. I wasn't supposed to be there, but I

had left Scott and Tom no option. I needed to be there for this
and had just jumped into the car as they left.

The porch groaned underfoot as we cautiously stepped up
to the front door. Tom leaned close to the window, peering
through its dusty panes, while Scott knocked on the door, three
times. His knuckles were barely making a sound against the
thick wood.

"Cocoa Beach police. Is anyone home?"

That's when we heard the scream. It wasn't very loud, but it
was enough to send chills down our spines. Big Tom paused; his
hand was frozen on the doorknob as the faint scream trickled
through the air. We locked eyes, and in one swift motion he
kicked open the door, causing it to swing wildly on its hinges
with a sharp crack. Splinters of wood scattered across the foyer
floor. We burst inside, guns blazing, ready for anything that
might come our way. We cautiously stepped forward and I was
hit with a musty smell that made my nose wrinkle. It smelled
like death in here. I couldn't see anything, so I raised my gun,
my heart racing in my chest.

"Cocoa Beach police! Is anyone here? Come out with hands
where we can see them."

My voice reverberated off the walls of the derelict house,
echoing through the darkness like a call to arms. I felt along the
wall for a switch, then flooded the hallway with light—old
photographs and fading wallpaper illuminated by an antique
lamp. We crept forward in unison, my heart thumping in my
chest as we listened intently for any sign of life. The air was so
thick it felt like I could reach out and touch it.

"Police! Come out with your hands up!" I shouted again,
the sound finally dissolving into eerie silence.

My heart thudded in my chest as we crept down the hallway, each door a possible danger. Scott held up his arm and
gestured for us to stop, indicating with a finger to his lips that

he'd heard something. We all went still, straining our ears for any trace of sound.

Then, we heard it. A soft call coming from the room at the end of the hallway. Without hesitation, we burst through the door, guns at the ready. It turned out it was the garage. But this wasn't your run-of-the-mill garage. The garage was filled with old boxes and tools, like most garages, but someone had built a separate cell-like area in the center. The walls were cinder blocks reaching up to the ceiling, and a metal door had been installed backward so it couldn't be opened from inside. There was a faint groaning coming from behind the door.

"H-help."

A wave of dread overtook me as I registered the faint, muffled cries coming from within the jail cell. We raced to the metal door and tugged at it desperately in a futile attempt to free whoever was inside, but it held firm. It was locked.

"Stand back," Big Tom said, pulling out a crowbar from one of the boxes beside us. He knelt down, fit it into the narrow gap between the door and frame, and with a single mighty thrust the door gave way, swinging open to reveal a small room filled with shadows. In the corner, a person was huddled in fear. His body was twisted in an awkward and unnatural position. I clasped my hand to my mouth as I realized who it was.

It was my brother; it was Andrew.

I sprinted across the room, my shoes slapping against the dirty floor. Andy lay lifelessly on the ground. His clothes were torn, and his face was covered in a mixture of dirt and blood. I screamed his name and dropped to my knees beside him. A wave of anger surged through me as I looked over my shoulder at my colleagues, silently begging them for help.

"Call an ambulance!" I shouted. "Call an ambulance now!"

Big Tom grabbed his phone and did as I told him to. His words became distorted in the background as I felt dizziness overcome me.

My brother's fingers dug into my flesh, and I winced as he yanked me down to his level. His lips were cracked and moving soundlessly, eyes wild with panic. He pulled me closer until his breath was hot in my ear.

"It's a trap," he gasped before his body went slack and his head lolled back. The world slowed to a crawl as I looked down at him, my heart racing. Pain throbbed through my body as I laid him down on the ground. His skin was cold and clammy beneath my fingertips. Tears began to pool at the corners of my eyes.

"Andrew?" I screamed. "Andrew?"

His eyes were rolling back into his head. His labored breaths quickly faded away, leaving a heavy silence. I looked up at Scott and Big Tom, their expressions hard as stone and illuminated by the flickering light from the garage.

"What do you mean it's a trap?" I choked out, my voice quivering with fear.

FORTY-EIGHT

BILLIE ANN

The sound of sirens grew louder and louder, piercing through the tense silence of the garage. We had opened the garage door, while waiting for them, and I could feel my heart pounding against my chest as the ambulance pulled up, its red and white lights flashing against the walls. My brother had a pulse and was breathing, but unconscious still. I had put him down gently on his back, and raised his legs above heart level and was supporting his neck and head on my knees, to obtain an open airway and make sure if there were any fluids they would drain out by his mouth and not into his lungs.

It seemed like it took them forever to get there, and with every passing second my brother's chances of surviving grew smaller. Without wasting any time, two paramedics rushed out of the vehicle, pushing a stretcher ahead of them.

"Over here!" I yelled, waving my arms frantically as I led the paramedics to where my brother Andrew lay motionless on the ground. His skin was a sickly shade of pale, and his eyes were closed shut. I could feel tears welling up in my eyes as I saw the paramedics rush into the garage, their bags and equipment clanging loudly against the concrete floor. They quickly assessed the situation, setting up the stretcher beside Andrew's still form.

"Please, hurry!" I begged, my voice breaking as I held on to Andrew's hand.

The paramedics nodded solemnly, their faces a mask of professionalism and concentration. They worked quickly, attaching wires to Andrew's chest and checking his vitals. The paramedics lifted Andrew's limp body onto the stretcher, efficiently and expertly.

I felt a wave of relief wash over me as they began to make their way back to the ambulance. I followed closely behind, my heart pounding in my chest.

Please don't let him die. Please.

As we emerged from the garage, the bright flashing lights of the ambulance seemed to blind me momentarily. I walked beside the stretcher, my eyes fixed on my brother's pale face, my hand still clutching his hand tightly. The paramedics were just about to lift the stretcher into the back of the ambulance when my ears registered the sound of gunfire.

The shots seemed to echo through the deserted streets, bouncing off the walls of the surrounding buildings. My heart leapt into my throat as the paramedics quickly set the stretcher back down on the ground, their eyes scanning the perimeter for the source of the gunfire.

"Get down!" one of them yelled, pushing me to the ground as more shots rang out, the sound coming closer and closer.

I looked up at the paramedics and could see the fear in their eyes. I scrambled to my feet. I knew I had to do something, had to protect my brother and the paramedics. I scanned the surrounding area, trying to figure out where the shots were coming from, but the sound was impossible to follow because of the echoes bouncing off the buildings and surrounding trees.

Without hesitating, I reached for my gun and pulled it out of its holster. Big Tom and Scott followed my lead, both of them taking out their own weapons as well. We formed a protective circle around the stretcher, our eyes scanning the shadows for any signs of movement.

Suddenly, the gunfire grew louder, and I saw a flash of movement out of the corner of my eye. I aimed my gun and pulled the trigger, the sound of the shot ringing through the air. Big Tom and Scott followed suit, shooting in the direction of the movement.

The exchange of gunfire lasted for what felt like an eternity but was probably only a few seconds. Everything seemed to be happening in slow motion as we exchanged shots with whoever was attacking us. I could feel the adrenaline coursing through my veins as I aimed and fired again and again. My mind was a blur as I fought to keep my focus on the task at hand. I knew that I had to protect my brother at all costs, even if it meant putting my own life on the line. I could hear the paramedics calling for backup, their voices barely audible over the sound of the gunfire.

I knew that I had to end this and end it fast. I took a deep breath, my fingers tightening around the trigger of my gun, and charged forward, firing as I went. Big Tom and Scott followed my lead, and together we advanced toward the source of the gunfire. The shots grew louder, and I could see the dim outline of a figure in the distance.

I aimed my gun and pulled the trigger again, the sound of the shot ringing in my ears.

It wasn't until everything grew eerily quiet that I realized the shooting had stopped. I looked around, trying to assess the damage. Scott had a bullet wound in his shoulder and was clutching his side. He had been shot. Panic set in. We had to get more help. Big Tom ran to him and attended to his wounds, along with one of the paramedics. They fought to stop the bleeding. My attention quickly went back to my brother, who was still fighting for his life on the stretcher. The paramedics were frantically trying to stabilize him, their hands moving quickly and efficiently as they worked to save his life.

The sound of approaching sirens grew louder, and I knew that backup was on its way. But at that moment, all that mattered was Andrew's and Scott's survival. I knelt down beside the stretcher, my hand still tightly clasped around Andrew's, as I prayed silently for him to pull through.

"Please don't leave me, Andrew," I muttered, the words barely audible over the sound of the approaching ambulances. "Please don't die."

The sound of approaching sirens grew louder and louder until a squad car pulled up next to us, and two police officers jumped out, guns at the ready.

"What's going on here?" an officer I knew by the name of Harrison demanded, his eyes scanning the area for any signs of danger.

"We were ambushed," I answered. "At least one shooter is behind those trees!" I yelled, pointing in the direction that I had fired my last shot. Without wasting another second, the police officers rushed toward the trees. Their footsteps echoed as they ran, their guns held firmly in their hands. I watched as they disappeared behind the trees.

Another ambulance arrived, and with the help of the paramedics, we quickly loaded both Scott and Andrew into the back of each of them. I climbed into the ambulance with Andrew, my hand still tightly clasped around his. The ambulance took off at breakneck speed, its sirens blaring as we raced toward the hospital.

FORTY-NINE

Then

Betty, Travis, and John walked into the resort's breakfast buffet, ready to grab a bite to eat before their long day of relaxation and fun in the sun and water. Betty looked around the room, taking in the sights and sounds of the resort's luxurious dining area. The smell of freshly brewed coffee and warm croissants filled the air, and the sound of soft music played in the background.

As they approached the omelet station, a new server greeted them with a smile. "Good morning, folks. What can I get for you?" she asked.

"I'll have an omelet with ham and extra cheese, please," Betty said, looking up at the new server.

As the server began to prepare Betty's order, she couldn't help but notice that the girl who had served them yesterday was nowhere to be found.

"Excuse me," Betty asked the new server. "Where is the girl who took care of us yesterday?"

The new server looked at Betty with a blank expression. "Oh, she's not coming in today."

Betty was taken aback. "Why not?"

Travis scowled at her. "Mind your own business, Betty. It's not our place to ask about the staff's personal affairs."

But Betty couldn't shake the feeling that something was off. Yet she kept her mouth shut, and the food soon arrived.

As Betty tried to enjoy her omelet, her mind kept wandering back to the missing server. She couldn't shake off the feeling that something was wrong. She kept glancing around the room, noticing the staff talking seriously with one another.

"Are you okay?" John asked, taking a bite of his toast.

"I don't know," Betty replied, her voice tinged with worry. "I just can't stop thinking about the girl who served us yesterday. And now she's not here, and no one seems to be telling us why."

Travis rolled his eyes. "Betty, it's really not that big of a deal. Maybe she just had a day off or something."

But Betty wasn't convinced. She watched as the staff continued to huddle together, their faces grave with concern. She couldn't help but wonder what was going on behind the scenes.

As the meal went on, Betty's nerves only seemed to get worse. Every time a staff member passed by, she would stare at them, trying to read their expressions. But they all seemed to be avoiding eye contact with the guests, including her.

Finally, as they were finishing up, Betty couldn't take it anymore. She stood up from her seat and approached the new server. "I'm sorry to bother you again, but can you please tell me what's going on? Is everything okay with the staff?" she asked, her voice trembling.

The server hesitated for a moment, then sighed. "I don't know if I'm allowed to say anything, but... there was an incident last night."

"What incident?"

The staff member hesitated, then looked around to make

sure no one else was listening. "One of our servers was attacked while walking back to her room. Someone found her down by the beach this morning. She's in the hospital now, but she's going to be okay."

Betty's heart sank. "Attacked?" she whispered back, horrified.

The staff member nodded. "Raped, and beat up, is what we have been told. We're all really shaken up about it. That's why your regular server isn't here today. We're all pitching in to cover for her."

Betty felt a wave of sympathy wash over her. She couldn't imagine what the server must be going through. "Thank you for telling me," she said softly, before returning to her table.

Travis and John looked at her expectantly.

"What was that about?" Travis asked.

Betty took a deep breath. "One of the servers was attacked last night," she said, her voice choked with emotion. "That's why our regular server isn't here today."

Travis' and John's expressions turned serious. "That's terrible," Travis said. "Do they know who did it?"

Betty shook her head. "I don't think so. The server is in the hospital, but she's going to be okay. That's all they told me."

The rest of their meal was a somber affair, with everyone lost in their own thoughts. But Betty couldn't shake off the feeling of unease that had settled over her. She couldn't help but wonder who could have done such a thing, and what was going to happen next.

Betty, Travis, and John returned to their room after breakfast, their minds heavy with the news of the attacked server. Betty paced around the room, her mind racing with questions about the incident.

Suddenly, there was a knock on the door. Travis sprang up to open it, and Betty saw three men standing outside, showing their badges. She recognized them as police officers, and her heart skipped a beat.

Travis went out into the hallway and closed the door behind him. Betty could hear muffled voices coming from outside. She stood frozen in the middle of the room, her mind racing with possibilities. She walked closer to the door and tried to listen in.

"Come on, guys," she heard Travis say. "I'm a colleague. You really believe a young server girl over me? A fellow cop?"

After a few minutes, Travis came back into the room, looking pale and shaken.

"What's going on?" Betty asked, her voice trembling.

Travis took a deep breath. "The police are investigating the attack on the server. It's nothing to be concerned about."

"Nothing to be concerned about? Why are they questioning you?" she asked, startled.

"They're questioning all the guests who were present on the property last night," he said. "Everyone who is staying here. It's normal procedure."

"But why did you need to talk to them in private?" Betty asked, looking at Travis with suspicion.

Travis hesitated for a moment, then sighed. "They asked me a few questions about my whereabouts last night. Apparently, I was seen in the area where the attack took place."

Betty gasped, her eyes widening with shock. "What? That's crazy! You didn't do anything, did you?"

Travis shook his head vigorously. "No, of course not. I just happened to be in the wrong place at the wrong time."

Betty looked at him, still unsure. "But why were they questioning you in private like that? If it's just normal procedure, they should have asked you in front of us."

Travis looked away. He sighed, annoyed. "I don't know. Maybe they just wanted to be discreet. They didn't want to cause a panic among the guests."

Betty didn't buy it. She knew there was more to the story

than Travis was letting on. But why was he keeping something from her? Because he knew more than he said? Or was it just to protect her?

She decided it had to be the latter. It simply had to be. Travis was a good man. He was her man.

"So, what happens next?" she asked while glaring toward John who was watching TV. They had promised to take him snorkeling today and he was waiting for them to get ready. She halfway expected Travis to tell her that now it was time to relax and enjoy the vacation, but instead he grabbed the suitcase and started packing.

"Now we go home. I don't want to stay one more second in this place. Not after what happened."

Betty nodded, still feeling uneasy about the whole situation. Travis was right. They needed to leave. There was no reason to stay. As Travis continued to pack, she couldn't help but wonder what was really going on. She knew Travis was keeping something from her, but she didn't want to push it. Not now, at least. Right now, she just wanted to get out of this place and go home. For a brief moment she thought about her sister and their wedding, and then about the article in her mail, then shook her head when remembering what her mother told her.

"This is not worth losing your marriage over. You have a good life. Travis is good to you, and you don't have to work. You're lucky, do you hear me? Don't ruin it."

She was right. As always, she was right.

"John, pack your things," she said and turned off the TV.

"But...?" the boy protested, but she sent him a look to let him know there was no discussing this. It was already decided. The boy didn't say anything else but started to pack his clothes and toys in his small dinosaur bag.

As they made their way to the lobby to check out, Betty couldn't help but notice the staff all huddled together, whispering and pointing in their direction. She wondered if they were talking about Travis and his conversation with the police officers. She felt a pang of resentment toward them. Who did they think they were? Judging her and her husband?

As they finally made it out of the hotel, Betty turned back to look at the building one last time. She was definitely never coming back here again.

FIFTY

BILLIE ANN

The paramedics hovered over Andrew, their blue-gloved hands moving quickly as they worked to keep him alive. Their voices were tense and urgent as they yelled out instructions to each other. I couldn't tear my eyes away from my brother's face, searching desperately for any sign of life or movement. I leaned in close, whispering words of encouragement into his ear, hoping that he could hear me and know that I was there with him in the ambulance.

Suddenly, Andrew let out a weak cough, his body convulsing as he struggled to take in air. My heart leapt in my chest as I saw signs of life returning to him. I could see him fighting to stay conscious, his eyes flickering open for a brief moment before fluttering shut again.

The paramedics quickly sprang into action, administering medication and adjusting their equipment to help stabilize him. I watched with bated breath as they worked, hoping that they could save my brother's life. It felt like an eternity before there was any sign of progress, but eventually, Andrew's breathing began to even out and his pulse stabilized.

"Please, Andrew, just hold on a little longer," I whispered under my breath. "We're almost there. We're almost at the hospital. You can make it. I know you can."

As I watched Andrew, a flood of memories rushed through me. Memories of us as kids, playing hide-and-seek in the woods behind our house. Memories of us as teenagers, sneaking out to parties and getting into trouble. But most of all, memories of us as adults, trying to navigate this complicated world together. Until he fell apart and I lost him to a world of drugs. I had missed so many years of his life.

Still, I couldn't imagine a world without Andrew in it.

The paramedics continued to work, their movements becoming more frantic by the second. And then, suddenly, there was a moment of stillness. The machines monitoring Andrew's vitals beeped in unison, and I held my breath, waiting for the outcome.

"W-what happened?" I asked. "What's going on?"

The paramedics exchanged grim looks, and one of them spoke in a hushed voice. "He's crashing."

I felt a lump form in my throat as I heard the paramedic's words. They looked at each other, their expressions conveying a sense of dread that made my heart sink. I closed my eyes for a moment, trying to process what was happening. It felt like everything was happening in slow motion, and yet at the same time, too fast for me to keep up with.

I looked back at Andrew's face, praying that there was still a chance for him. Suddenly, one of the machines beeped loudly, and the paramedics rushed to his side, frantically adjusting their equipment.

I watched them work, my mind racing with all the possible outcomes. I didn't know if Andrew would make it, but I refused to give up hope. He had fought so hard to stay alive, and I couldn't let him go now.

And then, just as suddenly as the machines had beeped, Andrew's eyes fluttered open. He looked at me, gasping.

"Billie Ann," he croaked, his voice barely a whisper. "I... I can't..."

Tears welled up in my eyes as I took his hand in mine. "Shh, it's okay," I said, trying to keep my voice steady. "You're going to be okay."

It was of course a lie. But it was one I wanted to tell him, and myself. Even if I knew that with the beating he had received he might survive, if he was lucky, but he was never going to be okay again.

The paramedics continued to work around us, trying to keep him stable, but I could tell that it was a losing battle. Andrew's breathing became more and more labored, his chest rising and falling in uneven gasps.

I knew that time was running out.

"Andrew," I said, my voice shaking. "I need you to hear me. I need you to know that I love you, and that I'm so proud of you. You're the strongest person I know, and I know that you can fight this."

Andrew's eyes met mine, and there was a glimmer of recognition in them. He squeezed my hand weakly, his breathing slowing down.

"I'm sorry," he whispered, his voice barely audible. "I'm sorry for everything. Tell Mom and Dad, I'm so, so sorry."

Tears streamed down my face as I shook my head, trying to push away the guilt and regret that threatened to overwhelm me. "No, Andrew, please don't say that. You can tell them yourself. When you're better."

But Andrew's eyes had already started to glaze over, his grip on my hand weakening. I could feel my heart breaking as I watched him slip away from me, his chest falling still.

"No," I cried out, tears streaming down my face. "Andrew, please. You can't leave me."

I clung to his hand, not wanting to let go. The paramedics pushed on his chest, and the monitors beeped back to life again. Andrew looked at me, barely holding on.

"Billie Ann," he said. "It's a setup."

"I know, I know," I said. "They shot at us when we tried to get out of the house, but we still managed to get you inside of the ambulance."

"No," he said, suddenly looking very seriously at me. He pulled my arm to get me closer. "No. That wasn't the setup."

"Yes, there was an ambush..."

"NO!" The sudden strength to his voice surprised me. He closed his eyes to gather himself and muster the energy to say what he needed to say.

"What? What are you trying to tell me?"

His voice was hoarse and raspy. "It's a diversion, Billie Ann."

"A diversion from what?" I asked, panic setting in. Was he hallucinating? Was he talking feverish talk? Or was he actually trying to tell me something important? I felt so confused.

He pulled my arm again. "Zack. Where is Zack?"

"Zack is with Joe, my ex. He's fine."

Andrew shook his head, his breathing becoming labored again. "No, no, he isn't. They led you here, so they could get to him."

"What are you talking about?" I asked as the ambulance arrived at the hospital. The paramedics opened the door and rushed my brother out of the back on the stretcher and inside of the hospital.

"What are you talking about?" I yelled after him, but he was gone. I was left standing there, watching as sliding doors closed behind them, my brother being rushed away, my mind reeling with everything that had just happened. Andrew's words echoed in my head, and I couldn't help but feel a sense of urgency. What had he meant by a diversion? And who was trying to get to Zack?

That's when my phone rang in my pocket and I took it out.

It was Joe.

FIFTY-ONE

BILLIE ANN

"Hi it's me. I've been trying to reach you. Do you have Zack? I want to say good night to him, and he's not answering his phone."

I was standing outside the emergency room, the rain pouring down as I listened to answer Joe's question, but not quite understanding what he was saying. It made no sense.

"What do you mean? He's with you," I said, trying to keep my voice steady. "He's spending the night at your place."

There was a pause on the other end of the line, and I could hear the rain pounding down harder on the roof above me covering the entrance. I closed my eyes and took a deep breath, trying to keep the panic at bay.

"No," Joe said, his voice rising with panic. "You sent Charlene to pick him up earlier? She said you wanted him home?"

I shook my head, confused. "What? No. I didn't send anyone to pick him up. I'm at the hospital, we found my brother, he's in there fighting for his life now. I haven't been home at all. And I most certainly haven't talked to Charlene. Not since our fight earlier. What's going on?"

Joe didn't answer, and I could only hear the sound of his breathing on the other end of the line.

"Then where is he?" he finally asked, his voice trembling. "I received a text from Charlene saying she was coming to pick him up. That you wanted him home, that you changed your mind. So I took him downstairs and let him run to her truck when she arrived. It was raining so I watched him while he ran to her and just waved at them."

"Didn't you talk to Charlene?"

"No, I didn't see the need to get all wet. Is Charlene not home either?"

"I don't know," I admitted, feeling the panic rising in my chest. "Like I said, I haven't been home for hours. I swear, Joe, I didn't send anyone to pick up Zack. I thought he was with you. He was supposed to be with you. Besides, Charlene is grounded and not allowed to use her phone. I took it from her and put it in the kitchen."

The silence on the other end of the line was deafening. I could hear the rain continuing to pound down on the roof above me. I felt my stomach clenching with worry. I kept hearing my brother's words echoing in my mind.

It's a diversion. Where is Zack?

"Joe, please tell me he's okay," I begged, tears starting to stream down my face. "Please."

"He's not here," Joe said, his voice breaking. "I don't know where he is. How can I tell you he is okay?"

My heart felt like it was breaking into a million pieces. My baby boy was missing, and I had no idea where he was or if he was safe. I closed my eyes and took a deep breath, trying to hold back the sobs that were threatening to escape me.

"Call Charlene," I said, determined. "If she texted you, she must have her phone. Ask her, Joe."

"I already did. She's not picking up either."

That's when my heart stopped.

I felt like the world was closing in on me, suffocating me with its weight. My son was missing, and no one knew where he was. And now my daughter wasn't picking up her phone? I tried to think rationally, but all I could feel was the panic and fear coursing through me like a rushing river. I needed to find my children.

"Joe, I need to call it in," I said, my voice shaking. "We have to report him missing. Now."

I heard Joe take a deep breath on the other end of the line. "Yeah. Yeah, you're right," he said, his voice sounding distant. "I'll keep calling Charlene and go to the house and see what's going on."

I nodded, even though he couldn't see me. "Okay. Okay, good."

I was pacing back and forth outside the emergency room, my mind racing with fear and panic. I didn't know what to do. My son was missing, and my daughter wasn't answering her phone.

I was about to lose my mind when I saw a familiar face—it was one of the paramedics from earlier.

"Excuse me, ma'am?" he said tentatively, holding out a phone. "This was found on your brother. They're asking for you."

I looked up at him, barely registering his words at first. My mind was so consumed with thoughts of Zack and Charlene that it took me a few seconds to grasp what he was saying.

"My brother?" I repeated, my voice hoarse. "What do you mean? Is he...?"

The paramedic shook his head quickly. "No, no, he's still in surgery. But they found this phone on him, and it's been ringing, so they gave it to me. The person on the other end said they need to talk to you."

I swallowed hard, my heart pounding in my chest. What on earth was happening? "Okay," I said, reaching out to take the phone from him. "Thank you."

I placed the phone against my ear. "H-hello?"

FIFTY-TWO

Then

Betty stood in her backyard, the sun setting behind the trees, a gentle breeze blowing through the leaves. She was nervous, but excited. She had invited Travis' new partner over for dinner, and the new partner was bringing her family along. Betty had never met her before, but from the way Travis had talked about her, she seemed nice.

As she waited for them to arrive, Betty prepped the grill and set out plates, utensils, and condiments. She wanted everything to be perfect. Just as she was about to light the grill, she saw a car pull up to the curb. When the doorbell rang, Betty took a deep breath and wiped her hands on her apron before opening the door. Standing there was a stunning woman with shoulder-length blonde hair, wearing a sundress and a warm smile.

"Hi, Betty. I'm so happy to finally meet you," the woman said, extending her hand.

Betty shook her hand and welcomed her inside, taking note of the man and young girl following behind her.

"I hope it's okay that I brought my husband and daughter. I didn't want to impose," the woman said.

"Of course not. The more the merrier," Betty said with a soft smile. "I'm so glad you could make it."

Betty smiled warmly at them and led them to the backyard where the grill was set up. As they walked, she couldn't help but notice how beautiful the new partner was. Her blonde hair cascaded down her back in soft waves, and her eyes sparkled in the fading light.

As they settled around the grill, Betty began to relax. The new partner and her family were so easy to talk to, and they all seemed to genuinely enjoy one another's company. They laughed and joked as they grilled burgers and hot dogs, enjoying the warm summer evening.

At one point, the young girl wandered over to Betty and tugged on her shirt.

"Can I help you cook?" she asked, her eyes wide with excitement.

Betty smiled and nodded, showing the young girl how to flip a burger and checking on her progress as she took on the responsibility of cooking dinner.

As the night went on, Betty found herself growing more and more fond of the new partner and her family. They were kind, warm, and easy to be around, and Betty couldn't help but feel a sense of connection with them.

As they sat around the firepit after dinner, sipping wine and roasting marshmallows, the stars twinkled above them, Betty found herself alone with the new partner, while the men shared a beer on the back porch. The little girl was playing with John in the living room. Everything seemed so at ease. So peaceful.

"I have to say, I'm really impressed with you," Betty said, looking into the new partner's eyes.

"Oh?" the new partner asked, a hint of a smile on her lips.

"You just seem so... together. So confident. I wish I could be more like that," Betty said, "I mean you're still young and all. I wasn't that together when I was your age."

"Oh, I'm not together," the partner said laughing. "I'm just very good at pretending to be. I'm a mess like most people, and to be honest a little lost from time to time, especially in my new position at work. Travis has been a great help for me. He has really been taking very good care of me."

"Are you new to this area?" Betty asked.

"No, I have actually lived here my entire life. Grew up here by the swamps, with my brothers."

"Oh, really? Travis and I have only been here a few years. Maybe I know your family? What was your last name again?"

She cleared her throat. "Wilde."

Betty's expression changed as soon as she heard the name. Her face became strained, and her eyes looked distant, as if she was lost in thought. Her smile faded, and a look of fear crossed her face. She froze, her eyes locked onto the new partner, unable to speak or move. She tried to keep her composure, tried to pretend like everything was okay, but she couldn't shake the feeling of dread that had settled in her stomach. She felt strange and distant, as if she was no longer a part of the conversation. The new partner noticed the sudden change in Betty's demeanor and furrowed her brows in concern.

"Is everything okay?" she asked.

Betty shook her head, trying to snap out of whatever thoughts were plaguing her. "Yeah, sorry, everything's fine. It's just that... Wilde is a name that I haven't heard in a long time."

Betty took a deep breath and forced herself to refocus. She looked up at the new partner and flashed her a small smile.

"Sorry about that," she said, "I'm fine now. Would you like some more wine?"

The new partner nodded, and Betty got up from her seat and walked to the kitchen to retrieve the wine bottle. As she returned, she saw that Travis had come back out with his beer in hand and was sitting bent forward, deep in conversation with his new partner. Betty couldn't help but notice the way Travis' eyes flickered to the woman's lips as she spoke, the way his body leaned in just a little bit closer to her, and gently placed a hand on her arm or shoulder every now and then, and they laughed. Oh, how they laughed together. Betty felt a pang of jealousy deep in her chest. She had never felt this way before, but something about this new partner made her feel territorial and possessive.

"More wine?" she asked as she approached them, holding the bottle up.

"Yes please," the partner said and raised her glass. Seeing his wife come closer, Travis leaned back in the chair and sipped his beer with a pout. Betty made sure she didn't leave them alone for even a second for the rest of the evening and kept a constant eye on them both.

No one was going to take her man from her. She would make sure of that. She had fought too hard to get to where she was. She had made too many sacrifices to let go now. No one was going to ruin what she had.

FIFTY-THREE

BILLIE ANN

I inhaled deeply, feeling my heart race as I attempted to steady my voice. The rain pelted down on the roof above me, making it difficult to hear the person on the other end of the line. I pressed the phone tight against my ear, trying to block out the noise. "Who is this?" I forced myself to sound confident, even though my stomach was churning with nerves.

The breathing on the other end of the phone got heavier, almost as if the person was trying to hold back their laughter.

"Are you having fun yet?" the voice said mockingly.

My jaw clenched as I stared at the nameless caller's number blinking on my phone screen. They were obviously trying to provoke a reaction from me. Fear crept up my spine as they spoke again, tauntingly.

"You don't remember me? Too bad. Because I remember you."

I knew now that this wasn't Jimmy; he couldn't have been responsible for what had happened over the last few hours, I was right about that. But this was someone I knew. A chill went down my spine.

"Who are you?"

"I thought you'd have that figured out by now, to be honest. I'm a little disappointed."

My throat tightened. My family didn't have any enemies that I knew of. Was this someone I had arrested? Someone who had a vendetta against me? The low, gravelly tone of their voice made my skin crawl. I took a deep breath and tried to steady myself before responding.

"You need to stop what you're doing to my family. This isn't funny," I said, my voice shaking slightly.

The voice on the other end of the phone grew quiet for a moment, and I could hear the sound of rain in the background.

"You don't think it's funny? I think it's hilarious," the voice said with an angry sneer.

I felt a surge of anger wash over me, and I clenched my fists.

"What do you want?" I demanded, my voice more forceful this time.

"What do I want?" the voice repeated, as if considering the question. "I want you to suffer. I want you to feel the same pain you caused me."

My heart skipped a beat as I tried to think of any person I could have hurt enough to provoke such a response.

"I don't know what you're talking about," I said, trying to keep my voice steady.

"You don't remember me, do you?" the voice asked, and I could hear the satisfaction in their tone. "That just makes this all the sweeter. As sweet as cherry pie."

My heart pounded against my rib cage, and my palms grew clammy as the realization sank in—this person was serious. They weren't joking. They had a vendetta against me, and I had no idea who they were.

Their voice trembled with anger as they threatened me. "If you think I'll back down now, you're wrong."

"Please, just tell me who you are," I pleaded.

There was a long pause on the other end of the phone before the voice spoke again. "I am Wilde."

My heart pounded as the words sank in. *I am Wilde*, like the person who hurt my brother had written on the ground. In blood.

"It's you," I said.

"Exactly. Now I have your attention perhaps?"

My fingers tightened around the phone as I hissed through gritted teeth. "What do you want?"

"You'll find out soon enough," he taunted, knowing how much it frustrated me not knowing his intentions.

"Why are you hurting my family?" I yelled over the sound of the pounding rain. "Why did you hurt my brother?"

"Play my game and you'll find out," he said.

"I'm not playing any game."

"Play my game!" he yelled. "I have played yours for years and years. Now it's your turn," he hissed.

"What are you talking about? What game..."

My heart skipped a beat, my body freezing in place. Through the phone receiver, I could hear faint sobs in the background. My mind raced as I recognized the sound.

Zack!

Panic surged through me as I frantically tried to make sense of what was happening. My boy was in danger.

"Where is my son?" I screamed into the phone, my heart pounding in my chest. There was no response, but I could still hear the sound of someone breathing heavily on the other end.

"Answer me!" I yelled, trying to keep the fear out of my voice.

The breathing grew louder and then suddenly stopped.

"Hello?" I said, my voice trembling. "Are you there?"

Silence.

The phone slipped from my trembling hand as I stared at the screen in shock. Tears blurred my vision, but I quickly wiped them away, trying to steady myself. Zack was in trouble, and I had to find him before it was too late. The sound of muffled sobs still rang in my ears from the call that just ended. Without hesitation, I called the Chief's number, knowing she was the only person who could help me now. I paced back and forth, heart racing with fear and adrenaline, as I waited for her to pick up on the other end. No one threatened my children without facing serious consequences. No one messed with my children and got away with it.

No one.

FIFTY-FOUR

BILLIE ANN

My fingers trembled as I turned off the ignition and fumbled for the door handle of my car. A firm hand gripped my arm, and I looked over to see Chief Harold's steady gaze.

"It's going to be okay," she said firmly, her radio crackling with confirmation of backup on the way. My heart raced while I thought about the motivation of this person trying to hurt me. Who was it, and why was this happening to me? Could it be someone I had put behind bars before? Was this revenge?

I took a deep breath and looked out the window. The cemetery loomed in front of us, the iron gate rusted and imposing. It was the last place I wanted to be, but if my son was here, I had to go in. They had traced the phone that called me to this spot. This was where I had heard my son cry for me.

"Let's go, we'll find him," she said, her voice firm and steady.

I nodded, taking a deep breath and stepping out of the car. We walked toward the gate, my heart pounding in my chest. The Chief led the way, her hand on her holster, ready for anything. Fear struck me, and I started to run, my feet pounding against the pavement, thinking only of my son, of Zack.

What if I'm too late?

As I ran deeper into the cemetery, the Chief following close behind, the silence was eerie and suffocating. The moon was full, casting an ominous glow over the gravestones. I shuddered, feeling a chill run down my spine.

Where are you, Zack?

I heard a twig snap behind us. I spun around, my heart pounding in my chest. The Chief had already drawn her gun, pointing it toward the sound.

"Who's there?" she shouted.

There was no answer, just the howling of the wind. We stood there for a moment, our eyes scanning the dark shadows cast by the trees. Then, we heard it again, a rustling in the bushes.

"Zack?" I yelled; my voice was shaky with fear.

Still, there was no answer. The Chief carefully approached the bushes. She crouched down, her gun trained on the undergrowth, and parted the leaves with her free hand.

I held my breath as she walked away from me. I turned to scan the row of headstones. And that's when I saw it. The tombstone with my name on it.

Wilde.

My heart skipped a beat as I stumbled toward the gravestone. It couldn't be real. I reached out my hand, tracing the letters of my name with my trembling fingers.

Then I began to dig. Frantically, I scraped at the dirt with my hands, tearing away chunks of earth as if my life depended on it. The Chief called out to me, but I ignored her. I had to find Zack. He was here somewhere, I knew it. As my hands hit his small foot and I pulled him out of the dirt, tears spilled down my cheeks, and I cried out his name.

"Zack, my boy."

I put him on the ground and started to perform CPR.

The Chief moved closer, her hand hovering over her

holster, ready to act in any way possible. We worked together, our hands moving in unison as we tried to save my son's life. I felt his chest rise and fall beneath my hands, his body slowly coming back to life. I pumped his chest, feeling the air escape his lungs with every push. The Chief was beside me now, her hand on my back, a silent encouragement. I could hear ambulance sirens in the distance, but I knew they wouldn't get here in time. I had to save my son.

"Come on, Zack. You can't leave me. You can't leave me now!"

Suddenly, Zack gasped for air, his small body shaking as he coughed up dirt. I pulled him into my arms, holding him tightly as he clung to my shirt. After what felt like an eternity, Zack's eyes fluttered open. He coughed and sputtered again, his small body racked with spasms. I pulled him close, holding him clutched in my arms.

"What... what happened?" he whispered, his voice raw and hoarse.

"I don't know, son," I replied, my voice choked with emotion. "But you're safe now."

The Chief stood up, her face grim. "We need to get out of here," she said. "Now."

Together, we made our way back to the car, my son shivering in my arms. An ambulance drove up just as we made it out, its sirens blaring. We handed Zack over to the paramedics, who took him into the back of the ambulance. I climbed in after him, holding his hand tightly, refusing to let go. The Chief climbed into the front seat of my car, starting it up and following us to the hospital.

The ride to the hospital seemed to take forever. I held on to Zack's hand tightly, praying that he would be okay. As we drove, I couldn't help but think about the tombstone with my name on it. Who could this guy be? Who had I upset so much that they'd take my child and try to destroy my family?

Finally, we arrived at the hospital. The paramedics rushed Zack into the emergency room, while the Chief and I watched helplessly. We sat in silence, waiting for news, our hearts heavy with fear.

Hours passed before a doctor came out to talk to us. He had a solemn expression on his face, and my heart sank. Joe had arrived there and was pacing back and forth angrily.

"Your son is going to be okay," the doctor said, and I let out a sigh of relief. "He was sedated and buried alive. He inhaled a lot of dirt, but we were able to clear his airways. He's going to be fine, but he needs some rest and observation."

I slumped in my seat, tears of joy streaming down my face. The Chief put a comforting hand on my shoulder, a small smile on her face.

"You did good," she said softly. "You saved his life. Our team is combing through the area around the cemetery all night, and hopefully we will have some answers in the morning. Unfortunately, they never found the shooter from the farmhouse. No prints, no suspect debris. It's possible it was the same person, but we could also be dealing with more than one."

My body shook with anger as I clenched my fists and turned to the Chief. "I swear, I'll hunt this sick bastard down and make him pay for what he's done. He messed with the wrong woman." My voice was filled with determination as I glared at her, daring her to doubt me.

FIFTY-FIVE

Then

When Travis first introduced his new partner, Billie Ann Wilde, to Betty, she had felt a pang of jealousy. After all, the woman was beautiful, intelligent, and seemed to have it all together. But Betty soon decided it was a waste of her time, trying to keep them apart, and remaining jealous. Instead, she decided to keep her enemy close, so to speak. She invited the woman over often for dinner or just a cup of coffee, and as they spent more time together, Betty realized that Billie Ann was also kind and genuine.

One day when she came to visit, Billie Ann sat down heavily on the couch, her hand resting protectively over her stomach.

"I have something to tell you," she said quietly. "I'm pregnant again."

Betty's eyes widened in surprise and concern. "Oh, my, that's wonderful news! But I can understand why you might feel overwhelmed."

Billie Ann nodded, tears welling up in her eyes. "Between

work and taking care of Charlene, I don't know how I'll manage it all."

Without hesitation, Betty offered her support. "Don't do it alone. Let me help. I can watch Charlene whenever you need a break or have appointments."

Relief flooded through Billie Ann, and she couldn't hold back her grateful smile. "That would mean so much to me, thank you."

As the months went by, Betty became like a second mother to Billie Ann's daughter, Charlene. The little girl would eagerly run into Betty's arms every time she saw her. "Aunt Betty!" she squealed happily.

"Hello, my sweet girl," Betty would reply, enveloping her in a warm hug.

Her own son John wasn't so cute anymore, even if she still loved him dearly. She enjoyed having young children in her life again.

As the due date drew nearer, Betty's phone rang every morning at ten a.m. sharp. She would listen to Billie Ann's groggy voice on the other end as she propped her feet up on the couch, a cup of decaf tea in hand.

"How are you holding up?" Betty asked softly.

"I feel like a beached whale," Billie Ann joked through a yawn.

"I bet you're getting tired," Betty said.

Each time, Billie Ann would let out a weary laugh and say "exhausted" before launching into tales of swollen feet and constant trips to the bathroom.

Betty even helped Billie Ann pack a bag with diapers, onesies, and extra clothes for the baby to take to the hospital. When Billie Ann went into labor unexpectedly, early in the morning hours, her husband Joe was away on business. Betty's phone rang at three a.m., and she immediately recognized Billie Ann's number.

"This is it," Billie Ann said, sounding terrified on the other end. "The baby is coming. I can feel it. Joe isn't even here! And my parents are out of town."

Again, Betty didn't hesitate before making the decision. Travis was still sleeping, and she snuck out of bed without waking him up, then said, "I'll be right there."

She threw on a pair of jeans and a shirt and rushed to the car. Without hesitation, Betty took Billie Ann to the hospital, then went back home and took care of Charlene, making sure she had breakfast and got dressed before dropping her off at school, before going back to wait for news at the hospital.

When Billie Ann finally gave birth to a healthy baby boy, Betty was the first one to see him. She took Billie Ann chocolates and a bouquet of flowers. As she held the newborn in her arms, she felt a sense of fulfillment and joy. She had never been able to have her own child, and holding this little bundle of joy made her feel like a proud grandmother. It almost brought her to tears.

Over the next few weeks, Betty spent more time with Billie Ann and her family than ever before. She helped out with the household chores, cooked meals, and helped Charlene with her homework or sometimes took her to the park to give her mother a well-deserved break. The more time she spent with Billie Ann, the more she realized how lucky Travis was to have her as a partner. She was smart, witty, and had a way of making everyone feel at ease.

Soon, Billie Ann went back to work, and Betty helped her out as much as she could, picking the kids up from school or daycare when Joe was working, or taking over a home-cooked lasagna when she knew both parents were too busy to cook.

She grew to care for the entire family, and that's why it was an even bigger shock when Travis one day came home early, slamming the door behind him, his face contorted with rage, as he yelled, "I'll kill the bitch! I'm gonna freaking kill her!"

FIFTY-SIX

BILLIE ANN

I sat there looking at my son, hooked up to machines that beeped steadily in the background. His chest rose and fell as he was pulled deeper into his sleep. The hospital room felt sterile and cold, the only source of warmth coming from the machines that monitored my son's vitals.

As I sat there, lost in thought, the door creaked open and in walked Danni. She rushed to my side, wrapping her arms tightly around me. She looked around the room, taking in the machines and wires that surrounded my son's bed.

"Did they trace the phone that called you?" she asked and pulled up a chair next to me.

I shook my head. "It was in the grave with Zack," I said. "The techs have it secured, but I doubt it will enlighten us much. This guy is clever."

Danielle squeezed my hand, her eyes softening with sadness. "We'll figure it out," she said firmly. "We won't rest until we do."

I leaned my head against her shoulder, feeling a small measure of comfort in her embrace. We sat in silence for a few moments, the beeping of the machines the only sound in the room. I closed my eyes, trying to will away the image of my son lying there, motionless and vulnerable.

The sound of the door opening pulled me out of the daze I had fallen into. I looked up and saw Joe coming into the room, his eyes blazing. I felt Danielle's grip on my hand tighten in response. I braced myself for whatever was about to happen.

"What the hell is going on here?" he bellowed, his voice echoing off the walls.

Danielle stood up, her hand still clasped in mine. "Joe, please calm down," she said, her voice measured and calm. "This is not the time or place for this."

Joe growled, his eyes darting between me and Danielle. "Why is she here? And why are you two acting like everything's okay?"

I stood up, my own anger beginning to bubble to the surface. "Joe, this is not the time or the place for this," I repeated, more firmly, my voice shaking slightly.

But Joe was beyond reason. He strode over to the bed where our son lay, his fists clenched at his sides. "Look at him!" he shouted. "Look what's happened to him because of you!"

I felt the tears well up in my eyes, but I refused to let Joe see me break down. "Don't," I said, my voice quivering with anger and fear. "Don't you dare blame me for this."

He took a step closer, his eyes boring into mine. "Don't blame you? Our son is lying in a hospital bed, hooked up to machines, because someone decided to hurt him. Because of you. And yet, you're sitting here with your new fling, acting like everything's just peachy."

Danielle stepped forward, putting herself between Joe and me. "You have no right to talk to her like that," she said, her voice firm. "She is here for her son, just like you are."

Joe scoffed. "Yeah, right. She's here for the sympathy. And you," he said, turning to Danielle, "you're just a home-wrecker."

My blood boiled at his words, but Danielle remained calm. "I'm not a home-wrecker," she said, her voice steady. "I'm here to support her, because I care about her. And I care about your son."

Joe sneered at her. "You don't know a damn thing about him."

"I know that he's your son," Danielle said. "And I know that he needs his parents to be strong for him right now."

Joe looked like he was about to say something else, but then the door opened again and a nurse stepped inside.

"Excuse me, I'm going to have to ask you to keep your voices down," the nurse said, her tone gentle but firm. "There are other patients on this floor, and we need to maintain a calm environment."

Joe glared at the nurse, but he seemed to realize that he was fighting a losing battle. He turned on his heel and stormed out of the room, the door slamming shut behind him.

I sank back down into the chair, my body trembling with a mixture of anger and fear. Danielle sat next to me, her hand gently rubbing my back. "Are you okay?" she asked softly.

I nodded, unable to find my voice. I knew that Joe was hurting, but his anger was misplaced. This wasn't the time or the place for him to take out his frustrations on me. Right now, all that mattered was our son, lying there in the hospital bed.

As the nurse checked on my son's vitals, I took a deep breath and forced myself to focus on the present. There would be time for dealing with Joe later. Right now, I needed to be strong for my son and for myself.

I turned to Danielle, who was still sitting beside me. "Thank you," I said, my voice barely above a whisper. "For standing up for me."

Danielle smiled, her eyes softening with kindness. "Of course," she said. "That's what I'm here for."

We sat in silence for a few more moments, both lost in our

thoughts. But then Danielle leaned over and pressed her lips against mine in a gentle kiss. It was brief, but it was enough to make me feel that I wasn't alone.

FIFTY-SEVEN

BILLIE ANN

It was close to the early morning hours, when I sat in the uncomfortable chair next to my son's hospital bed, staring blankly at the white walls around me. Danielle was still by my side, holding my hand, but had dozed off in her chair. Meanwhile my mind was completely consumed with worry for my son. The only thing that kept me from completely losing it was trying to figure out who had done this. I had been in touch with the team and updated on leads. Finally, they all believed me, that it wasn't Jimmy, and they were reinterviewing Angela, my aunt, and other family members to try and find out who would do this. I had tracked down every convict I had ever arrested who might harbor a grudge against me and my family. But all of them were still in prison.

Suddenly, the door opened and a gentle voice interrupted my thoughts. "Excuse me," the nurse said softly, "but I wanted to let you know that your brother is awake and better. He's out of the ICU, so you can visit him whenever you want. He has been asking for you."

I looked up at her, momentarily confused. My mind had been so focused on my son's condition that I had almost forgotten about Andrew. But as the nurse's words sank in, a wave of relief washed over me. My brother was better. That at least was something.

"Thank you," I said gratefully, standing up from my chair. "I'll go see him right away."

I woke up Danielle and told her I was going to see my brother really quick and then come back. There was a guard at the door, so they were safe. She grunted something half in her sleep, and I put a blanket over her and kissed her forehead. As I made my way down the hallway toward Andrew's room, I couldn't help but feel guilty about how little I had seen him these past years. It wasn't only my fault, since he hadn't exactly called or shown up, not after the big fight with my parents. I knew he wasn't well, that the drugs had taken over his life, but I still felt like I could have done more. I could have been there more for him. And now that he was awake and better, I realized how much I had missed him.

I pushed open the door to my brother's room, and my heart swelled with relief as I saw him in the bed, looking much better than he had the last time I had seen him. He was hooked up to various machines, and his entire body was in a cast, but he was awake and alert.

"Hey, bro," I said softly, walking over to his bedside. "How you feeling?"

"I'm all right," he said, smiling weakly. "Just glad to be alive. How's Zack?"

I took a deep breath, suddenly feeling a lump form in my throat. "He's still hanging in there," I replied, my voice catching slightly. "It's been touch and go, but they say he will be okay, so that's what I choose to believe. I'm worried about you too."

He exhaled. "Yeah, they say I might never walk again. Several fractures on the spine and all that."

I nodded, feeling awful. "Did you see his face? The guy who took you and hurt you?"

"Nah, he was wearing a mask. The one from those movies, the ones our mom wouldn't let us watch when we were younger, you remember?" I nodded. "But it was a woman who coerced me to go with her. I think she might just have been someone paid to get to me, but it might be a lead?"

"I will definitely look into that," I said. "Anything else you can help us with? Estimated age of the kidnapper? An accent? Any defining features?"

Andy shook his head, his expression pained. "I'm sorry, sis. I wish I could do more to help."

I shook my head, sitting down in the chair next to his bed. "Just getting better is enough. We need you around."

There was a moment of silence between us, the machines humming softly in the background. I looked at Andrew, really looked at him, and saw the toll the drugs had taken on him. He looked so fragile and vulnerable, and I couldn't help but feel a surge of protectiveness.

"I'm sorry," he said suddenly, breaking the silence. "For everything. For not being there for you when you needed me. For not being a good brother."

I put a hand on his arm, feeling tears prick at the corners of my eyes. "It's okay," I said softly. "There's still time."

"How are Mom and Dad?" he asked.

I shrugged. "Struggling. They lost a grandson and a nephew. Another grandson is in a mental institution. Another is in a coma, and still no sign of waking up. They almost lost their son too."

"I'm sure they didn't care much about me," Andrew said.

"They care more than you think," I said. "Both of them."

"I wish we had never gotten into that stupid fight."

"What was it about?" I asked. "They never told me. One minute you were there, and the next you left. I asked them a gazillion times what it was about, but they refused to tell me."

"It doesn't matter now," he said, his eyes avoiding mine.

"I think it does. Don't I deserve to know what could possibly be so serious that I wouldn't see you for years?" I asked.

He swallowed. I could see his eyes well up. "I was desperate. I needed money for another fix. I grabbed Dad's computer and went into his web bank to transfer money to myself."

"Oh no, Andrew. You stole from them?" I said.

He nodded, looking away. "I had done it before without them realizing it."

"So, that's what made them angry at you?" I said.

"Yes, well... I can't really blame them."

I looked at him, feeling sadness in me. "How did they find out? Did they see you do it?"

"No, actually I revealed myself," he said.

"How so?"

"There was something I didn't understand. When I looked at his account there was money going out of it as a recurring payment called 'college' and that made me puzzled. None of us went to college anymore, and neither did any of their grandchildren. At least not then. I asked them about it, and they wouldn't answer."

I wrinkled my forehead. "So, what does that mean?"

"I don't know," he said. "I got angry because they refused to tell me. I accused them of lying. Then they asked me to leave because I admitted to having tried to take money out of their account. I decided to never return."

I sat there, stunned. My mind was racing, trying to process what my brother had just told me. I couldn't wrap my head around it.

"I know," Andrew said, his eyes filled with regret. "I should have told you what happened. But I was so messed up back then, I was so embarrassed, I didn't know how to deal with it. I just wanted to forget about everything and numb the pain."

I nodded, understanding now why he had turned to drugs over his family and loved ones. It was his way of coping with the pain and the guilt. My heart ached for him. I watched him as he dozed off into a deep sleep, my mind racing with a million thoughts. Who was this woman who had lured my brother, and who was this person paying her? I felt like the voice on the phone had sounded familiar but couldn't put my finger on it.

Did I know this person? Was it someone close to me?

FIFTY-EIGHT

Then

Betty's eyes followed Travis as he paced back and forth, his fists clenched at his sides and angry mutters escaping his lips. The slam of the front door had echoed through the house, followed by the clatter of keys hitting the kitchen counter. She set down her coffee mug and the crinkled newspaper, worrying as she observed her husband's erratic behavior.

"What's going on?" she asked, standing up from her chair.

Travis stopped his pacing and turned to face her, his eyes blazing with anger. "I hate her, I hate her so much," he growled.

Betty walked away from the table and approached him cautiously. She had seen Travis angry before, but something about this was different. "Who? Who do you hate?" she asked, trying to keep her voice calm.

Travis let out a frustrated sigh and ran his hands through his hair. "That bitch. Billie Ann."

"Your partner?" she asked, puzzled. Travis had always been so fond of Billie Ann. Why was he suddenly acting like this?

"Is there any other Billie Ann around here?" he hissed. "Yes of course it's her. I'm gonna kill her if I ever get my hands on her again."

"Why? What did she do? Travis, what did Billie Ann do?"

Travis turned to face her, and Betty immediately wished she had just kept her mouth shut. The anger was written all over his face and she could see just how much he was hurting.

"She has accused me of rape. Can you believe it?"

There was no way Betty could have kept her mouth shut anymore. She was practically hyperventilating as she asked, "What? What are you talking about?"

Travis ran his hands through his hair and pulled out a kitchen chair. He sat himself down and looked at his wife. "She has accused me of raping her."

"What have you done?" Betty asked, finally understanding. "Did you sleep with her?"

"No, I did not sleep with her," he snapped. "But she tried."

"What?" Betty took a step back. "This can't be."

"You're darn right it can't be."

"Travis, she's just lying. She's trying to get you in trouble because she's jealous."

"She wants the promotion, that's what she wants," he said with a snort. "She came on to me, I could hardly get her to leave me alone. I told her I'm a married man and I'm not a cheater, so I had to tell her no. She didn't like that, she didn't like that at all. She's trying to get me fired by making me look like a sexual harasser. I'm going to kill her."

"Is that why you're home early?"

"They sent me home," he said. "I'm suspended while there's an investigation, apparently. As if my word isn't good enough for them. After all these years I have spent on them and been loyal to the uniform. I can't believe it. They take her word over mine?"

"That's ridiculous," Betty said. She grabbed a beer from the fridge and handed it to him. "This is not the end of it. We will

get you a good lawyer, and we will fight it. And Billie Ann
better never set foot in this house again, as long as I live here.
You are my husband and I believe you."

Travis took the beer and chugged it down. He wiped his
mouth with the back of his hand. "That's right, baby."

"No one's gonna take my man away from me. I'll make sure
I tell her that. What are you gonna do?" she asked, worried.

"I'm gonna find the lying bitch and tell her I'm not putting
up with it. Stay here, I'll be right back." Travis got up from his
chair and headed toward the door.

"No, Travis, don't!"

Betty watched in horror as the door slammed shut behind
him. She grabbed her cell phone and started calling his number,
but she knew before it started ringing that it was no use. Travis
had already left the house and was on his way to find Billie
Ann. And there was nothing she could say or do to stop him.

FIFTY-NINE

BILLIE ANN

I freeze as Travis barges into my house without permission. He doesn't even bother to knock before he's storming in, his eyes blazing with fury. Before I can even ask what he's doing here, he's on me, his fingers closing around my throat.

I gasp, struggling to breathe as he lifts me off the ground with ease. His fingers dig into my flesh, leaving angry marks as I kick and flail, trying to escape his grasp. But Travis is too strong, too determined.

"You think you can do this to me?" he spits, his face twisted with rage. "You think you can accuse me of raping you?"

"You did," I gasp, my voice barely audible as his grip tightens. "Please, let me go."

But Travis only sneers, his eyes darkening with malice. "You're not going anywhere," he growls. "Not until you promise to drop the charges. I swear I will kill you if you don't. I'm not gonna let you ruin everything I have worked for."

"Let me go," I struggle to say, and yelp when he yanks me forward by my hair, my head jerking to the side.

"And if I don't?"

I'm so scared I can barely speak. But I'm also angry. He

raped me, one night when we were alone at the station after dark, working late. Put his hand over my mouth and pushed me down. "You know you want it," he kept telling me. "You know you want this as much as I do." But I didn't. And I defied him by telling our superior about what happened.

Travis lifts me higher, the toes of my shoes scraping against the ground. I'm afraid that he's going to throw me across the room, but instead he slams me against the wall.

My body groans against the impact, and I press my hands against the wall, trying to calm my breathing.

"W-what do you want from me?" I manage to stutter, my eyes darting to the side as Travis towers over me. "You raped me! I'm not gonna lie for you."

Travis' eyes flash with fury, and he quickly grabs the back of my neck and slams me against the wall again. His lips curl up into a grin, and his eyes burn into mine. "You're fucking lying," he snarls.

"I'm not," I whimper, my eyes darting away from his. "You raped me. It's the truth."

Travis' eyes narrow, and he quickly yanks me away from the wall. I cry out as he pulls me forward, his fingers gripping my neck.

I shiver, fear coursing through my veins. Travis' eyes nearly light up with anger, and he grabs me by the arm before shoving me across the room.

My back crashes against the glass table, and I gasp as pain rips through my body. Travis' eyes widen, and he quickly approaches me, his hands closing in on my throat.

"I knew you were fucking me over," he hisses, his fingers tightening around my throat.

"No!" I shriek, my hands flying to his. I claw at his fingers, desperately trying to yank him away from me.

"Travis, stop!" I scream as Joe runs in, his eyes widening as he sees Travis trying to kill me.

He tries to pull Travis away from me, but he's too strong.

"No! You're ruining my life!" Travis shouts as he spins around, his hand catching Joe in the jaw.

Joe's head snaps backward, and he groans as he falls to the floor. Before Travis has a chance to go for him again, I thrust my foot into his side. He doubles over, and I quickly kick him between the legs.

"Fucking bitch," he hisses as he grabs at his crotch, his eyes wide with pain.

I quickly scramble away from him, my hands flying to my throat as I choke. I'm wheezing, struggling to breathe as my eyes dart to Joe. He's sitting on the floor, his eyes wide as he stares at Travis.

"You'll pay for this," Travis growls as he rubs his crotch.

I don't say a word. I'm too scared, too shocked to even say anything. Instead, I watch him leave, Joe helping me up as Travis stumbles out of the house.

I'm shaking as I sink to the floor. Joe places a hand on my shoulder, and I'd throw it off if I could. I'm too shocked, too overwhelmed by everything. This isn't supposed to happen. After I came forward with what happened, everything was supposed to be all right. Travis would be locked up, and everything would be good.

"I-I'm so sorry," Joe stutters as he helps me up. "I'm so sorry."

"It's not your fault," I whisper as I sink to the floor. "It's all my fault. I'm to blame."

* * *

The machines in the room beeped, slowly and steadily, telling me that my son was still alive. My heart ached and tears rushed to my eyes, but I swallowed them down. I hadn't thought about what happened for years, but now it was on my mind constantly. Ever since the phone call with the person talking about my son, and revenge as sweet as cherry pie. I only knew one person who liked cherry pie more than anything. My former partner, Travis. My partner who was supposed to protect me, but instead raped me. It was his word against mine back then, since we were alone when it happened. He then accused me of hitting on him constantly, and his wife was backing him up saying I was flirtatious at their house with him in front of her. People believed him over me, and I ended up doubting myself and what really happened. It was an awful time in my life. One I wanted to forget, but never could. I could still see his face when closing my eyes. Those eyes I would never forget as long as I lived. I would still dream about him at night, waking up bathed in sweat.

He had been let go after I reported him, but that was that. Asked to retire. But there were no criminal charges against him, since I couldn't prove that I didn't consent to it. He argued that I wanted to have sex with him. He argued that the bruises on my cheek from him hitting me were part of a sex game we had played. I had asked for him to hit me, he said. My Chief back then didn't want trouble. He wanted this affair gone. So, he asked him to retire, and then he sent me away. My rapist was still out there, and that terrified me. He and his wife had tried to hurt me before. Was this their work as well? Had they hurt my son?

SIXTY

BILLIE ANN

The Chief's office was like a cave, with shadows clinging to the walls and a single desk lamp casting a weak yellow light. I perched on the edge of a hard chair, twisting my nervous hands in my lap while she studied me with piercing eyes.

"Are you okay?" she asked, her voice soft but firm.

Her gentle yet commanding voice cut through the oppressive silence, pulling me out of my thoughts. I looked up at her, tears threatening to spill from my eyes. "No, Chief. I can't seem to shake all what has happened from my mind, but I have had a lot of time to think, and I have a theory."

The Chief's rigid posture softened as she leaned forward, her piercing gaze narrowing.

"Go on," she commanded.

I swallowed hard and forced out the words, barely above a whisper. "Do you remember my old partner? I told you about him?"

The Chief's face remained stoic, but I could see the hint of recognition in her eyes. Her unreadable expression told me she was waiting for more information.

"Yes, I read your file. And I think I told you when I came

here, that I wanted you to know I fully believe your side of the story. I also remember talking to you about those emails we found from him last year, that made us believe he was somewhat involved in the kidnapping of your friend Danielle."

"Well, I think he might have had something to do with this too," I said, my words coming out in a rush. "I just don't know how."

The Chief sat back in her chair, her eyes still fixed on me. "Explain."

I took a deep breath, steadying myself. "The man is in a wheelchair. He can't have killed my nephew or my cousin by himself."

"Remind me again, how did he end up in a wheelchair?"

I swallowed hard and looked down. "He was hit by a car. This was after he retired. But that has made me rule him out when thinking of who wanted to hurt me and my family. But what if he isn't alone?"

"You mean his wife? What was her name again?"

"Betty."

"You think she might have helped him? That she killed those children, and she kidnapped your brother and hurt him? Your brother is a pretty big guy."

She gave me a skeptical look. "Do you think she might be capable of such a thing?"

"I do, and I don't," I said. "I know she hates me. After I reported Travis, she approached me outside of the police station and told me I was ungrateful, that she didn't understand how I could do this to them, when they had treated me like family. Stuff like that. I felt awful, but I had to do it, you know? I cared about them both. She was right, they had helped me out so much."

"Still doesn't justify what he did to you," Chief Harold said. "You did the right thing reporting him. Your Chief should have charged him and not just asked him to retire. What he did was not okay."

I felt such relief when hearing my Chief say these words. For so many years I had felt this deep guilt over having reported my former partner. I had questioned myself whether or not it was the right thing to do. But what I didn't tell her was that it was Joe that had hit Travis with Charlene's truck. After he tried to kill me at our home, and I ended up telling Joe it was Travis who had raped me, he snapped. It happened one day many years later, when he saw him walking in the street in our old town, as he was there on business. I had found this out later, and then had him arrested for it. Of course she would know if she looked at his records, but it didn't seem like she had.

Joe still resented me for what happened back then. But the charges were dropped when Travis and Betty disappeared. We found out that for years they had been helping our former Chief hide a child he had kidnapped. Travis and he were best friends, and when it was discovered, Travis chose to run away. I could only interpret that as a confirmation that he knew about the kidnapping.

"The only solution is they must have had help somehow," she said. "But from who?"

My eyes grew wide, as a thought occurred. "I think I know."

SIXTY-ONE

Then

"I can't eat this crap!"

Travis slammed his fist into the table, and Betty jumped. She looked at him, feeling anxious.

Now what? What was wrong this time?

"But it's your favorite," she said. "Chicken parmigiana."

He hissed at her. "That's not my favorite. This tastes like toilet water. I want something else. Now. I'll watch TV while you make it."

He grabbed the wheels of his chair and rolled away from the table.

Betty stood motionless in the kitchen, her hands shaking. She had taken so much care in preparing the meal, had made sure to buy Travis' favorite food, yet he had been disappointed. Again. She knew it wasn't his fault; it was this whole thing with the accident and the resulting depression. It was taking a toll on their marriage. She couldn't blame him for it. Yet it was hard for her not to take his outbursts personally. She thought back to this morning, when he had refused to get out of bed or even look at her. That was the worst part. She took a deep breath, determined not to let him ruin the night. It wasn't easy, but she was determined to stay strong. She grabbed the pan of chicken parmigiana, threw it in the trash and started over.

While she cooked him a steak and mashed potatoes with gravy and string beans, she heard the familiar hum of the TV coming from the living room. Travis was watching a show he liked, something about cowboys and horses. She allowed herself a small smile as she thought about how content he was at those moments. Maybe, for one night, he could forget about his troubles and find some joy.

She plated the food and took it out to the living room. She watched as his eyes lit up when he saw it.

"Now that is my favorite meal," he said, taking a bite and savoring it.

"Glad you like it," Betty replied with a faint smile.

He thanked her and went on to tell her all about the show he was watching, and she listened intently and responded with the same enthusiasm.

It was in that moment that Betty realized how much she loved Travis, despite his mood swings and outbursts. He was her partner, her best friend, and the love of her life. She knew that she would do anything to make him happy, even if it meant cooking the same meal over and over again until it was perfect. As the night wore on, they finished their dinner and talked about their plans for the weekend. Suddenly, Travis reached for her hand.

"I'm sorry for earlier," he said. "I know I can be difficult sometimes."

Betty squeezed his hand. It was rare that he became himself, like the good old Travis she had known and loved, but in those moments when he did, she remembered who he was and how wonderful he could be.

"It's okay, Travis. I know you're going through a tough time."

"I don't deserve you," he said, his voice choking up with emotion. He slumped his head.

Betty leaned over and lifted his chin up with her finger, then kissed him gently on the lips. "Yes, you do. And I'm always here for you, no matter what."

They stayed like that for a while, holding hands and watching the show on TV, until Travis fell asleep. Betty grabbed a blanket and put it over his legs, then looked at him, her heart aching. Oh, how she longed for the man he used to be. That powerful strong man, who never let anything get to him, who refused to let life get him down. He had been a big man, one people in town respected and looked up to. The head of the homicide department with eight detectives serving under him. He had taken down more murderers than anyone in the department. Ever. He was a legend. He won awards for his work and was a highly decorated hero as well.

And this was how he was going to end his days? Strapped to a chair?

It wasn't fair by any means.

Betty cleaned up after dinner, and she walked into the kitchen, feeling the tears press behind her eyes. She had cried so much over what happened to Travis, she had barely any more tears left.

She wanted to make it right. At least get the bastard who ran him over.

That's when the phone rang. She looked at the display then picked up. It was the guy—Bob—that she knew at the DMV. She had gotten ahold of the security photos from the ATM by the street where Travis was hit, and she had sent them to him. The police didn't seem to care since Travis wasn't very popular after those insane accusations his former partner had come up with, just to destroy him. So even if Betty went down there almost every day to make sure they were working on finding out who hit Travis, they still hadn't found out anything, and she knew they weren't even trying. So, she had decided to act on her own.

"Yes?"

"I got what you are looking for. I have a name," Bob said.

"Yes?"

"The truck is registered to someone named Wilde. Billie Ann Wilde."

Everything stood still for a few seconds as she pieced it all together. "Of course," she said.

Then she hung up. Betty stood for a while with the phone in her hand, till she realized she was shaking. She had wanted this, she really did, but now that it was happening, she felt anxious. Would getting justice for Travis really bring her the relief she so desperately needed?

Of course, it will, silly. Of course. Only then can you both move on.

SIXTY-TWO

BILLIE ANN

I parked my police cruiser in front of my childhood home north of Orlando, the driveway still lined with the same palm trees. The smell of freshly cut grass filled my nose as I stepped out onto the pavement, and memories flooded back of playing tag on the lawn with my siblings. The faded paint on the front door reminded me of the times we would race to see who could touch it first after school. Nostalgia overwhelmed me as I gazed at the familiar house that held so many happy memories.

As I walked closer, the Florida heat hit me like a brick wall. I walked toward the front entrance, noticing the overgrown weeds and untrimmed grass. It seemed like my parents had let the yard go a bit lately. It wasn't like them.

Memories flooded my mind as I walked up to the front porch, recalling the countless times my brothers and I had played in the yard, and gone gator hunting in the nearby swamps. I remembered the many bruises and scrapes I had gotten from roughhousing with them, but I wouldn't have traded those moments for anything.

The familiar aroma of garlic, onions, and simmering sauce wafted toward me as I pushed open the front door. It was like stepping into a time machine—the smells of my childhood home enveloped me, and I felt like I had never left at all. I took off my shoes and wandered toward the source of the enticing smell.

But being back there also brought back some bad memories that now hit me like a brick wall. I could still hear Peter's voice from the night of our big argument. The anger in his eyes as he told me to stay out of his life. The hissing sound coming from his lips when I had finally been honest with him, when I told him I couldn't just watch anymore as he destroyed our family.

I poked my head into the kitchen, knocking lightly on the doorframe. My mother stood at the stove, her back to me as she stirred a bubbling pot of stew. I could see her shoulders shaking with sobs. Cooking was always her go-to when she was upset or worried, and the fragrant smell of spices filled the room, like they had when I was growing up. She turned to me and tried to smile, but it faltered when she saw the concern in my eyes.

"Mom, are you okay?" I asked, taking a step closer to her.

She looked at me, her eyes red and swollen. "Oh, honey," she said, pulling me into a tight embrace. "It's just so much right now."

I wrapped my arms around her, burying my face in her soft, floral-scented hair. It was a familiar embrace, one that always brought me comfort. I felt hot tears welling up in my eyes as I thought about growing up in this house. My mother's gentle touch and soothing voice made me feel like I was a child again, safe and loved.

She released me, and her tearstained cheeks made my heart ache. "I'm sorry," she said, wiping her eyes with the back of her hand. "I can't seem to stop crying. First Charlie and now Jeremy. And Alex... she's still battling for her life. And Zack? What's happening?" She took a deep breath and looked up at me with a sad smile. "It's just too much." I nodded in understanding, feeling the weight of our family's struggles as well.

"I know, Mom. It's been a lot. And Andrew too. He's better though."

She chuckled and shook her head, ignoring me mentioning Andrew. "You look tired, sweetie. Have you slept at all?"

"Not a lot. Mom, someone is trying to hurt our family. Do you have any idea why?"

"It almost feels that way, huh? Do you want some stew? It's done," she said, a concerned look in her eyes. "You look like you haven't been eating much either."

"It's okay," I said. "I'm not hungry and I'm actually here to talk to Dad. Where is he?"

She shook her head. "He's not here. He left this morning and I haven't heard from him. He's not dealing well with the loss of his grandchild and nephew. It's really taken a toll on him. He was up last night most of the night pacing around. I sure hope he'll be back in time for dinner. We're going back to the hospital to be there for your aunt later. I am taking her some of this stew, so she can get some real food, instead of the hospital food she has been living off lately. And then we're going to Peter and Angela's afterward to take some food for them as well, since they're so grief-stricken they can't cook, and have barely been eating. This is the time for all of us to come together and help out where we can. I told our church to start a prayer chain and pray for us. What do you need your dad for? Maybe I can help?"

I stared at her, my mind racing with thoughts. "Do you mind if I borrow his computer in the office for a minute?"

She stared at me, puzzled, then shook her head. "Of course not. You know where to find it."

I nodded and I made my way to the office, the hardwood floor creaking under my feet. As I walked through the house, I could hear my mother's sobs echoing in my ears. I knew how hard it had been for her. My heart ached for her.

I found my father's office and sat down at his computer. I

logged in using his password and opened his web bank. Then I started looking through his transactions. It didn't take me long to find what I was looking for. I grabbed my phone and called Big Tom.

"What's up, boss?" he said. "I just got back from visiting Scott at the hospital. They say he'll be out by the end of the week, so that's good news. Might take a while before he's ready to get back to work though."

"That's wonderful news," I said. "But that's not what I'm calling about. I need you to check out something for me."

"Of course, anything."

"If I send you the information for a bank account, can you find out who it belongs to?"

"Sure. Shouldn't be that hard."

"Awesome. I'll send you the info in an email right away."

I hung up the phone and sent the information to Tom. Then leaned back in my father's leather office chair, contemplating what I had just done. I knew that if my father found out that I was snooping through his bank account, he would be livid. But I had to do it. The college fund Andy had mentioned was playing on my mind. I had to find out if my suspicions were true. I wondered what to do if they were. Part of me really didn't want them to be.

SIXTY-THREE

BILLIE ANN

After what felt like an eternity, Tom's name flashed on my phone screen. I snatched it up and pressed it to my ear, each beat of my heart quickening with anticipation.

"Hey, Tom?" I said, trying to mask the eagerness in my voice.

"Yeah," came his gravelly response.

"You got something?"

"I did. Just got off the phone with the bank."

There was a brief pause on the other end of the line before Tom spoke again. "The name on the account is John Walker."

My heart dropped into my stomach as I processed the name. John Walker. It was a name that I never thought I would hear again. I quickly pulled up a search engine on the computer and typed in the name, my hands shaking with anticipation.

As soon as I saw the first image that popped up, I knew that my worst fears had been confirmed. It was a picture of a man that I knew all too well. There he was, staring back at me from the screen.

"Holy s..." I whispered, my eyes widening.

"What's wrong?" Tom asked, his voice filled with concern.

"It's worse than I thought," I said, my voice trembling. "Much worse."

"What do you mean?"

"I need to go," I said. "I need to find my dad before it's too late. Before someone else dies. Stand by for backup if I need it."

I didn't wait for him to say anything, I didn't have time to explain. Instead, I hung up, then stormed back into the kitchen, where my mother was setting the table. She looked up.

"You're staying for dinner, right?"

"Mom, where is Dad? I need to know right now, where is he?" I almost screamed at her. She looked at me startled at my sudden aggression.

"I... I don't know," she said. "He said he was going for a drive, that's all."

"His phone," I said. "Did he take it?"

She nodded, still holding utensils in her hands. "Yes, he always takes that awful thing everywhere. Constantly staring at it, scrolling with his finger, it's so darn annoy—"

"Thank you," I said and stormed back to the computer. I opened Find My Phone and saw where it was located. Then my heart dropped.

The phone was located in the same house where we had found Andrew all beaten up. This could be no coincidence. I knew that I had to act fast before someone else ended up dead. I grabbed my keys and headed out the front door, my mom trailing behind me frantically asking what was wrong.

"Not now, Mom. I need to go."

I didn't have time to explain, and I didn't want to risk her safety by involving her in this dangerous situation. I got into my car and sped off toward Merritt Island, about an hour drive away from my parents' house.

Every second felt like an eternity as I weaved in and out of traffic, my mind racing with different scenarios of what was going to happen once I got there.

When I arrived at the farmhouse, I parked my car and cautiously approached the entrance. The gate was slightly ajar, and I slid into the property. It was still blocked off with police tape, but someone had removed it from the patio, and the sticker on the front door was split in halves. And the lights were on in one of the windows. I could hear muffled voices coming from inside. I took a deep breath and pushed the door open, stepping inside.

SIXTY-FOUR

Then

Betty's knuckles tapped rhythmically against the wooden door of John's dorm room. She could hear him fumbling around inside before the door swung open, revealing his surprised face. Without hesitation, she threw her arms around him in a tight embrace, holding on for dear life as if she hadn't seen him in years.

"Mom, what are you doing here?" John said, as he hugged her back.

"Can't a mom visit her son at college?" she said.

Betty stepped back to take a look at her son. He had grown so much since she last saw him, and she was proud of the man he had become. She then stepped into his dorm room and looked around, taking in all the little details that made it feel like home to him.

John's cozy room was a carefully organized space. His bed, with its dark blue comforter smoothly tucked in, took up most of the room. The desk, situated beside the window, was meticulously arranged with papers and textbooks stacked neatly in a row. A compact mini-fridge hummed under the desk, stocked with snacks and drinks. Above his desk hung a framed photograph of Betty and Travis, their smiles captured forever on the wall by John's bedside.

Betty strolled to the window, taking in the bustling campus scene below. She watched students scurry to class, their backpacks weighing them down. A warm sun shone overhead, and a gentle breeze whispered through the palm trees, causing their leaves to dance. Beaming, Betty turned back to John and made her way to his side. "You've created a lovely space here, John. It's inviting and snug," she complimented with a grin.

"Thanks, Mom. I actually enjoy being here. It's kind of like having my own little space," John replied as he leaned against his desk.

Betty nodded and looked around the room once more before sitting on John's bed. She patted the space next to her, gesturing for John to sit down. John joined her on the bed, and they both sat there in comfortable silence, just enjoying each other's company.

Betty then turned to John and asked, "So, how are your classes going? Are you keeping up with everything?"

John smiled and replied, "Yeah, Mom, everything's going well. I'm keeping up with all my work and my grades have been good so far."

"That's great to hear, John. I'm so proud of you," Betty said, a smile on her face. "And what about your social life? Have you made any new friends?"

John chuckled. "Nah. I don't really need anyone. I want to focus on school."

"That's smart, John. Make sure to always put your studies first," Betty said with a serious tone.

"I will, Mom. Don't worry," John reassured her. "You know me."

She nodded. "I do. By the way I have found out who hit

your dad with the truck. I finally have a name."

John's expression changed from relaxed to alert in an instant. "Really? Who was it?" he asked, his voice laced with anger.

Betty hesitated for a moment before answering. "It was his former partner. You know, the same one who got him fired because of all those false accusations she made."

John's jaw clenched. "I knew it! The bitch. I can't believe she did that. Like she hasn't hurt us enough?"

"I know, John. It's a terrible thing," Betty said, her voice filled with sadness.

John nodded, but Betty could tell that his mind was racing with thoughts of revenge.

Betty noticed the look on her son's face and placed a hand on his shoulder. "Don't do anything rash, John. We'll let the police handle it."

John took a deep breath and threw out his arms. "You're gonna let them take care of it? After what they put Dad through?"

Betty smiled. "Yeah well, it's the right thing to do."

"The right thing? How is that the right thing? This woman has been hurting our dad over and over again, and they've done nothing. Nothing!"

"Calm down, son. I know you're mad, but there isn't much we can do about it. Billie Ann Wilde had it in for us from the beginning. I just didn't realize it till it was too late."

"What do you mean?" he asked with a small snort.

"Well, her entire family has a history with our family so to speak. And I guess she was angry because of you going away to college and her family paying for it. Perhaps she thought it would mean less money for her? Her inheritance. Who knows?"

"What are you talking about?" John asked.

"This. I'm talking about this and you going here. Who did you think paid for it?"

SIXTY-FIVE

BILLIE ANN

I gripped the handle of my gun tightly, feeling its familiar weight and cool metal against my palm. The old farmhouse door let out a loud creak as I pushed it open, cautiously stepping inside. My eyes quickly adjusted to the dim light, and I saw my father sitting on the worn-out couch, his head buried in his hands. His broad shoulders shook with deep, gut-wrenching sobs. My heart dropped into my stomach as I slowly made my way toward him.

"Dad," I called out softly, but he didn't respond.

Tears welled up in his eyes and spilled down his stubbled cheeks as he looked up at me.

"Oh, Billie Ann," he choked out, "it's all... It's all my fault."

I stepped closer, resting a hand on his trembling shoulder.

"No, Dad," I reassured him. "It's not your fault."

But he continued to cry, mumbling brokenly, "Yes, yes, it is. Charlie, Jeremy, Alex, and even Andrew and poor Zack. It's all because of me. I did this to our family."

My dad's face was etched with pain, and I couldn't help but feel my heart breaking for him. I sat down next to him on the couch and put my arm around his shoulders. "Please, Dad," I pleaded. "It can never be your fault."

But before he could respond, a voice from behind me made us both jump. I turned and saw Betty Walker standing in the doorway with a gun pointed at us. My body froze in fear as I watched her finger twitch on the trigger.

"Drop the gun," she said. Then added sarcastically, "Please."

I put the gun on the floor cautiously.

"Kick it over here," she said.

I gave it a kick and it slid across the wooden floor. Betty picked it up. "We've been waiting for you."

As Betty held the gun on us, I could hear the sound of creaking wheels approaching from outside. The noise grew louder and louder until it felt like it was right on top of us. Suddenly, the farmhouse door swung open, and Travis came into the light, sitting in his wheelchair, a smirk on his face.

"Well, well, well. Look who decided to join the party," Travis said, his eyes glinting with malice.

I could feel my heart pounding in my chest as Travis rolled his wheelchair closer to us. Betty kept her gun pointed at my dad and me, but I couldn't take my eyes off Travis. He was the one who had caused all of this, the one who had orchestrated the deaths of our family members.

"What do you want from us, Travis?" I asked, my voice trembling slightly.

Travis chuckled. "What do I want? I want to see you suffer, Billie Ann. I want to watch you and your dear old dad beg me for your lives."

I looked at my dad. His head was still down, his shoulders still shaking. I turned back to Travis. "Why don't you just kill me, Travis? It's what you want, isn't it?"

"Oh, I will kill you," Travis replied. "When the time is right. But first, Billie Ann Wilde, you're going to watch your dad die."

He gave me a sickly sweet smile and nodded toward Betty. Betty stepped closer, gun stretched out in her hand.

"Stop," I said and jumped in front of the gun, blocking my dad. "Enough of all this nonsense. It is me you want, not him. He didn't do anything wrong. I'm the one who reported you for the rape and had you fired. Take it out on me, not him."

"Oh, but he has his share of suffering too," Betty said and looked at my dad. "You never told them, did you?"

"He didn't," I said. "But I know."

My dad lifted his gaze and looked at me. "You do?"

"Yes. It was you who had an affair, not Mom. For all these years I thought it was her. But you were the one who cheated. And you had a child with her. A child whose mother was a drug addict, and who died of an overdose. And then he went to live with the Walkers, who adopted him. My brother grew up in their house, and I didn't even know who he was when I came to visit, when Travis became my partner. I'm the one who should be angry. I was robbed of those years of having a brother."

"Oh, you weren't robbed by us," Betty said. "Your dad is the one who robbed so much from all of you."

SIXTY-SIX

Then

Betty sat in the driver's seat, her hands gripping the steering wheel tightly. Her eyes were fixed on the house in front of her. The house stood tall and elegant, with a grand entrance and perfectly manicured lawn. The exterior was made of exquisite stone, with intricate details and large windows that reflected the sunlight. She turned off the engine and glanced over at her son John, who was sitting in the passenger seat. He looked up from his phone and followed her gaze out the window.

"What are we doing here, Mom?" he asked, his voice laced with curiosity.

Betty didn't answer right away. She took a deep breath and let it out slowly, trying to calm her nerves. She knew what she was about to do was risky, but she couldn't help herself.

"Look at that house, John," she said, pointing a finger toward the bungalow. "Do you see it?"

John nodded. "Is this where he lives?"

She smiled. "Yes, this is where your biological father lives."

"But it's so close to our house?" he said. "How come he never came to see me?"

"He was busy with his other children," she said.

"Like Billie Ann?"

"Yes, she was a teenager when you were born."

Betty looked at the house, just as the door opened and Sean Wilde walked out. He was holding hands with a small child, a boy, and they were laughing and giggling.

Betty's heart skipped a beat as she saw Sean. She remembered the last time she had seen him, the way he had looked at her with such hatred and disgust when she asked him for money to send his own son to college, and if he didn't, she would tell his family his little secret. He had paid a check every month when John was younger, but that had stopped when he turned eighteen. Betty had other plans; she wanted her son to get an education, so she approached him. Sean hated her, she knew that much. But she couldn't let that stop her now.

"John, I want you to do something for me," she said, turning to her son.

"What is it?" John asked, looking at her quizzically.

"I want you to get out of the car and go talk to your father," Betty said, her voice firm.

"But, Mom, I don't know him," John protested. "I don't even know what to say."

"Just go say hello, John," Betty said, placing a hand on his shoulder. "I'll be right here in the car. It's time for you to meet your father."

John hesitated for a moment, but then nodded and got out of the car. Betty watched anxiously as he approached Sean and the little boy. They stopped laughing as John came closer, and Betty held her breath, waiting for what would happen next.

As John reached out to shake his father's hand, Sean's face contorted with surprise and disbelief. He stared at John, his mouth hanging open in shock.

Betty watched from the car, her heart pounding in her chest. She knew this was a risky move, but she had to do it. She rolled down the window so she could hear the conversation.

"I don't know who you are," Sean said.

"I'm your son," John said. "John. My mom's name was Marianne. She... she died. I grew up with the Walkers across town."

Sean pulled the young boy closer and seemed to be sheltering him with his hands, as if he believed John was dangerous.

"I don't know what you're talking about. Please just leave us alone. I'm on my way to the park with my grandson."

"But... you're my dad," John said. "Aren't you happy to see me?"

"I don't know who you are," Sean said and began to walk away. "Please just leave us alone."

He tried to walk past him, but John stopped him. "You have sent me money my entire life? I thought that meant you cared about me? How can you say you don't know who I am?"

Sean looked at the young child holding his hand. "Listen, Charlie," he said. "Can you run inside and ask Grandma what time she wants us home for dinner, please? I forgot to ask."

The boy nodded eagerly and ran back into the front yard and up the stairs. Sean turned to face John. Betty listened carefully.

"Listen, boy," he said, grabbing John's collar. "I paid that money so I never had to see you again. My family doesn't know you exist, and I need it to remain that way. Do you hear me? You need to get out of here, fast, before anyone starts asking questions. You were nothing but a mistake. An accident, and I have been paying for it ever since. I will not let you ruin my family with this. Now get out of here."

John's face fell as he heard Sean's words, and Betty's heart broke for her son. She knew this would be a difficult conversation, but she had hoped for a different outcome.

"Please, Dad," John said, his voice barely above a whisper.

"I just wanted to meet you, to know who you are. I'm your son. I'm a Wilde."

"I told you, I don't know who you are," Sean said, releasing John's collar. "Now leave before I call the cops."

Betty watched as John walked back to the car, his shoulders slumped in defeat. She opened the door for him, and he climbed in, tears streaming down his face.

"I'm sorry, John," Betty said, her own voice shaking. "I thought it would be different."

"I just wanted him to know me," John said, wiping his eyes. "Why doesn't he want to know me?"

Betty sighed. "These people, the Wildes, are nothing but trouble. They have ruined so many lives. Someone ought to teach them a lesson."

As she spoke, Betty's eyes lingered on Sean's retreating figure. She knew she couldn't let him get away with this—not after what he had done to her and her son. A fire burned inside her, a fire fueled by years of pain and resentment.

"Mom, what are you thinking?" John asked, sensing the change in his mother's demeanor.

Betty turned to him, her eyes blazing. "I'm thinking it's time to show the Wildes what happens when you mess with us," she said, a dangerous edge to her voice.

"What do you mean?" John asked, a hint of fear in his voice.

"I mean we're going to teach them a lesson they won't forget," Betty said, a smile spreading across her face. "We're going to make them pay for what they've done to us."

John looked at her with a mixture of fear and admiration. And in this moment, she knew she had him on her side. John could help her get the revenge she so desperately wanted. And justice for all the suffering they had gone through due to them, to the Wilde family.

SIXTY-SEVEN

BILLIE ANN

"Your dad never wanted anything to do with his son, Billie Ann," Betty said. "And it broke his heart. Seeing him play with his grandson, knowing that he wanted you and your brothers, but not him, broke John's heart. And mine too."

"So, you made him murder my nephew and cousin and torture my brother?" I asked, anger boiling inside of me.

"Actually, he did all that by himself," Travis said. "We just watched. We just wanted you. We just wanted to hurt you for what you did to me, to us."

I looked down at the gun in Betty's hand, wondering if I could somehow grab it from her, or at least slap it out of her grip. But I had to think about my dad. I risked them killing him, if I missed or made a mistake.

My mind raced, trying to come up with a plan. I couldn't let them get away with what they had done, but I couldn't risk my dad's life either. I took a step forward, trying to make Betty and Travis nervous.

"You don't want to do this," I said, my voice steady. "You're just angry, and you're taking it out on innocent people."

Betty raised the gun, pointing it at my head. "Shut up, Billie Ann. This is your fault. You ruined our lives."

I took another step forward. "No, you ruined your own lives. You chose to take revenge instead of finding a way to heal and move on. You can still make things right."

Travis laughed. "Make things right with what? You think we can just forget about everything that's happened? That we can just forgive and forget?"

I took a deep breath, trying to remain calm. It was clear that Betty and Travis were dangerous, and I needed to figure out the best way to get out of this situation alive. "Okay," I said, slowly raising my hands. "You got me here. What do you want from me?"

Betty smirked, her grip tightening on the gun. "We want you to suffer," she said. "Just like we did. Just like your brother did."

"I'm so sorry for what happened to Travis, for the accident," I said, trying to appeal to their sense of reason. "But I didn't do it. I didn't know about it till way after it had happened."

Betty's eyes narrowed. "You're lying," she said. "We know you were involved. We have proof."

I swallowed hard, trying to think of a way out. "What kind of proof?" I asked, stalling for time.

Travis rolled his wheelchair forward, a cruel smile on his face. "It was your truck that hit me and placed me in this darn chair for the rest of my life."

Betty shook her head. "You're the one who hit him, Billie Ann. You were the crazy driver that hit him and left him there to die."

I turned to Betty, trying to stay calm. It was Joe that had hit him with Charlene's truck. I had him arrested when I found out, and he had never forgiven me for that. He had been so mad when he realized it was Travis who raped me, and one day he saw him in the street, a free man despite what he had done, and

Joe had simply snapped. It was wrong of him, but he had done it out of love for me.

"That's not what happened, Betty," I said. "I know you're upset, but you need to understand that I didn't drive the truck when it happened; I wasn't the one driving."

Betty raised the gun, pointing it straight at my head. "Don't lie to me!" she yelled. "We saw the picture. We saw it all!"

My mind raced, trying to think of a way out. I stared at the gun in Betty's hand. I narrowed my eyes, trying to find a solution.

"You're just like your brother," Travis said, his voice turning from laughter to anger. "You're a liar and a cheater. You deserve to die."

Travis reached for something behind him and pulled a rifle out of the wheelchair. He turned the gun, pointing it straight at my dad.

"Put down the gun," I said, my voice dripping with fear. "Please don't do this. I'm begging you. Don't make me watch you kill my dad."

Travis grinned, his face lighting up with excitement. "You're right," she said. "You are begging, and that"

He didn't get to say anything else, as the sound of sirens approaching in the distance filled the house. Travis and Betty exchanged a look.

"What? You didn't think I would call for backup before I came inside?" I asked.

Betty's eyes filled with rage as she glared at Travis. "What are you waiting for?" she said, pulling her gun away from my dad and pointing it at me. "Shoot her. Kill her now."

Travis raised his rifle, leveling it at my chest. I stared straight into his eyes, unable to believe that he would kill me.

"No," I whispered, tears springing to my eyes. "Don't do this, Travis."

Travis shook his head. "I have to," he said.

I turned away, closing my eyes. "Please don't," I whispered.

"Open your eyes," Travis said. "I want to look into your eyes as you die."

I opened my eyes, watching as my dad jumped from the couch and wrestled the rifle out of Travis' hands. Then it went off.

"Dad," I screamed, running to his side. "Are you okay?"

Blood was gushing from his abdomen, and it terrified me. Betty stared at him, mouth open. Then I kicked her hand and the gun went flying.

My dad moved fast despite being hurt. He grabbed the gun and pointed it at her head. And that's when Travis slammed into him. His wheelchair fell forward, and he was on the floor. My gun was within reach. I ran to it, picked it up and pointed it at him.

"This is it. It ends here."

"Billie," my dad said, his voice raspy. I knelt down by his side and touched his face. I kissed him on the cheek and pulled him into my arms.

"Don't die," I pleaded with him. "Please, don't leave me."

He smiled, the kind of smile that he always had. He stroked my back, and I cried into his shoulder. Then after a few moments, my dad took a deep breath, and he stopped moving.

"No, Dad," I wailed, shaking his shoulders.

But he was gone.

"No!" I screamed, tears falling from my eyes.

Betty and Travis stared at me, looking shocked at what they had just witnessed. But I didn't care. I didn't care how mad they were, or how much they wanted revenge. My dad was gone, and I knew it was because of them.

I stood up, pointing the gun at Betty. My hand was shaking as I walked closer, finger on the trigger.

The front door burst open, and two SWAT team officers burst into the room. "Freeze!" one of them yelled.

"Drop your weapon."

I reluctantly put the gun down, tears streaming from my face. "My father," I said, looking at the officers. "Call an ambulance. He's been shot."

Big Tom came in with the rest of the SWAT team and rushed to me. "Billie Ann, are you hurt? Are you okay?"

I sniffled, looking at my dad, then shook my head. "It's not over yet."

SIXTY-EIGHT

BILLIE ANN

The car hugged the curves of the narrow, tree-lined road, and my grip on the steering wheel tightened as I approached the secluded cabin. My heart thumped wildly, a mix of fear and adrenaline coursing through my body. Tom sat in the passenger seat, his normally jovial expression replaced by one of grim determination.

"And you're sure about this?" he asked.

"Yes. I recognized the cabin from when Scott went through John's Instagram profile. It belongs to Travis and Betty, his parents. I've been there before, when my family and I were invited up here with them for a weekend. He goes here to fish from time to time. It's on a lake."

"And you're sure it's John Walker, the same John Walker who received money from your dad, and who killed Charlie and Jeremy and hurt Alex, Zack, and Andrew?"

"Yes, that same John Walker. Betty and Travis' adopted son." I let out a deep sigh. "And my brother."

"Half-brother," he corrected me.

"Still the same to me."

As we approached the cabin, I could see him pacing back

and forth on the porch, a gun in his hand. I pulled the car over to the side of the road and got out, taking a deep breath before making my way toward him.

"Tyler," I called out, my voice shaking only slightly. "Let Charlene go. You don't have to do this."

Tyler, or John as his real name was, turned his head toward me, a wicked smile spreading across his face.

"Oh, I think I do," he sneered. "And you won't be able to stop me."

"I won't let you hurt my daughter!" I yelled out. "Not while I'm still alive!"

"I want you hurt. I want you to suffer," he yelled. "Our dad chose you. Not me. You always had everything. I had nothing. I want you to know what it feels like to have nothing."

"I know this must be hard for you," I said. "Going through what you have. But hurting more people, more family members, won't make you feel better. We can end this right now."

I walked up the stairs, pointing my gun at him. He lifted his to stop me, but I was way faster. I pulled the trigger, and he screamed out in pain as the bullet tore through his arm, causing the gun to fall from his hand.

"I always was the fastest shooter among my brothers," I said, picking up his gun. "No reason that should change now."

"You bitch," he said while on his knees.

"Where is she?"

"Wouldn't you like to know?" he asked with a grin.

I reached down and looked into his eyes. Then I pressed a finger into his bullet wound in his arm, and I squeezed it as hard as I could. He let out a scream of pain and fell flat down on the porch.

"Let's try again. Where is my daughter?" I asked.

He didn't say anything. I kicked him in the stomach.

"Where is she?" I demanded.

"She's out back," he replied with a pathetic whimper. "You can go take a look."

I signaled for Tom to handle John, while I went through the cabin and into the back, where the yard reached down to the lake.

I gasped as my eyes took in the sight before me. Charlene was tied securely to a large tree, weeping softly as she struggled to free herself.

"Charlene!" I called out, then ran to her.

"Mom!" she cried out. "Mom, save me! Mom, save me!"

I pulled out a pocketknife and cut the ropes that tied her and pulled her into my arms as she cried out in relief.

I looked into her eyes.

"It's all right, Charlene. We've got you now. Everything is going to be all right now."

Charlene held me tightly as she cried, and I kissed her hair.

"It's okay, baby girl, you're safe now," I whispered.

I turned around and grabbed Charlene's hand as we made our way back into the house, when I heard a loud scream coming from the other side. I let go of Charlene and ran out to the front porch, where Tom was on the floor, holding his stomach while blood was gushing from a wound. "He had a knife, the little bastard. Get him."

I pulled the gun, just as John jumped into his truck and started the engine. I aimed at his windshield and fired just as he drove off. The glass shattered, but John kept driving.

"Son of a bitch!" I yelled, then ran back into the house. "Charlene!"

"I'm here!" she called out from the kitchen.

I ran to her and put my arms around her once more.

"I love you, Charlene," I said through tears. "I love you so much."

"I love you, too, Mom," she said, hugging me back. "I'm sorry for everything. I didn't know... I should have listened, but I didn't... and all of a sudden, he pulled a gun on me, and brought me here... and..."

"Come on," I said, wiping the tears from my eyes. "Let's get the hell out of here. Next time he won't get away from me."

Charlene and I ran out the front door. I put my hand on Tom's shoulder.

"Tom? Tom, can you hear me?"

He opened his eyes and nodded.

"All right, that's good," I said, "You're going to be okay," I said as I checked his wound. It was deep, all right, but didn't seem to have hit any of his major organs. It would leave a scar, but it would heal. As we waited for the ambulance to arrive, I held my daughter tight in my arms and realized how badly I was shaking. John had gotten away, but I was going to catch him. One way or the other. If it was the last thing I did.

EPILOGUE

Two Months Later

I stood in the center of the courtroom, my heart thumping in my chest so loudly that I was sure everyone in the room could hear it. The judge had disappeared for what felt like an eternity, and the anticipation had been gnawing at me, leaving me in a state of near panic.

Finally, the door at the front of the room opened with a creak, and everyone in the courtroom rose to their feet as the judge made his entrance. He was tall and imposing, his long black robe trailing behind him as he walked to the bench, and his stern gaze swept over the room.

As he settled into his seat and looked down at me over the rim of his glasses, my hands began to shake. I had been waiting for this moment for so long, and now that it was here, I was terrified of what he was about to say.

"Ms. Wilde," the judge began, his voice deep and commanding. "After careful consideration of all the evidence presented in your case, I have decided to grant the full custody of your three children to your husband Joe Harper. My decision is based on the fact that I have seen no evidence to support your claim that you are able to fully protect them."

My heart sank as the words left the judge's mouth. It felt like the air had been knocked out of my lungs. The thought of losing my children to Joe was unbearable. I couldn't imagine not being there for them every day, not being able to hold them whenever they needed me.

As the judge continued to speak, my mind wandered to all the things that had led to this moment. The fights, the accusations, the hurtful words thrown back and forth like daggers. I knew that I had made mistakes, but I also knew that I loved my children more than anything in the world.

The judge's voice brought me back to the present. "Ms. Wilde, I understand that this is a difficult decision, but I believe it is the best one for your children's well-being. As I understand it the person who has been putting you and your family in danger is still out there, he's still on the loose. While that is the case, I need to make sure your children are safe. That is my biggest priority."

Tears streamed down my face as I tried to process what was happening. I knew that I had to accept the judge's ruling, but it didn't make it any less painful. Before coming to the courthouse, I had stopped by the hospital to check on my dad, who was going through another surgery later today. But he was alive. The paramedics had acted fast when getting to the house, and they had managed to revive him. My mom was a mess, my brother Andrew in a wheelchair, and my oldest brother Peter barely keeping himself alive after losing his son. Scott had returned to work, and so had Big Tom, but they had both been hurt and that made me feel awful. Maybe I really was bad news for all the people around me? Maybe the children were better off without me?

The only really good part was that both Travis and Betty Walker were behind bars, waiting for their trial, and the evidence we had been gathering was piling up, enough to lock them away for a very long time, hopefully.

"Your Honor," I said. "I'm an outstanding member of society. I am a cop, a detective. I can very well protect my children."

He looked at me from above his glasses again. "Ms. Wilde. Just within the past year, your youngest was buried alive, your oldest kidnapped. Your middle child has turned to drugs. I simply fail to see how you are able to protect them and give them the secure upbringing they are so desperately in need of. That is also why I have decided to grant the house on Crystal River Drive to your husband. So the children won't have to change address as well. They have been through enough, don't you think? I will grant you supervised visits, until further notice."

I couldn't believe what I was hearing. It was true that the past year had been horrific for my family, but I had done everything in my power to protect them. The judge's decision felt like a harsh punishment for something that wasn't entirely my fault.

I took a deep breath and tried to compose myself. "Your Honor, I understand your decision, but please, I beg you to consider my children's feelings in all of this. They love me, and I love them more than anything in this world. Please don't take them away from me."

The judge's expression softened slightly. "Ms. Wilde, I understand that this is a difficult time for you, but my decision is final. I urge you to use this as an opportunity to better yourself and work on becoming the type of person who can provide your children with the stability and safety they deserve."

My heart shattered as the judge's words echoed in the silent courtroom. With that, the judge banged his gavel, signaling the end of the hearing. I watched as the courtroom emptied, my eyes never leaving the judge's face. His verdict had left me feeling broken and helpless, unsure of what my future held. But

I knew that I had to keep fighting for my children, to prove to the world that I was capable of being the mother they needed.

As I left the courtroom with tears still streaming down my face, I saw Joe waiting for me with a smug expression on his face.

"I told you, you were never going to win this," he said, his voice dripping with contempt. I felt a hand on my shoulder. It was my lawyer, looking at me with compassion in his eyes.

"Come on, let's get out of here," he said. "I'll drive you home."

I nodded numbly as he guided me out of the courthouse and into the afternoon sunlight. The world felt different now, as if the colors had been muted and the air had grown thick with sadness.

But even in the midst of my despair, I refused to give up hope. I would fight for my children, no matter what it took. And one day, I knew that I would find a way to bring them home where they belonged.

A LETTER FROM WILLOW

Dear reader,

Thank you for choosing to read *In Her Grave*. If you did enjoy it, and want to keep up to date with all my latest releases, just sign up at the following link. Your email address will never be shared, and you can unsubscribe at any time.

www.bookouture.com/willow-rose

I hope you loved the story, and if you did I would be very grateful if you could write a review. I'd love to hear what you think, and it makes such a difference helping new readers to discover one of my books for the first time.

The inspiration for this story came to me when I one night had a nightmare that I saw a tombstone with my own name on it. As I woke up, I couldn't stop thinking about it, and that's when I thought, *But what if it was my own child that someone buried down there?* And so the story began to shape in my mind.

I knew this book was going to be about Travis and Betty and especially Betty and how she grew to become who she is and why she is so angry at Billie Ann. But also how she found excuses for her husband's behavior simply because it was too painful to admit to reality. Here's an article about someone going through something similar when realizing her husband was a rapist, yet deciding to stand by him.

https://www.theguardian.com/society/2012/oct/12/husband-rapist-shannon-moroney-book

Also, the idea for the cell inside of the garage was taken from a real story. A woman in Oregon was kidnapped and held captive in a cell the man had built out of cinder blocks inside of his garage. You can read more here:

https://www.usatoday.com/story/news/nation/2023/08/02/oregon-kidnapping-woman-escapes-cinderblock-cell-fbi/70514576007/

Thank you to my wonderful editor, Jennifer Hunt, who always makes sure my books are the best they can possibly be. As always thank you for all your support and reviews. They mean the world to me. As long as you read, I will write!

Take care,

Willow

KEEP IN TOUCH WITH WILLOW

www.willow-rose.net

facebook.com/authoroleary

x.com/madamwillowrose

instagram.com/willowroseauthor

bookbub.com/authors/willow-rose

PUBLISHING TEAM

Turning a manuscript into a book requires the efforts of many people. The publishing team at Bookouture would like to acknowledge everyone who contributed to this publication.

Audio
Alba Proko
Sinead O'Connor
Melissa Tran

Commercial
Lauren Morrissette
Hannah Richmond
Imogen Allport

Cover design
The Brewster Project

Data and analysis
Mark Alder
Mohamed Bussuri

Editorial
Jennifer Hunt
Sinead O'Connor

Made in United States
Orlando, FL
23 June 2024

48201505R00174